D0403536

ALSO BY TARA ISABELLA BURTON

Social Creature

Strange Rites: New Religions for a Godless World

The

WORLD
CANNOT
GIVE

Tara Isabella Burton

SIMON & SCHUSTER

New York   London   Toronto   Sydney   New Delhi

Simon & Schuster
1230 Avenue of the Americas
New York, NY 10020

First Simon & Schuster hardcover edition March 2022

SIMON & SCHUSTER and colophon are registered trademarks of Simon & Schuster, Inc.

For information about special discounts for bulk purchases, please contact Simon & Schuster Special Sales at 1-866-506-1949 or business@simonandschuster.com.

The Simon & Schuster Speakers Bureau can bring authors to your live event. For more information or to book an event, contact the Simon & Schuster Speakers Bureau at 1-866-248-3049 or visit our website at www.simonspeakers.com.

Interior design by Ruth Lee-Mui

Manufactured in the United States of America

1 3 5 7 9 10 8 6 4 2

Library of Congress Cataloging-in-Publication Data has been applied for.

ISBN 978-1-9821-7006-6
ISBN 978-1-9821-7008-0 (ebook)

To Dhananjay:
my most serious, and attentive, reader

Part I

MICHAELMAS

1

LAURA CRIES EASILY.

She cries at poems when the slant rhymes surprise you. She cries at old movies where people are in love but can't acknowledge it for self-abnegatingly heroic reasons, like being married or having to lead the French Resistance, and she cries at the lonely light of early mornings. She cries when she pieces together the etymologies of words, and she cries when people sing the exact right harmony and their voices lattice so that she hears only one perfect, unearthly sound.

Laura even cried in the middle of History, once, the time they were reading about how people in the Middle Ages who made art depicted human beings as ordinary-size, but angels as impossibly big, like houses or towers, and the textbook author said it was because people in the Middle Ages really did see angels all around them—not scientifically, sure, but psychologically—and the notion that once upon a time a person could just look around and see angels, everywhere, struck Laura as so impossibly beautiful that she erupted into weeping and then had to lie and tell everyone it was menstrual cramps, because as soft and susceptible as Laura Stearns is, even she knows that in the real world, you can't go around crying about angels unless you want people to think you're one of those nuts who stand outside the Bellagio with picket signs that say *The End Is Near*.

It's not that Laura doesn't know she's too sensitive. She knows her parents, her teachers, her school counselor all call her *young for her age*. (Laura is sixteen. She feels so old.)

One day, they tell her, she will have to develop that necessary carapace that other people seem to be born with by default, the one that means things no longer make you cry.

Only then, Laura thinks, she wouldn't love things so deeply. She wouldn't love Sebastian Webster the way she does. She doesn't know who she is, not loving him.

Sebastian Oliver Webster knew things. He understood about angels, about heroes, about lattices of voices. He understood about beauty and meaning, and about World-History, which he always capitalizes. He understood about green morning light, and also about slant rhymes—*All Before Them* is full of them, hidden in his prose—and every time Laura rereads it she starts crying on page seventeen and doesn't stop until she's slammed it shut. Laura has read *All Before Them* fifteen times.

It's the ending that gets her.

It's dusk, late in term time. A spring storm's blowing in along the coast. It's 1936. Robert Lawrence—he's the character Webster based on himself—walks into the St. Dunstan's chapel. He tries to pray.

Most of the plot is resolved by this point. Gus has already had his affair with his headmaster's wife; the boys have all dared each other to jump off Farnham Cliff. And Robert Lawrence has already beaten up poor Shrimpy Masterson in the Falmouth woods.

It's not that Robert's a bad person. Laura always has trouble explaining this part. It's just that Robert wants so much, and so deeply, and more than anything Robert wants this experience he calls a *shipwreck of the soul*, even though Webster never explains exactly what this means.

Laura isn't sure what it means, either, although the words together make her heart seize, but, anyway, it's the only thing Robert wants, and so it's all Robert can't have.

Not that he doesn't search. He tries drugs, religion, sex. He falls in love with this townie named Peggy. He breaks Shrimpy Masterson's nose in the woods. Laura has to skip that scene whenever she rereads it, because it hurts too much to get through.

But anyway, anyway, the ending. It's dusk; it's 1936; the sky is splitting open. Robert's still trapped in what Webster keeps calling the *whole sclerotic modern world*, where nothing means anything, where everything Great or Pure or World-Historical (Webster's styling; only now Laura uses it too) that was ever going to happen has happened already, long ago, where nobody's soul ever gets dashed on rocks.

And Robert—he's sitting there in the chapel, his head in his hands, looking up at this stained glass mosaic of the Virgin Mary as the Stella Maris, her lantern aloft like she's some kind of lighthouse, but anyway, Robert's staring up at her, aching to feel it, incapable of feeling it, and then all of a sudden he hears little Shrimpy Masterson sing.

Webster leaves this part ambiguous. That's his genius. He doesn't tell us if Robert finds God, or if he does what *kind* of god he finds, or whether the thing that finally breaks Robert open is supposed to be Shrimpy himself, or the sound of the Magnificat, or the sight of the storm-split sky darkening through Mary's lantern, but anyway, anyway, Robert experiences, at last, the *shipwreck of the soul* he's spent the whole book looking for.

Finally, Robert gets it.

He falls to his knees.

It came to him, at last, Webster writes, *the truth he had always known, within himself, unvoiced. He realized*—and Laura is convinced that this is the single most beautiful phrase in the English language—*the rocks and the harbor are one.*

Two pages later Robert sets off on a stolen boat into the sunrise, and even though Webster doesn't tell us what happens to him Laura likes to imagine that he ends up how Webster ended up in real life: stealing away from St. Dunstan's one May midnight in 1937, getting baptized by some Irish Catholic priest in Boston; talking his way into a berth on a transatlantic freighter to go fight in the Spanish Civil War, dying on a battlefield six months later, leaving behind nothing but a handwritten manuscript of such wild-eyed genius that, eighty years later, Laura feels sure he is the only person in the world who could ever understand her.

Not that Laura experienced anything she could confidently describe as a *shipwreck of the soul*, nor does she know, exactly, how she'll be able to tell when she does. She knows only that she, like Robert Lawrence, wants to have one more than anything in the world, and that the closest she's ever gotten is reading *All Before Them* for the very first time.

Laura wonders often about what Sebastian Webster's shipwreck was like. She wonders whether it came quickly, like a thunderclap, or gradually, like dawn. She wonders whether once it came, he wrote the whole novel, in a single feverish week, ablaze with certainty, or whether he wrestled over every word, the way Laura wrestles whenever she tries to explain herself to the people that she knows.

She wonders whether he knew, running off from St. Dunstan's under the cover of moonlight, that he was doomed to die on the battlefield, or whether it came as a shock to him when some Spanish soldier bayoneted him in the back. She wonders if you can have a shipwreck of the soul in a place like Henderson, Nevada, or in a time like the present, or if you have to be lucky enough to live in a place and a time where people are fighting World-Historical battles you can die in. She wonders if you can have a shipwreck without dying.

Maybe, she thinks, once you have one, death doesn't scare you, anymore.

• • •

Laura likes to think she and Webster would have been friends.

If she had only been there, with him, back then, at St. Dunstan's (oh, if only she'd been a boy!)—she'd know exactly what to say to him. She has the whole scene in her head. They'd sit, together—maybe at Farnham Cliff, just like Robert's always doing with Gus, gazing out over the rocky coastline, counting the mother-of-pearl oysters that wash up with the wreckage of vanquished boats.

Maybe they wouldn't even have to talk. Maybe he'd just take her hand, and press it to his lips, and they would watch the moonlight overflow onto the black water, and he would simply understand, by virtue of his mystic shipwrecked soul, all those things Laura never has words for.

But Sebastian Webster is dead. What's left of him is buried in the crypt under the St. Dunstan's chapel, where the spires cast their shadows toward the sea, where the student body sings Evensong every Friday night, just like they did in Webster's day.

They've admitted girls since the sixties.

That's why Laura's heading there right now.

Laura has been awake for twenty-four hours. She has flown from Las Vegas to New York, and then from New York to Boston. Her suitcase is heavier than she is. She has taken the train from Boston to Portland, shivering with glory, shuddering, texting her parents every few hours just like she promised, because although after months of deliberation they have at last agreed to let her go to St. Dunstan's, she knows they expect her to get lost in baggage claim and call them, begging to let her come home and spend junior year at Green Valley High after all. She has taken the bus from Portland to Weymouth, reciting the names of the dormitories to herself, because if she forgets just one St. Dunstan's will disappear.

Laura is standing at Weymouth's bus stop, which is really just a lamppost, waiting for the cab that will take her to campus, three miles north along the coast. Laura's heart is a hummingbird.

Laura isn't even tired. Laura can't stop smiling. It is the first day of Michaelmas term.

Laura's parents have reminded her—so many times—that St. Dunstan's is a real school, populated by real people, with real classes and real athletics and real college matriculation statistics. Even at St. Dunstan's (they have reminded her) she will not find Sebastian Webster himself, with his hollow cheeks and his dark hair slicked back high on his forehead and his fingertips striated with ink, crossing Devonshire Quad in the salt-tinged morning mist. Even at St. Dunstan's (Laura knows this part by heart) she will have to study hard, and read assiduously; she'll finally have to enroll in extracurriculars. She might even have to make some friends.

Laura knows all this. She can't bring herself to believe it. Deep down, Laura knows that St. Dunstan's can't possibly belong to the real world, to that *sclerotic modern world* Robert Lawrence despises.

After all, Laura has seen the pictures.

God, she has spent so many hours googling pictures!

She has seen how the fog still hangs dark and thick on Farnham Cliff, where a memorial statue to Sebastian Webster now stands. She has seen the chapel: its stark spires, its lighthouse Madonna illuminated by the riotous sunset reds, Sebastian Webster's bones interred below. She has watched and rewatched and paused and gasped and started up again so many videos of the choir singing Evensong at chapel, the way they do every Friday night. Surely, Laura thinks, nobody could sing Evensong at chapel every Friday night without it shipwrecking your soul, at least a little.

She has spent all summer wondering about the people she'll find there. She wonders if anyone loves Webster like she does; whether anyone requested—as she did—a room in Desmond Hall, because that is where Webster wrote and slept and wrote, back when Desmond was a dorm for boys. She knows they will be smart, probably much smarter than she is—God, she *hopes* they are a million times smarter than she is, so long as they're patient enough and willing to tell her what to read next, and what to think about it, and what it all means.

Her roommate in Desmond is a girl from outside New York City called Bonnie di Angelis. She has been at St. Dunstan's for two years already. This makes Laura nervous. Maybe Bonnie is used to the spires, and the salt fog, and the sight of the black water. Maybe Laura will seem childish. Lots of people find Laura childish.

Laura wonders if she should hide her copy of *All Before Them* in her suitcase, instead of carrying it, face forward, against her chest. Maybe turning up with a copy of *All Before Them* in your arms is a thing only freshmen do.

Laura breathes in the Weymouth air. She scans the town—the bobbing fishing boats at the dock, all the wooden houses with their flaking paint and nautical colors, the Wayfarer Hotel with its big glass windows revealing its overstuffed Victorian living room.

Laura's lips taste like salt.

Laura cranes her neck all through the drive. Twice she asks the driver to slow down so that she can take it in more reverentially: the narrow country road that snakes along the coastal path, with woods on one side and a sheer cliff drop along the other. She wants to ask him to stop, once they get close to Farnham Cliff, so she can see the Webster statue face-to-face.

She doesn't dare.

Then the car turns inland.

It's all here. Here is the old chapel, fog clinging to its spires like smoke; here is Carbonell Library with its little dome, across the quadrangle from the sprawling red brick of Mountbatten Hall, where the offices and classrooms are, trellised with leaves that have turned red, too, giving the whole building the look of a bonfire. Here are the dorms—Desmond and Lyndhurst and Latimer for the girls; Morris and Unger and Cranmer for the boys. Here is Jarvis Lighthouse, in the distance: half caved in.

Laura tries to hide her tears from her Uber driver, a middle-aged man with a baseball cap and an earring; he beams at her in the rearview mirror.

He tells her not to worry. He's driven hundreds of students just like her up to the academy over the years. More than a few have cried.

Homesickness. It passes. By summer she'll be crying when she leaves.

"I'm not homesick," Laura says. She wipes her eyes with the back of her hand.

She has been homesick, all her life, for here.

Laura registers at Mountbatten. She gets her room key. She breaks her suitcase handle. She lugs it by the zipper all the way across Devonshire Quadrangle. She almost drops her book.

She drags her suitcase up three flights of stairs. She kicks it down the hallway. She stands, breathless, in front of room 312, where STEARNS/DI ANGELIS is emblazoned by the door.

DI ANGELIS is decorated already with gel-pen flowers and a curlicue over both *I*'s.

Laura is deciding whether to knock or just push open the door when she hears a voice inside.

"Can it *be*?"

It is loud and high and nasal. Laura cracks the door open.

"Another year," the voice goes on. "Another set of memories. Another ripening of the autumn leaves and of our hearts."

Laura opens the door.

A blond girl in a rowing blazer is lounging on the bed by the window.

She is staring straight at Laura.

"The lessons we've learned here," she goes on intently, "will shape us for the rest of our— *Fuck!*"

She sits straight up.

"Cut!"

Laura stands flummoxed on the threshold.

"Sorry," says the blond girl, "I know. I know. *Gross.*" She beams and rolls her eyes at the same time. "But . . ." She winces. "It's just . . ."

"You're in the shot."

Laura whirls around.

A scowling, scraggly girl with chunky pigtails is sitting cross-legged on Laura's bed, next to the door, holding a phone. She's filming. She glares at Laura.

"I . . . ," Laura fumbles.

"We're almost done," the blond girl says brightly. She turns back toward the girl on the bed. "Come on, Freddy, just one more. Please?"

"You said that an hour ago."

Bonnie keeps smiling. Bonnie starts over.

"Another year. Another set of memories. Another ripening of the autumn leaves and of our hearts."

She swoops across the bed, turning her face to the window.

"What we learn *out there*"—she gestures, grandly, toward the water—"will create the people we become, *in here*." She folds her hands against her heart. "I can't wait to share my journey of *becoming* with you all." Her chin shoots up. "*Cut!*"

"Was that too on the nose?" Laura doesn't know which one of them she's talking to. "I feel like that's too on the nose.

"It's straightforward," the ugly girl says. "People like straightforward."

"*Journey of becoming?*" Bonnie wrinkles her nose. "It's clunky. What do *you* think?"

"Me?" Laura is conscious that Freddy is still glowering at her.

"You're impartial," Bonnie says. "What do you think? Is *journey of becoming* too clunky?"

Laura hesitates. "It's a little clunky."

"Originally I was going to say *bildungsroman*," Bonnie says, "but I feel like that's maybe—I don't know—pretentious? Like, I want it to be a *little*, like, literary, you know, I mean like *smart*, but not, like, *obscure*. I don't want it to look like I'm trying too hard."

"You *are* trying too hard."

"She's right, though." Bonnie pouts. "It's clunky. 'Journey of becoming'—Christ, what was I thinking?"

"I—"

"What's something better?" She fixes her eyes, unblinking, on Laura. "Like—a journey that changes you? But in English."

"A pilgrimage?" Laura tries.

The girl's face lights up. "Pilgrimage," she says. "That's good."

Freddy snorts. "It's not a pilgrimage if you don't *go* anywhere."

Bonnie ignores her.

"From the top," she says.

"Don't hate me," says Bonnie when they finish. "I know. *I know.* It's awful. We're all supposed to be present, and in the moment, and, like, living for the 'gram." She shrugs. "But my problem is that I never *remember* anything. I'm like a hummingbird." This makes her trill. "I *have* to have a record or—" She sticks out her hand. "I'm Bonnie," she says. "That's Freddy. Barnes." She grins. "My enabler."

Freddy doesn't acknowledge this.

"I'm—"

"Oh, I know who you are," says Bonnie brightly. "I Insta-stalked you over the summer. You're from Vegas, right? *Love* that."

"Actually, it's about sixteen mi—"

"You're really pretty. You have really full lips. Are those the real lines?"

Laura has never thought of herself as pretty. She is short and chubby and her hair is dishwater blond. "I think so."

"You're lucky. I have to draw mine in. My lips are like pencils. Freddy?"

Freddy hands her the phone. Bonnie scrolls through the photos.

"You see? You can barely even see them. And God, my *arms.*"

"It's the angle," says Freddy. "Probably."

Bonnie cocks her head at the video.

"Is it good enough, do you think?"

"I think you look beautiful."

"You're sweet."

"Just put it on your Story," Freddy says. "Then you won't have to worry. By the time you hate it, it'll be gone."

Bonnie wrinkles her nose.

"But that's the *point*," she says. "I want something, you know, permanent. I know, I know, it's trite. My boyfriend, Brad—well, he's not really my boyfriend—anyway, he says it's trite. But, like, I think there's something beautiful, you know, in capturing, like, one perfect moment, but forever. Plus, it's good for your career."

Bonnie explains the whole thing. She has nine thousand followers on Instagram.

"Eight thousand, nine hundred, and ninety-six," Freddy cuts in. "You lost a few yesterday."

She has a deal, already, with this small clothing company that does this kind of preppy-tweedy-streetwear fusion look that's getting really big. They send her free stuff, sometimes, so long as she posts herself wearing it on campus. It's more authentic, showing someone wearing it on a real boarding school campus, even though St. Dunstan's isn't one of the *really* prestigious ones. It's not that Bonnie wants to be an influencer, or anything like that. Influencing isn't Bonnie's *passion*. Bonnie wants to be an artist and do mixed-media stuff, or experimental interactive stuff, like that lady who sat naked staring at strangers for three minutes each, only in this day and age if you don't have a fan base, nobody is willing to take a chance on you, or give you a book deal or a gallery show or anything, and you need twenty or thirty thousand followers to do that, and everybody loves the whole boarding school aesthetic, and besides, it's a kind of art, too, isn't it?

"When she gets twenty thousand," Freddy says, "they'll start paying her."

"Not that I care," Bonnie cuts her off. "I hate money."

Laura keeps nodding, politely, hoping nobody will ask her to weigh in.

"I want to film a segment at Evensong," Bonnie says. "People *love* Evensong. Those robes! But Brad won't let me. He says—"

"Evensong!" Finally, something Laura knows. "I can't wait to—"

Freddy snorts from across the room.

"Oh, it's *gorgeous*." Bonnie grabs hold of Laura's hands. "You'll love it. I'm *sure* you'll get asked."

"Asked?"

Bonnie's eyes widen. "I mean," she says, wiggling an eyebrow. "By a boy. Or a girl. I don't judge."

"It's the hottest date night at St. Dunstan's," says Freddy. She doesn't look up from her phone. "It's the only date night at St. Dunstan's."

Bonnie explains the whole thing. Someone picks you up at your dorm, you walk together at sunset, and then once it's dark you can hold hands without anybody seeing. Back in first year, when Bonnie was dating Gabe Meltzer, he used to bring flowers to Desmond every week, only he'd try to finger her in the back row, which Bonnie felt was a little bit sacrilegious, even though Bonnie, personally, feels the presence of the divine everywhere, not just in chapel, so there's no logical reason why a chapel should be more sacred than, say, the rare-book room at the top of Carbonell Library, and Bonnie has had sex plenty of times in the rare-book room at Carbonell Library.

Laura tries, too late, to rearrange her features. Bonnie notices and briefly looks stung.

"It's not like they use it for anything *else*."

One day, Bonnie says, Brad will pick her up here, too. Only, they're not official yet, because it's complicated, because Brad has commitment issues, what with his parents being divorced and all. Anyway, Bonnie says, she's not bitter about it, because Brad is in the chapel choir—he has this gorgeous tenor voice—so it's not like they'd even get to sit together.

"You'll love it."

Laura has never pictured other people at Evensong. Evensong has always been for her and Webster alone.

"I . . . I'm really excited about the music." Laura tries not to think about fingering. "I—I mean—I love choral music."

Freddy snorts again, louder this time.

"Sure you do," she says.

"Don't listen to Freddy," Bonnie says. "She doesn't like the choir." She lifts her chin. "She's a philistine. The music's *gorgeous.*" She taps Laura a little too hard on the shoulder. "I'm just glad that you're not one of those boring people who objects."

"Why would I object?"

"Because they make you go."

"Mandatory church," Freddy says. "Worked for the Spanish Inquisition."

"It's not *church,*" Bonnie says. "It's . . . it's . . . tradition."

"It's *in* a church, isn't it?"

"It's a chapel," says Bonnie. "It's not the same." She bites her lip. "Anyway, *some people,*" she nods toward Freddy without looking at her, "think it's *oppressive.*"

Freddy shrugs.

"The donors like it," Freddy says. "So it doesn't matter what we think."

Not that people haven't *tried,* Bonnie points out. Like Isobel Zhao. Last year, Bonnie sniffs, Isobel Zhao ran for student council president—even though she was only a sophomore at the time, and everybody knows nobody runs until junior spring—on this whole platform of abolishing Evensong, or at least making it optional, which as far as Bonnie is concerned is the same thing, since the whole point is that everybody goes, whether or not they believe in God, because it's a nice thing to do, and anyway Isobel Zhao got 40 percent of the vote, which was less than Anton Gallagher, who won, but still worrying all the same, as a sign of the times.

"I think it's tragic," Bonnie says. "Nobody cares about tradition anymore." She sits up straight. "Except *choir*, of course."

Freddy grimaces.

"Do *you* sing?" Laura tries once more to steer the conversation back to safe ground.

"I'm in the Dewey Decibel System," Bonnie says too quickly. "That's the a cappella group, you know. And I have so many *other* interests." She clears her throat. "My art. And junior year—it's the most important one, for colleges. I have to prioritize my academics." She swallows. "Besides, it'd be weird for Brad. You know what they say about couples spending too much time together. . . ."

"You're not a couple," says Freddy.

"Come on, we're *almost* official."

"You've been saying that since March."

"Freddy's just mad because she's going to die alone." Bonnie sniffs. "Anyway, *I'm* excited. I want to see the new chaplain. Reverend Tipton. *Lloyd.* Apparently he's *British.*" She waits.

Laura makes an ambiguous noise. Bonnie seems satisfied.

"I heard they poached him from Eton. It was all very sudden, you know, after Heeno—Reverend Heenan—died . . . they were scrambling to find someone over the summer. Poor man." Bonnie allows, at last, a reverential pause. "I mean, he was *really* old, so—*fuck!*"

Bells echo from the chapel.

"We're late! Look!"

Bonnie motions out the window.

The sun is setting. People are already crossing Devonshire Quad. The fog has lifted, and the sky is vermillion, spiked with gold thread.

"I was *going* to change." Bonnie looks mournful.

She goes to her closet and picks a pair of precarious stilettos. She squeezes them on.

She totters toward Laura and Freddy.

"Come on," she says.

She seizes them: balancing, pendulous, between them.

"Let's go."

Laura enters the chapel. She forgets everything else.

Laura has been worrying about so many things—fingering, and dates, and flowers, and people who want to abolish Evensong, and what people do in the rare-book room of Carbonell Library, Bonnie's love life, Freddy's sneers. None of them seems to matter very much now.

After all, Laura thinks, how can a person care about such irrelevancies when a person is entering a soul-shipwrecking place?

It's just as Webster said.

Here is the organ; here the marble patterns on the floor. Here is the organ loft; here the lectern shaped like an eagle; here the stained glass window where St. Peter is a fisher of men; here the one with Noah's ark; here all the fishermen's saints, because St. Dunstan's was once for fishermen's sons; here—Laura's heart leaps—is Mary the star of the sea: her homecoming expression, her lighthouse arms.

"I know. Right?" Bonnie shoves her way into the front pew.

The sun is gone. The candles flicker. Their shadows are like lace.

"Look." Bonnie leans in to Laura's ear. "That's *him*. Isn't he *gorgeous*?" She points up front toward the altar, where the choir stands in the stalls: two rows of three each, all in black robes, covered by white surplices, staring straight ahead.

"Brad!" she burlesques a whisper. "Over here." Bonnie windmills her arms into a wave.

A boy in the front looks up. He is short and boxy, with thin lips and large, cowlike eyes.

His mouth twitches when he sees them. He raises his hand awkwardly, in a syncopated wave.

The girl next to him grabs him by the shoulder.

He freezes. Her nails dig into his arm.

His smile dies.

The girl purses her lips so tight Laura worries she'll swallow them.

Brad lowers his arm. He stares off into the middle distance. The girl keeps her arm there.

Laura keeps looking at her.

She is tall—three easy inches on Brad—and severe-looking, pale enough that Laura can make out the blue of her veins. Her hair is long and black and straight; her eyes are arctic blue. Under her robes Laura can make out a pair of black lace gloves. Her back is straight enough to snap.

"Who's that?" Laura whispers.

"Virginia Strauss," Bonnie says. "Choir president."

"What's the matter with her?"

Virginia slowly returns her hands to her sides.

"She's just . . ." Bonnie chews her lips. "Serious."

Virginia adjusts her music on the prie-dieu.

"Does she like Brad or something?"

Freddy snorts. "Virginia Strauss," she says, "doesn't like anyone."

"That's not—" Bonnie tries. "I mean, she's nice. Once you get to know her."

Freddy just stares at her.

"That's what Brad says. She's a good friend, deep down. She's just . . ." She searches the rafters for a word. "Guarded."

Virginia clears her throat.

The boys all stand to attention. They take up their music. They are all perfectly still.

A man in a collar shuffles up the nave.

He is in his early thirties, with horn-rimmed glasses and a nervous, slightly twitchy expression. He is also—even Laura picks up on this this—good-looking.

Bonnie squeals. "That is *not* Reverend Tipton!"

He makes his way to the lectern.

"I didn't know they let people who look like that be priests." By now Bonnie is shouting.

"It's fine," Freddy says. "He's a Protestant."

Reverend Tipton adjusts his collar.

"*O gracious light . . . ,*" he begins.

"Oh God, and he's *British,*" Bonnie coos, as Laura strains to hear the rest.

"*Pure brightness of the everliving Father in heaven,*" he goes on, stammering on every third word.

"*O, Jesus Christ, holy and blessed!*

"*Now, as we come to the setting of the sun,*

"*and our eyes behold the vesper light,*

"*we sing your praises.*

"*O God: Father, Son, and Holy Spirit.*"

Virginia crosses herself before Reverend Tipton does. The boys mirror her.

Bonnie accidentally elbows Laura in the ribs doing it, too.

Then they start to sing.

THE WORLD CANNOT GIVE

. . .

Laura doesn't know how to explain this part, either.

It's not just that they're *good*—*good* is such a dull word for it! Laura has heard good music before, on Spotify, or even sometimes live from the Las Vegas Philharmonic; she knows already that good music inverts her; this isn't that—no, not that this *isn't* that: this is more of *that* than she has ever known, but also this is something else entirely.

It's how they're all singing different notes, that are also somehow all the same; it's how they're at once so grand and exultant, swelling up their chests on *for he hath rejoiced*, and also so soft when the line of the music dies; it's how Laura can hear all their voices, irreducibly distinct from one another, and also how what Laura hears is a single sound, unbroken, and in the end it's the strangeness that gets her, because Laura is aware that two opposing things can't possibly be true at the same time but, also, right now, they are.

And, God, Laura thinks, watching the six of them sing, it's how they're not professionals or disembodied voices on a speaker, doing it; they're just people, ordinary people, real and frail and the same age as she is; like this is a thing a person like her could do.

No wonder, Laura thinks, Robert Lawrence shipwrecked his soul.

Laura wants to do this, too.

Virginia sings the solo line.

For he has regarded, she sings, in her wild, alien soprano, *the lowliness of his handmaid.*

Laura can't stop watching her.

Virginia's eyes are closed. Virginia has turned her face upward to the light. The veins in Virginia's throat throb every time she changes register.

She looks, Laura thinks, like one of those illustrations she has seen of medieval saints in ecstasy, throwing back their heads while St. Michael plunges a flaming spear into their hearts. She sings, *For behold, from henceforth, all generations shall call me blessed,* like this is a thing that is happening to Virginia personally, like God has put the Messiah into her womb.

Laura has never seen anyone more beautiful in her life.

They keep singing. Laura doesn't breathe. She reaches out and grabs Bonnie's hand, even though she doesn't even like Bonnie that much; only, tears are clotting the corners of her eyes; only, Laura has to hold on to stop the world from spinning; only, tears are streaming down Laura's face, and she doesn't even try to stop them.

Then: the sound of an explosion.

Someone screams. For a wrenching second Laura remembers the headline of every news story she's ever read about people who bring guns to school, only then the electric guitars start up, and the girl who screamed titters in embarrassment; then comes the distortion, the riff, the growl.

The sound is coming from every speaker in the chapel.

Then, the disembodied voice:

What is this that stands before me?
Figure in black which points at me.

It takes everyone a second to get it.

"What the *fuck*?" a girl hollers from the back.

A few boys start laughing.

Bonnie's head whirls around. "Show some *respect*!"

The choir is silent. Reverend Tipton is pacing in impotent confusion. The music keeps blaring, and somebody screams about how Satan's sitting, how Satan's smiling, how the flames rise.

"Black Sabbath." Freddy Barnes smirks into her palms. "Nice choice."

A couple of people have started filming.

"Dis-*grace*-ful," Bonnie whispers. "And on his first day!"

Ozzy Osbourne keeps shouting about how Satan's coming, how everybody's running scared.

Virginia finally looks up.

Brad is standing, reedy and inutile; the rest of them, too, are lost in shock, and even Reverend Tipton is blinking increasingly violently, as if this will stop the speakers somehow, but Virginia is already halfway down the nave.

She marches all the way to the back of the chapel. She doesn't blink once.

A girl is standing by the door, leaning catlike against the back of the wall.

Half her head is shaved. The other half is pink. She's wearing scuffed leather boots held together with duct tape. She's grinning.

Laura averts her eyes.

The girl meets Virginia's gaze.

Laura swallows.

Virginia reaches down and yanks the power cord from the wall.

There is a final, thundering crash as the speakers overload. Sparks carve out the darkness.

Virginia returns to the altar in silence.

She elbows her way past Brad into the stalls. She lifts her chin. She starts to sing.

Glory be to the Father, and to the Son, and to the Holy Ghost.

The boys look at one another. Then they join in.

As it was in the beginning, is now, and ever shall be. World without end. Amen.

"Disgusting," Bonnie repeats all the way back across Devonshire Quad.

Some people, she says, just get off on destroying things. That's the problem with Isobel Zhao, or people like Isobel Zhao—always looking to criticize, to tear things down; they don't care about St. Dunstan's, or Evensong, or beauty or art at all. They have no reverence for what's gorgeous in the world.

"And poor Tipton!"

He must be heartbroken. His very first Evensong, ever, at St. Dunstan's, all the way across the Atlantic, and look at the sort of welcome he gets.

"I should write him a welcome card," Bonnie says. "Make sure he knows we aren't *all* philistines, here."

"I thought it was funny," Freddy says.

"That's because you have no *soul.*"

They get back to Desmond. Freddy leaves them on the second floor.

Laura sits on the bed in silence, listening to Bonnie chatter.

She suddenly feels so hideously lonely.

It's not that she disagrees with Bonnie, exactly. It broke her heart, too, in some sense, that someone could listen to music like that—oh, she thinks again, that *music!*—and want to profane it, for nothing more than a silly prank, and yet somehow Bonnie's garrulous outrage makes her feel even more at sea than the prank itself.

Webster, she tells herself, would have understood.

She nods at Bonnie a little while longer, as Bonnie frets about poor Brad, and how hard it must have been for *him*—working as hard as he does on the choir, to have people disrespect his efforts like that—and if anybody needs admiration and respect and an attentive audience it's a child of divorce with commitment issues, and then Laura can stand it no longer.

"I'm going to take a shower," she says.

Bonnie barely looks up. "Suit yourself," she says.

Laura spends twenty minutes in the shower, even though she's clean after five. After, she brushes her teeth as slowly as she can manage.

Behind her, someone turns off one of the showers.

Virginia Strauss steps out toward the sink.

She is wearing a towel. Her hair goes down to her waist. She has five inches on Laura. Her hair smells like figs.

"You're blocking my toiletries box," she says.

"Sorry." Laura realizes, too late, that she has toothpaste in her mouth. It dribbles onto her chin.

Virginia starts to brush her teeth.

Laura overflows with all the things she wants to say to her. She wants to ask her what it was like, singing like that, and whether she really *was* in ecstasy or whether she just looked that way; and whether it's intentional, the way the end of every line sounds like dying; and whether she chose Stanford's Magnificat in C on purpose, because of Webster, or whether that was just one of those coincidences that makes you believe in the enchanted order of the whole world; and also whether she has ever been as lonely as Laura has always been, before coming here; and whether she is less lonely now, but Laura knows you cannot ask a stranger any of these things, so she sighs and then she stammers and then at last she expels, so lamely, "That was a really beautiful service."

Virginia just looks at her.

"I mean, other than the prank." Laura can't stop herself. "I mean, even with the prank, the music was still so *gorgeous*. I mean, I—I'm sorry that that happened to you. It's wrong, doing something like that, ruining the atmosphere, not that it was ruined, obviously, but—"

Virginia spits into the sink.

"That atmosphere?"

"I mean, you know, the music, and the . . ."

"It's a service of worship. It's not supposed to be *gorgeous*."

"I didn't mean . . ."

"If you want gorgeous music"—Virginia wrenches the faucet shut—"I suggest you go listen to the Dewey Decibel System."

She leaves Laura, fumbling, in the middle of the bathroom floor.

Laura composes herself in the mirror, trying not to cry.

What an idiot you are, she tells herself.

Only an idiot would use a gossipy hashtag of a word like *gorgeous* to describe something as rapturous as Evensong. Only an idiot would try to talk about *atmosphere*, as if St. Dunstan's were nothing but an Instagram background. She should have said something about Webster at least, or at least correctly identified the Magnificat they'd sung as being by Stanford, something—anything—to convey that, even if she isn't the kind of person who can sing with such savage clarity, then at least that she appreciates when other people do.

Finally, finally, she's found someone who gets it: who understands about souls and shipwrecks—and she's already ruined it. She doesn't begrudge Virginia her rudeness. Laura knows she deserves it. She's no better than Bonnie—making everything profound foul and dull and performative.

Laura's face still burns. She welcomes the shame.

It's reminding her how much better she can be.

Next time she sees Virginia, she tells herself, she will be ready. She'll have prepared. She will show Virginia that she understands Evensong, in all its rapturous and inhuman glory, that she knows that it is so much more than *atmosphere.*

By the time Laura gets back to room 312, Bonnie is already in her pajamas, poring over videos of the prank on her phone.

Laura gets into bed. She puts in her earbuds. She hunts for a recording of the Stanford Magnificat, one that sounds, even a little bit, like the way Virginia sounds when she sings it. She raises the volume, loud enough to drown out Bonnie's intermittent and disapproving sniffs.

Laura listens to it on repeat until she falls asleep.

2

LAURA SPENDS THE NEXT WEEK STALKING VIRGINIA.

Not that she speaks to her. She doesn't dare. Anyway, she barely gets the chance. She sees her only in glimpses. There she is, bent over coffee and textbooks at Keble at breakfast time; there she is, galloping across Devonshire Quad, with sheet music flying from her spidery arms; there she is, sitting straight-backed in Assembly.

Anyway, Virginia is never alone.

The choirboys—all handsome; all ebullient; all terrifying—are always with her. She holds court with them at the head of the table, or at the center of the picnic blanket. Her eyes are always sharp. She rarely smiles.

The boys' presence only highlights Virginia's uncanny anachronistic femininity: her stiff black skirts and her black silk blouses, with Peter Pan collars closing halfway up her throat; her knotted black fur collars and her inevitable black lace gloves, and the kind of thick black stockings that even Laura knows haven't been in fashion since the '80s, at least. Her hair is always long, and loose, tumbling over her collarbones; her makeup is always daintily applied. She sits, when she sits, with her ankles crossed.

But, Laura soon discovers, Virginia doesn't *sound* like a girl. Her voice is loud and throaty—so unlike the eerie soprano of her singing voice—carrying across Assembly, or Keble, dominating the indistinguishable hum of the boys' voices. Her laugh (Laura is astounded the first time she sees her laugh) is guttural. She cuts people off mid-sentence. When she talks she thumps on the table for emphasis.

The boys don't seem to mind.

When she talks, they turn their faces up, like plants tendrilling to the light. They sit motionless after mealtimes, their plates empty and their hands in their laps, until Virginia decides it's time to go, and then they pick up their trays with a single military thud and file out after her. They fetch coffee for her, without her asking, and throw their blazers over her shoulders when the wind blows inland from the coast.

Laura, aided by Bonnie's exhaustive compendium of gossip, feels like she knows them. There's Brad, of course, and his roommate, an astoundingly handsome, broad-chested senior called Anton Gallagher: who narrowly beat Isobel Zhao for student council, who (Bonnie breathlessly whispers) wakes up at four thirty every morning to make raw-garlic shakes for breakfast in the Morris Hall kitchen because he read online that it's good for a person's concentration. The mournful-looking senior is called Ralph Ervin; who's from Chicago, who is (Bonnie says) writing a roman à clef about his time at St. Dunstan's and whose mother is a once-famous actress he refers to only as Sadie. The fastidiously dressed junior is Barry Ng, who got his start as a church organist in San Francisco and who (Brad told Bonnie once) is a kind of musical genius, who can play pretty much every sonata ever written without even looking at the music and is probably going to Juilliard one day. Then there is twitchy little Ivan Dixon—a sophomore; a baby—who was homeschooled in Montana by a couple of evangelicals who don't even believe in evolution, and who was only allowed to come here at all because his parents heard St. Dunstan's had mandatory church.

"When he got here, he didn't even know how babies were made," Bonnie chirps. "Brad had to make him a PowerPoint."

Laura knows she can never dare approach them as a group. She pins her hopes on running into Virginia in Desmond. She takes increasingly long morning showers, listening for Virginia's footsteps, but succeeds only in using up all the hot water on the floor, making an accidental enemy of a shivering, limp-haired senior called Yvette Saunders who snappishly informs her that this is rural Maine, not the Ritz-Carlton, and she should probably start acting like it. By Wednesday afternoon, Laura concludes despairingly that Virginia might as well not live in Desmond at all.

Social media is no help. Virginia doesn't even have Instagram.

At last Laura finds an excuse to mention Virginia's absence to Bonnie. She tries to be oblique and worries, immediately, that she's been obvious.

Bonnie doesn't notice.

"Oh, she's *never* in the dorms. She gets up, like, crazy early. Like, *fives*-early."

Five o'clock at St. Dunstan's, Bonnie explains, is the official line of demarcation between *night*, when leaving your dorm means risking expulsion, and *morning*, when you can go anywhere you want, so long as it's technically in Weymouth.

"It's why everyone picks it as a time to fuck," Freddy adds. "Even if you get caught, the worst you'll get is early curfew."

Only: Virginia Strauss doesn't fuck.

"She *runs*." Bonnie sighs. "That's why she's so thin." She blows out her lips. "God, the *discipline*!"

Virginia runs every morning, Bonnie says. Sometimes also at night. She comes back at curfew, just as the bell rings. She goes straight to her room and studies until morning, which is how—everyone at St. Dunstan's knows this—she's the only person in the whole school to get straight As every term.

"Brad says she doesn't sleep," Bonnie says. "Maybe it's just cocaine," she adds as a hopeful afterthought.

Laura doesn't set an actual alarm—she can't risk Bonnie's curiosity—but spends the night in fractious semi-somnolence, and by the next morning, at four forty-five, she is bleary-eyed but awake, listening to Bonnie gurgle contentedly in her sleep.

Laura goes to the window. She opens it. She waits. She inhales the salt of dawn—if she cranes her neck, she can just about make out the water. She lets the breeze settle on her tongue. She watches the black, stark emptiness of Devonshire Quad, punctuated by those few, furtive figures sneaking between dorms. Light splinters across the sky.

At five o'clock exactly, Laura sees her, slipping out the Desmond door.

Her hair is tightened into a bun, which makes her look even taller and spikier than usual.

Laura leans a little farther out the window.

Virginia looks up. Laura stumbles back from the window so quickly Bonnie moans in consternation. But Virginia remains still, implacable, scanning the horizon.

She snaps into motion; then she is gone: beyond Laura's field of vision; toward the woods that lead to Farnham Cliff, and the Webster statue, and to the coastal road beyond, leaving the quadrangle strangely bereft.

Laura creeps back into bed.

She can't make herself sleep. She stares at the ceiling, trying to piece Virginia together: her stark beauty, and the sound of her voice, and that sharp way she said *atmosphere* and that glorious way she sang *my soul*; her face in ecstasy and the bun tight upon her head, and the way the boys all seem to worship her, and her grades, the fact that she does not sleep, her voice at Evensong. Laura has the inchoate sense that these are all twined together, somehow; you could no more dissociate Virginia's ecstasy from her cruelty than you could take salt out of the sea.

Laura wonders what it would be like to sing with her.

"I mean, *technically*," Bonnie says, later that morning, when Laura wonders, with studied nonchalance, if choir holds auditions. "You *could*. If you wanted." Technically, *all* extracurriculars are supposed to be open to everyone, at least for auditions. The faculty makes the decisions. Bonnie wrinkles her nose. "But Heeno never bothered." She giggles. "Brad says he was completely deaf by the end of last year. Virginia would pick, and he'd just sign the forms. Brad says—"

Laura is no longer listening.

Probably it's better that way, she tells herself. Probably getting close to them would ruin it. They'd have to be real people, if she got to know them, and then they wouldn't be characters in Webster any longer.

How much better, she thinks, just to be able to watch them every week, like some rapt, adoring ghost; better to listen to them, to close her eyes and pretend that she is in Webster's world—without having to convince them to love her back.

It's not so different, she thinks, from reading Webster.

Laura doesn't mind sitting alone: on the quad, at the library, in Keble for dinner, avoiding Bonnie's line of sight. She puts in earbuds. She reads. She looks out the window and watches the light change on the chapel spires. She's even happy.

Laura has gotten so comfortable with this silence that by the end of dinner, she doesn't realize that somebody is calling to her as she walks out of Keble Hall.

"Oi!"

Laura whirls around in confusion.

"New girl!"

Isobel Zhao is sitting at a stall table in the Keble foyer. Her pink hair is slicked back with gel; the shaved side has started to grow in. A redheaded girl in a blue polka-dot dress is sitting next to her.

"Wanna take a stand against oppression?" Isobel's grin is inscrutable.

"I—uh—sure?"

Isobel slams down a clipboard.

"Sign right here."

In seventy-two-point font:

On the second line, a little smaller:

Campaign to Abolish Mandatory Evensong

It has forty-eight signatures.

"Fifty, and we get to present it in Assembly. I've read the bylaws. They don't publicize it, of course. That's how they get you. But they have to hold a hearing—and the faculty have to vote."

"Always read the bylaws." The redheaded girl grins.

"Abolish Evensong?" Laura's heart sinks.

They both nod.

"I mean . . ." Laura tries to buy time. "Why?"

"Why?" Isobel twirls the words. "Why, in this progressive and enlightened—relatively enlightened, I mean, obviously; the world still sucks—in this progressive and relatively enlightened age of ours, are we formally required"—she closes her eyes—"*to humbly confess our sins to an Almighty God*?" She opens them again. "I mean—come on." She slides the petition across the table.

"I . . . kind of like it," says Laura, and then immediately regrets her own cowardice.

Isobel is undeterred. "Nobody's stopping you," she says. "You want to go, go. Be my guest."

"What matters is the choice," the redheaded girl cuts in. "It should be optional. Like drama. Or sports."

"Hence the *M*." Isobel taps *Mandatory* with her pencil. She considers Laura.

"Look," she says, "let's be real. The *only* reason it's mandatory is because the alums love it. Our bougie-ass donors would have a conniption if St. Dunstan's no longer had"—she chews through a mid-Atlantic accent—"the *last of the traditional prep school chapel choirs* in the country. It's, like, tourism for them."

"So they can relive their lost youth," adds the redheaded girl.

"Whereas we *actual* youths think it's weird and gross to have to pretend to pray once a week. And—like, this school's *for* the students, right?"

Laura doesn't say anything.

"Right?"

"I mean"—Laura tries to think of an inoffensive refusal—"but . . . the tradition?"

Isobel kicks out her boots. "Please," she snorts. "*Tradition*'s just a fancy word for dumb shit people are too lazy to change."

The redheaded girl murmurs agreement.

"*We're* not lazy," Isobel adds, with an ambiguous grin. "We're revolutionaries."

Laura is still not entirely sure how much she's joking. She's not sure Isobel knows.

Laura weighs her options. She knows she can't sign Isobel's petition—not when Evensong is the only thing that makes her feel close to the St. Dunstan's of Webster. And yet, she can't quite justify not signing it, either, because of *course* a person shouldn't have to go to church if they don't want to, even if the donors love the music.

She has the sense Isobel won't be satisfied with incoherence.

"I, uh," she begins carefully, "I mean, I'd want to give it some serious thought, obviously. I definitely don't want to—"

Isobel is no longer looking at her.

Virginia has just entered the foyer. Brad and Anton flank her.

"Oi," Isobel calls. "Strauss!"

Virginia pretends not to hear.

"Strauss!" Isobel calls again, like she isn't even afraid of her. "How'd you like to take a stand against oppression?"

The redheaded girl digs her fingernails into the back of Isobel's hand.

Virginia turns.

"Isobel," she says slowly, between clenched teeth.

Laura lowers her gaze.

"Fight the power?" Isobel is enjoying herself. "Bring down the man? Rage against the machine? Live free or die?" She taps the clipboard once more. "All you have to do is sign!"

"Jesus!" Anton takes a step toward her. "Not this shit again."

Virginia says nothing. She considers Isobel with a tight, cold expression.

"Come on, buddy," Isobel says. "Live a little. Two more signatures, and we can duke it out onstage like men. You plus Strauss makes fifty."

"You really never let up, do you?" Anton turns back, in appeal, to Virginia. "She never lets up!"

Virginia says nothing. Laura takes another step back, out of her field of vision, and realizes too late that she has trapped herself against the wall.

Anton rolls his eyes. "If you hate it here so much . . ."

"We don't hate it here." The redheaded girl tightens her grip on Isobel's hand. "We actually *care* enough to want to make it better. You should try it sometime."

Anton rolls his eyes.

"Sure, better, yeah. Getting rid of our history—what a real improvement."

The redhead sniffs. "We just don't think people should be *forced* to *worship* at . . ."

"What, you think you'll touch a crucifix and melt?"

"Think about it." Now she has leaped to her feet. She's still holding Isobel's hand. "Think really hard. What *possible* reason could people like us have for being uncomfortable in church?"

"Like Reverend Tipton cares about your sex life!"

"It's not about Reverend Tipton, Anton, and you know it! It's about this whole goddamn—"

"I hate, I despise your festivals," says Brad suddenly. "I take no delight in your solemn assemblies." It is the first thing he has said since they've come in.

Everybody stares at him for a moment, baffled.

"Amos," he says.

He puts his hands in his pockets. He looks at his shoes.

Isobel leans her elbows on the table.

"Honestly, Strauss, I don't see your problem," Isobel says, shrugging. "I'd have thought this'd be heaven for you. No shitty plebes ruining your precious Evensong?" She cocks her head at Virginia.

Virginia doesn't change her expression. "Give me a pen."

Anton and Brad look at her in confusion. They fumble in their pockets simultaneously.

"She's right," Virginia says. Her voice is sharp and clipped. "This *should* go to debate."

Virginia takes Brad's pen. Anton flushes. Virginia steps forward.

"If you're going to go around," she says, "spewing moronic things about chapel, you should have to defend them. And not just by playing pranks on freshmen."

She signs in a single calligraphic slant. She considers the sheet. "Forty-nine," she says. She looks up. "You!"

Her gaze falls on Laura, still trapped against the wall.

"Me?"

Virginia holds out her pen.

Laura takes it. She steadies her hands.

"Go on—sign!"

Laura signs.

Virginia is still watching Isobel. Her expression is inscrutable.

"I look forward," Virginia says at last, "to watching your debate."

She is gone before Isobel can reply. The boys shuffle after her.

"God," Miranda says when they've gone. "What a cunt!" Her cheeks are scarlet.

"Miranda, don't!"

"Sorry. She's a dick. Better?"

"That's not what I meant." Isobel considers the paper. "She got us to fifty."

"She didn't do it to be nice—"

"Who cares?" Isobel starts shuffling papers. "We've got fifty." She looks up at Laura. "Thanks."

"I mean—I didn't really do anything."

"You signed. I'm grateful. I'm Isobel, by the way." Isobel launches out her hand. "This is Miranda. She's my cultural attaché." She puts her other arm around Miranda's shoulder.

"I'm Laura."

"You're new, right?"

Laura nods.

Isobel considers her. "You can't be a freshman, though."

"New junior."

"Good," Isobel says. "I'd feel pretty guilty offering cigarettes to a freshman."

"I . . ." Laura succumbs to Isobel's force of will. "Thank you." She's never smoked before. "But—*here?*" The quad is so full of people.

Isobel and Miranda trade glances. They turn back to Laura together.

"*We* smoke in the woods," Isobel announces, as if this confers superiority. "By Farnham Cliff. Campus security never goes there." She checks her phone. "It's only seven. We've got three hours until curfew. I'll spot you *two*, even." Isobel considers. "Never let it be said I'm not hospitable."

Isobel and Miranda take Laura across Devonshire Quad. They pass the sports fields; they cross the woods.

The sun is setting now; the birches shot through with rose. They follow a single narrow trail, where repetitive footfalls have trammeled the leaves. The smell of brine is stronger here than inland; the salt on the wind lacerates Laura's lips. Isobel keeps her arm around Miranda's waist.

"What dorm are you in?"

"Desmond."

"Got a roommate?"

"Bonnie di Angelis?"

"Yikes." Isobel exhales. "Hope you own earplugs."

"She's not so bad," Laura says, more out of pity than conviction. "I mean, she's . . . nice."

"Ugh, *nice*."

"Poor Bonnie," Miranda murmurs.

Isobel speeds up. "*Poor* Bonnie—really?"

"People are awful to her!"

"Please. Bonnie deserves exactly what she gets. If I spent my days running around, doing *Dead Poets* cosplay to get the attention of a couple of privileged assholes, I wouldn't expect a world of sympathy when it turned out they didn't like me."

"She just wants to be their friend," Miranda says. "It's not a crime to want to be liked."

"It is when you're wanting to be liked by bad people," Isobel says. She turns to Laura. She raises her voice. "Bonnie di Angelis"—Isobel takes a deep breath—"is willfully complicit in the reification of the morally bankrupt class-wankery that is the white-boarding-school aesthetic." She turns to Laura. "Ever heard of commodity fetishism?" Then, to Laura's relief— "Watch out!"

They've come to the end of the woods. There is a narrow path of barren land, about three feet wide, and then a rough sheer drop that juts straight into the ocean.

It is the first time since her arrival at St. Dunstan's that Laura's seen the water up close: the staggering vastness of the dark; the sky, the water melding into each other. It's just like that scene, the one eight chapters in, that Laura knows by heart, the one where Gus and Shrimpy and Robert dare one another to jump off this exact cliff, into the churning waters below, the one where Gus breaks his arm, and Shrimpy almost drowns, and Robert makes it to the surface but spends the next fifty pages half wishing that he hadn't, because if he can do this, then he can do anything, even kill somebody, and the idea makes him feel so horribly alone.

Laura watches the foam rear against the cliffs.

"Never do this drunk," Isobel says. She goes toward the end of the cliff, scooping Miranda with her at the waist. She nods toward the downhill slope. "There's a few cliffs down *there*," she says. "They're safer. And down there's Bethel Beach, if you ever want to swim—though I wouldn't; you'll freeze your tits off." She turns in the opposite direction. "And *there's* . . ."

"Jarvis Lighthouse!"

"Someone's been reading the brochure."

Isobel takes a cigarette out from her bag.

"You *do* smoke, right?"

"Uh-huh," says Laura.

"Don't ever play poker."

"Don't corrupt the child!"

Isobel twines her fingers through Miranda's. "I'll have you know," she tells Laura, "Miranda corrupted *me*. Robbed me, straight out of the cradle. I wasn't even out yet." She looks back at Laura. "So, Laura Stearns, how'd you like to try your very first cigarette?"

Laura decides.

"I'd like that very much," she says.

Isobel brings Miranda's hand to her lips. "You see," she chirps. "She *wants* to be corrupted."

"Who doesn't?" Miranda leans her head on Isobel's shoulder. Isobel lights Laura's cigarette.

Laura immediately hacks up phlegm.

"Careful!" Miranda pats her on the back.

"Guess Strauss is right about us after all." Isobel's smile twitches. "Wreaking havoc wherever we go."

Laura has spent five whole minutes not vexing herself over Virginia. "Why do you hate her so much?"

Miranda's ears turn pink.

"I mean," she says. "How many reasons do you need? She's a self-centered, narcissistic, manipulative . . ."

But Isobel just grimaces. "The problem is," she says at last, "she's repressed. And repression—it warps people. Fucks with them in ways you can't imagine." She blows out a puff of her cigarette. "Honestly, it's tragic."

"Please! You can't give *Bonnie* shit, then turn around and defend—"

"Well, it's true," Isobel says. She straightens her back. She shakes out some ash from her cigarette. "She wasn't like that before."

"They were roommates," Miranda cuts in. "In Latimer. Their freshman year. Until, you know, she found Jesus. And, God forbid, Jesus sees her living with a—"

"That shit's a cancer," Isobel says suddenly.

"What is?"

"God. Fuck that guy."

"I . . ." Laura waits for a thunderbolt. None comes.

"Haven't you heard?" Isobel puffs out more smoke. "We're all going to burn in hell—the gays, the feminists. Probably the Catholics, too.

Poor Miranda—you're fucked." She strokes Miranda's hair. "My father thinks she's my roommate, you know. And a Protestant."

Laura isn't sure what to say. "I'm sorry."

"No worries," Isobel says. "He's old. I'm over it." She puts out the last of her cigarette on a rock. "I just have a pretty low tolerance for people *our* age, in this day and age, who go around blowing their tops off about hell."

"Virginia thinks that?"

The idea is so strange to her. Hell is an idea *other* people have, the people with picket signs outside the Bellagio, or on street corners, or maybe in the sweaty megachurches Laura's family always drives past on their way to Costco.

"She doesn't." Miranda makes a face. "Not really. She's just trolling. She thinks it makes her special—"

"No." Isobel is no longer smiling. "She believes it." She swallows. "You can say one good thing about Virginia Strauss—she's a serious person. She's just got some fucked-up ideas. And some fucked-up enablers."

"You mean—the boys."

"Dipshits," Miranda scoffs. "They blow so much smoke up her ass it's a wonder she can sit down."

"What's wrong with them?"

"What *isn't* wrong with them?" Isobel snaps. "Virginia—she may be a zealot, but you can respect her. This stuff matters to her. Them? They're just—bored, rich idiots with a hard-on for anything that predates the civil rights movement." She leans against a birch tree. "When the revolution comes: first against the wall. Mark my words." She makes a little gun with her fingers. She shoots into the waves. "Pew pew."

Laura feels a little braver. "Last week at Evensong . . . How did you do it?"

"Chapel laptop. Our friend knows the admin passwords."

Miranda starts to giggle. "God, their *faces* ..." She does an uncanny impersonation of Anton, flailing in his choir robes.

"Desperate times," Isobel says, lighting another cigarette. "Guerrilla tactics. *Vive la révolution.*"

"God, that poor priest!" Miranda's laugh fades. "I did feel bad for him. Almost."

"Please," Isobel says. "Heeno was senile. He probably thinks we're still in Vietnam. This new guy's, what, thirty? He has no excuse." She considers. "Lloyd Tipton." She chews the words. "Poor dumb bastard. You know, he's not even smart enough to lie about his name on Tinder."

"*What?*"

Isobel raises her phone. "I mean, I'm sure they're all on it. How else do you get laid in a town of two thousand? But the rest of them know to use fake names, so disgruntled assholes like us don't troll them." She shows Laura the screenshot. *Lloyd, 31.*

Miranda cranes out her neck. "Ugh, check out the bio."

"*Looking for a poetically minded young lady for seaside walks, candlelit dinners, and claret. Must love Keats.* Look—he even used his *Oxford graduation* as one of the photos. Complete cringe."

"Aren't priests supposed to be celibate?" Laura asks.

"Just the Catholic ones," Miranda says. "Not that they listen."

"Too busy fucking little boys."

"You're not going to message him, are you?" Laura can't help feeling a little sorry for Lloyd Tipton. She has the vague sense that, if she were ever brave enough to be on Tinder, she'd probably be completely cringe herself.

"God, no," Isobel says. "Strictly stalking purposes. Maybe a screenshot or two, if I feel puckish. Besides, I can sit back and relax." She smiles, half to herself. "Strauss'll eat him alive." She looks up. "Oh, look, our favorite fascist."

They are right in front of the Webster statue.

It is the first time Laura has seen it up close. It looks just like the picture of him, the only surviving one there is, on the back of her copy of *All Before Them*: a blaze-eyed schoolboy with full, womanish lips and a strangely mystical expression.

"*Come, shipwreck my soul,*" Isobel reads the inscription. "How sweet."

She puts out her cigarette on the statue base. Then she draws, with the remainder of the ash, a small but unmistakable Hitler mustache over Sebastian Webster's lips.

"There," she says. "Much better."

Laura swallows down her horror. "I don't understand," she says. "What's wrong with Webster?"

Miranda and Isobel both turn their gaze on her at the same time.

"Christ," Isobel says. "Don't tell me you're one of those."

"One of what?" Laura asks, with a sinking feeling that she *is*.

"Blah blah blah, poetic genius, blah blah blah, *prep school prophet*, blah, blah, teen mystic, blah, blah, Catholic, blah blah boats, blah blah Spanish Civil War."

"It's not even that good," Miranda says.

It is too late for Laura to stop herself. "But it's wonderful!" She sees the looks on their faces.

"Seriously?" says Isobel. "What's so good about it?"

"I . . ." It is the only thing in the world Laura is sure of. "I mean, it's about love, and beauty, and growing up!"

"Please. It's about rich white boys who feel sorry for themselves for being too young to die in World War One."

"It's *not!*" Laura is horribly aware of how foolish she sounds, but she cannot bring herself to sacrifice the point. "It's—about—about how some things are worth dying for."

"Sebastian Webster"—Isobel's nostrils flare—"died fighting for Franco. If a fucking *fascist dictator* is your idea of *worth dying for* then, yeah, happy to stay alive, thanks."

Laura flushes.

She knows, of course, in some vague and theoretical way, that Webster *technically* died fighting on the Francoist side—but that has always seemed to her beyond the point, somehow, like caring whether someone in the War of the Roses fought for Lancaster or York.

"But . . ." Laura tries. "Isn't the point that he died for what he believed in?"

They look back at her, unimpressed.

"So what did he believe in?"

Laura doesn't have an answer for this one, either.

"You know what your problem is, Laura?" says Isobel, with the blithe assurance of someone used to telling people what their problems are. "You're young. When you're young, you want to make excuses for everyone."

Laura is pretty sure that she and Isobel are the same age.

"The thing about growing up," Isobel says, "is that you learn that sometimes, bad people are just bad people. And most people, in the end, are bad people."

"Except us." Miranda winks. "We're awesome."

Laura doesn't say anything.

"Don't worry." Isobel pinches Laura's arm, trying to force a smile. "I bet you're a good person, too, where it counts."

Laura doesn't say anything to that, either.

·   ·   ·

It is eight thirty by the time they get back to Devonshire Quad, smelling of briny breeze and cigarette smoke. Isobel and Miranda turn onto the path to Latimer Hall.

"The missus and I," Isobel says, "are going to retire." She touches Laura's shoulder. "Remember what I told you." She taps a fist on her chest. "*Vive la révolution!*"

They leave Laura alone in the middle of the quad.

It can't be true, she thinks. Whatever Sebastian Webster was or wasn't, she thinks, he *couldn't* be a bad person, at least not in the way Isobel means. Laura has read *All Before Them* so many times. She has memorized so many of its pages. Nobody who wrote like that, Laura thinks, stirring herself into further certainty the more she thinks it, who wrote with such intensity, with such beauty, with such pure and violent faith in the goodness and sanctity of things, could ever be a bad person.

Laura lingers on the quad. She shivers a little in the wind.

She can't go back to Desmond. She couldn't stand Bonnie's trilled interruptions encroaching on the worry in her soul.

The light is still on in the chapel. The great oak door has been left open, although the room is empty. The electric lights cast the stained glass in a warm, embery glow.

It's a relief to be alone. Alone, Laura can sit in the pews; alone she can gaze up at the lighthouse Madonna, the one Sebastian Webster loved so much; alone she can love it, in her jealous, hangdog way, without worrying whether that makes her a bad person, too.

Isobel is wrong, Laura decides. She *has* to be wrong.

Laura wonders if Isobel is wrong about Virginia Strauss.

She sits for a while, breathing in the stagnant air, which still smells like candle wax.

Then she notices the door.

The little iron grille door behind the altar, the one leading to the stairwell down to the crypt, the one that has been locked every time Laura has been in here, is finally open.

Laura's heart beats a little faster.

She tiptoes across the marble floors, crossing the altar. She averts her gaze from the Stella Maris. She doesn't know why. After all, she tells herself, it's not like she's doing anything wrong, just walking through a door that happens to be open.

She tiptoes down the spiral stairs, steadying herself against the stone. Her hands press moss. The dank, wet smell of mildew gets stronger and more pungent as she descends. Her eyes adjust to the absence of light.

Laura turns a final corner into the crypt.

The room is dark. A single candle flickers in the corner of the room, illuminating a few carved marble inches. Laura takes a few tentative steps into the shadows. She feels along the marble walls of the crypt, making her way toward the candle.

Then a figure stirs in the darkness.

Laura yelps.

"*Jesus!*"

"Oh my God! I'm so sorry. I—"

The lights flicker on.

Virginia Strauss is staring at her.

She is standing, between the candle and the light switch, in a long black dress that goes all the way to her ankles. A string of beads wraps around her fist. Her eyes are red. "What do you want?"

"I'm so sorry. God, I'm so—I mean—I didn't know anyone was down here. I just— I'm sorry. I'll go."

She turns back toward the stairs.

"Wait." Virginia is peering at her with new interest. "What are you doing here?"

"I wanted to see the crypt." Laura swallows. "It's been locked since I got here, and then I saw the door was finally open...."

"That's because I'm the only one with the key," Virginia says. "Choir president privilege." Her mouth twitches in what Laura hopes is a smile. "I'm guessing you're not here for Heeno?" She cocks her head toward a smaller, newly carved memorial stone in the south wall.

"No," Laura says. "No—I'm here for ... for *him*."

She nods at the slab. She can make out the letters, now, immaculately etched into the marble: SEBASTIAN OLIVER WEBSTER, 1917–1936.

Virginia traces her fingers along the stone.

"Nineteen," Virginia says softly, "and he still accomplished more than most of the people here will in their entire lives." She glides her tongue along her lips. "Telling, isn't it?"

"You ..." Laura wants to say, *So you love him, too.* But the word *love* feels so ordinary, and so dissolves on her tongue.

"He understood things," Virginia goes on; then Laura can exhale. "I mean—about what matters."

"Exactly!" Laura says. "That—that bit in the chapel, at the end. It makes me cry every time I read it. The line about the harbor and the rocks!"

"*The rocks and the harbor are one*," Virginia says. She arches a challenging eyebrow. "He's out of fashion, you know, these days. Maybe you've heard."

Laura remembers Miranda and Isobel.

"I—I know people—don't like the Franco thing," Laura says. "I mean, I know, that part looks bad. But—that's not the point, though, is it? I mean, he wasn't a fascist or anything." She looks at Virginia with something like appeal. "Was he?"

"Of course he wasn't," Virginia snaps. "He was a mystic—and he wanted to fight for people who still believed in mystics. He was on the side of transcendence. That's all." She leans against the crypt wall—almost possessively, Laura thinks, as if it belonged to her. "You've been talking to Isobel Zhao."

Laura makes a noncommittal noise.

"The problem with Isobel Zhao," Virginia says, "is that she has zero sense of transcendence."

Laura can't tell if she's joking, either.

"She's been infected," Virginia hesitates, just for a moment, "by the *sclerotic modern world.*"

Laura nods, too quickly, so that Virginia will know she has gotten the reference.

"She can't understand, you know, what it means to have a calling that subsumes politics. She wants to be World-Historical, too. In her way. Even if she pretends she doesn't. But she doesn't get what it means, not really. She wants to apply today's standards to Webster—as if he weren't a totally singular person." She sighs, like it's obvious. "It's not her fault, of course. If you don't have a grasp of the absolute, all you have to go on is the vagaries of the present. And then it's relativism, all the way down."

"Right," Laura says, trying and failing to keep up. "Relativism."

"Obviously, you *can't* be any kind of realist without a metaphysical grounding."

"A metaphysical grounding?"

"You know. God."

"Oh. Right." Laura tries to find a tactful way to put it. "I heard that you were super . . . I mean, that you're really . . ."

"Really what?"

"Christian?"

"Oh." Virginia's gaze falls on her hands. The rosary is still twisted in her fingers. She smiles. "No."

"But—"

"Not technically." She twirls the rosary some more.

"Technically?"

"I haven't been baptized, yet."

"But . . . you believe?"

"In God, you mean?"

"I mean in everything. Jesus. Heaven." Laura shudders. "Hell?"

"If there *is* a God," Virginia says, "there has to be a hell. It's the only thing that makes sense. Every force has got to have an equal and opposite force. If you take Good and Evil seriously. Which I do." She cocks her head at Laura. "Maybe that's unfashionable, too." She smiles again, and once more Laura is conscious of exactly how beautiful she is.

"I mean . . ." Laura tries to put her thoughts into words. "For really evil people, I guess. Like Hitler or someone." This makes her think of Franco; this makes her blush.

"Hideous, isn't it?" Virginia says. "The whole idea. Eternal suffering." She twists the rosary tighter. "That's how I know I can believe in it. That it's not just me projecting what I *want* to be true onto God. I think when something really horrifies you, it's more reliable than if it just feels gooey and nice and dull."

"But, you don't think that, like, I don't know, Isobel and Miranda are going to . . ."

"I would not deign," Virginia says, with lofty tightness, "to speculate as to the fate of Isobel Zhao's soul."

She leans her full weight against the crypt wall. "What's your name?"

"Laura."

"Laura what?"

"Stearns."

"Where are you from, Laura Stearns?"

"Henderson. Nevada."

Virginia's face is blank.

"Near Las Vegas?"

"Vegas." Virginia smiles. "Really?" She looks Laura up and down, as if trying to place her in the taxonomy of sins. "Sin City?"

"I mean . . . it's not really like that. I know people *call* it that—but . . ." Laura feels a sudden, strange pang of protectiveness. "There were a lot of beautiful things there. Even if they *were*—I don't know, tacky or something."

Virginia's gaze flickers over her. "And you read Webster." It isn't a question.

Laura is relieved to be back on the subject. "I just—I mean, he makes you *see* things. He makes you feel like things matter."

Virginia nods. "Before I read Webster," she says, "I didn't believe in anything. I was a total nihilist." She smiles at this, too, archly, and Laura has the sudden sense that Virginia might be laughing at herself, at least a little. "I probably owe him my soul."

She watches Laura watching her. She waits, for a moment, taking in Laura's gaze, her dark mouth twitching against the whiteness of her skin.

She suddenly leans forward, pressing her purple lips against the crypt wall, right over the *S*, keeping her eyes on Laura the whole time. Then she pulls back, patting the stone with idle affection.

"Sometimes," she says, "I think he's the only man I'll ever really love."

Laura still isn't sure whether or not she's joking.

Virginia closes her eyes. "It's why I like to come down here," she says. "When I want to be alone. Or to pray."

Laura's eyes fall on the beads. "You pray at Evensong, though?"

"It's different," Virginia says. "With all those people. It's less personal. It's obviously more of a performance—even if you don't want it to be."

"The other week"—Laura remembers her earlier humiliation—"when I said *gorgeous*, I didn't mean, in some, you know, *aesthetic* way—"

"I was awfully rude to you, wasn't I?"

It isn't an apology. Laura doesn't mind.

"It's just that I hate it," Virginia goes on, a little louder, "when people don't take things seriously." She is no longer smiling. "It makes me furious. It feels like a violation, somehow. When people take something that's meant to be great and serious and about God, and turn it into something petty and silly and—and—pornographic."

"I'd never do that!"

"I thought—you know. That you were like di Angelis." Virginia grimaces. "Wanting to make it into something to show off, and post about, and make part of your *brand*. I saw you sitting together."

"She's my roommate," says Laura. "I mean, they assigned her to—"

"Bonnie di Angelis," Virginia announces, "is the embodiment of everything wrong with the world today. Honestly, it's sickening. It's—it's like the whole horrible spirit of the age, embodied in a single, infuriating person! Do you know, she tried to do a photo shoot in the crypt once?" She falls silent, meditating on Bonnie's many failings.

"It wasn't like that for me," Laura says, too quickly. "It's just, when you sang, that bit of the Stanford Magnificat. God, it was the most"—she will not say *gorgeous*—"transporting thing I ever heard." Laura tries to reproduce the melody. *"My soul doth magnify the Lord."* It echoes off the crypt walls.

Virginia looks up at her.

"Do that again," she says.

Laura does it again.

Virginia closes her eyes. She considers.

"That part's too high for you," Virginia says. "You're an alto."

"I'm sorry," Laura says. "I wouldn't know. I've never—"

"You've never trained?" Now Virginia is peering at her.

Laura shakes her head.

"Come with me," Virginia says.

She blows out the candle. She turns off the light. She marches up the stairs.

"Where are we going?"

"Organ loft."

They cross the altar together. Laura scurries to keep up.

She catches a glimpse of the marble baptismal font.

"Virginia?"

"What?"

"You said you hadn't been baptized."

"Right."

"Why don't you? If you believe."

Virginia is two paces ahead of her.

"I haven't found anyone I trust to baptize me."

Virginia is already at the bottom of the stairs at the front of the chapel, the ones that lead up to the wooden mezzanine over the door.

"What, was I supposed to let Heeno do it? That senile idiot. You know, he admitted in one of his sermons he didn't even believe in the literal Resurrection. Of Christ, obviously," she adds, seeing Laura's befuddlement.

"Called it a *metaphor*. A metaphor! He wasn't a serious person at all. I bet *he'd* never have the nerve to go off and die in Spain. Or anywhere, for that matter. Just died of a heart attack like everyone else. Nobody dies for metaphors."

Virginia strides up into the loft.

"Tipton, though," she says, sliding a sheaf of music off the dusty piano bench. "You know he's got a doctorate? From Oxford. Oxford! I googled him. He wrote his thesis on the Pelagian heresy. Now that's serious." She opens the organ cover. She fingers the keys. "He's someone I'd let baptize me," she says softly. She plays a note on the organ. "There. Sing that."

Laura does.

Virginia looks up at her. "How well do you know the Stanford Magnificat?"

Laura has listened to it 346 times. "I mean—I've heard it on Spotify. . . ."

"Listen, if I sing this . . ." Virginia sings the first line, in her high, trilling soprano. "Can you sing this at the same time?" She plays the alto melody.

"I can try."

"Sit."

Laura can feel Virginia's breath against her cheeks.

"On the count of three," Virginia says. "One, two . . ."

They sing it together: *My soul doth magnify the Lord*, Laura's deep voice and Virginia's light one. The strangeness comes over Laura once again: how two different melodies can become at once single and disparate; something that overflows, as if there is too much of itself for a single note to bear. They go on to *And my spirit hath rejoiced in God my savior*; then, Laura is no longer Laura, but only a vessel for whatever overflowing thing is passing through her, and the sound is both hers and not hers, and she is and is not part of it, and Virginia's hair smells like candle wax, and Laura thinks, This, this is the sound Robert Lawrence heard; this is the thing that could shipwreck your soul, if you only let it; it is a thing her body can do.

"I'm sorry," she tries, hurriedly wiping tears with the back of her hand, "I just . . ." She wipes a globule of snot with her sweater sleeve.

"You really love it, don't you?"

Laura nods.

Virginia looks up at her. Her gaze is so much softer now. "Not even the boys," she murmurs, "love it like that." She inhales. "You have a good voice," she says, with more firmness. "Untrained, but good. Surprisingly good."

She slams the organ cover down.

"Stay after Evensong tomorrow," she says. "For rehearsal."

"*Rehearsal?*"

"For choir," says Virginia. Then: "Unless you don't want to . . . ?"

"Of course I want to!"

"Good. Then it's settled." Virginia stands. "It *will* work you hard, though. You're not afraid of hard work?"

Laura can barely breathe. "I want hard work."

"Remember that," Virginia says, "when you start to hate me."

The bells have started pealing from the chapel tower.

"Curfew," Virginia says. "Don't be late. Mrs. Mesrin is a stickler. She'll put you on a week of early curfew if you're two minutes past eleven."

Laura has forgotten that such things as curfews exist in this world.

They descend the loft steps together, and together go out into the crisp September night. Then Virginia strides wordlessly ahead across the quadrangle and heads toward Desmond Hall alone.

Laura scurries across the quad, trying and failing to make sense of her joy. She has forgotten, by now, the unsettling sourness of her walk with Isobel and Miranda. Now she thinks only Virginia—of Virginia's ferocity and Virginia's otherworldly certainty and that strange, sure way Virginia has of talking about World-History and Good and Evil, as if they are as real and immediate and relevant to the here and now as Keble Hall or curfew. She talks, Laura thinks, like the things they have read about matter. She talks, Laura thinks, folding the knowledge joyfully away, like Webster.

And the singing! Laura tries to call back the feel of the sound in her throat, against her tongue, on her lips. They had sounded so *right* together (not *gorgeous*, she thinks; never *gorgeous*). *She* had sounded right. She sings the alto melody again, under her breath, as she swipes her key card against the Desmond doorway, as she glides up the stairs, imagining Virginia singing the soprano line.

She barely hears the curfew bell, still ringing across campus. She barely registers the moans coming from her room.

She opens the door.

"Oh my God!"

Bonnie is lying, splayed out, on her bright-pink-and-green bed. A pink candle flickers on the bedside table. Bonnie is wearing peach lingerie: a bra, panties, and even those fiddly garters that clip on to the back of roll-up stockings. She's gaping into the camera of her phone.

Laura slams the door shut. "I'm sorry," she calls uselessly through the door. "Sorry."

"Oh, you're fine!" Bonnie chirps, opening the door. She hasn't bothered to put on clothes. "Come on in!"

She bounds back onto the bed.

"Don't worry," Bonnie says. "I'm not embarrassed. I think we should celebrate our sexuality. You know, to reclaim it." She blinks rapidly. "If you ever want the room to yourself, you know, just ask. I won't be mad or anything. Orgasms are good for you." She fixes Laura with her gaze. "They make you live longer."

"I . . ." Laura remembers, suddenly, what Virginia said about Bonnie being the spirit of the age. She can't really imagine Bonnie being the spirit of anything. "Thanks?"

Bonnie unscrews her iPhone from the tripod.

"Anyway," she says. "Don't worry. I *wasn't* masturbating." She considers. "I mean, I *was*, a little, but it wasn't for *me*." Bonnie giggles. "It was for *Brad*." She says this as if it is something they are both complicit in. "I like to send him videos sometimes." She catches a glimpse of herself in the wall mirror and lingers. "To show him what he's missing. We don't get to see each other a lot, you know. Because of choir, and schoolwork, and everything. It's a nice way to remind someone you exist. Everybody does it."

"Sure," says Laura carefully, trying to suggest sympathy without interest. "Of course."

Bonnie doesn't register this. "Some people," Bonnie says, "think it's degrading. Or anti-feminist. Or something. But *I* don't. I think there's something beautiful in making something like that for someone. It's like making yourself into a work of art. You know?"

The silence crisps into awkwardness, and Laura realizes that Bonnie is staring at her, waiting for her to answer.

"Yeah," says Laura. "Yeah, sure, totally."

Bonnie breaks out into a smile. "I *knew* you'd understand," she says. She fiddles with her phone. She takes a deep breath. "I'm scared. Dare me."

"What?"

"Say I dare you."

"I dare you?"

Bonnie grins. She closes her eyes. She touches her phone. "There," she says at last. "I sent it." She exhales.

She turns to Laura.

"He's a good person, you know," she says. "He doesn't think he is. But he is. *I* see that. It's just—hard for him. With *her.*"

Laura realizes, with new interest, that Bonnie is talking about Virginia.

"What do you mean?"

"They're best friends," Bonnie says. "Ever since freshman year. I mean—I'm not jealous, or anything. Everyone *knows* Virginia isn't into guys. Or people at all, really."

Laura registers this.

"I think he feels weird about dating if she doesn't," Bonnie says. "Like he's betraying her somehow. Because she *won't*. He says he thinks of her like his kid sister. He's protective. It's one of the things I like most about him."

Laura can't imagine Virginia needing protection from anyone.

"But soon," Bonnie says. "Soon," she says again, more firmly this time. She blows out the candle.

Laura lies awake thinking about Virginia.

She ponders Miranda's loathing, Isobel's grudging respect, Brad's protectiveness, trying to weigh how they could possibly all be directed toward the same person, let alone toward a person who hardly seems like a person at all.

Laura's hour in the crypt has unsettled her. Only, when she thinks of those moments, singing, Virginia's hair falling over her tiny lace-edged wrists on the organ keyboard, Virginia's hair falling over Laura's shoulders, she thinks only that Virginia Strauss, as terrifying as she is, must be the most wonderful person in the world.

Maybe, Laura thinks, wonderful people are always a little bit terrifying. World-Historical people must be. If she met Sebastian Webster, she'd probably be terrified of him, too.

It's like what Virginia had said about hideous things, how the things that horrify you are the ones you know to trust.

Maybe, she thinks, that's how she knows she can trust Virginia.

Laura stays awake, too shot through with joy to sleep, until the first breaking-in of dawn. Then she goes to the window. Then she waits. Then she watches, breathless, as the Desmond door opens and a slim figure emerges and then gallops toward the woods, and the water, alone.

3

LAURA SPENDS THE NEXT DAY WAITING FOR EVENSONG. SHE CAN'T pay attention in Latin, nor in Calculus; by Topics in European History, she is so rapt in anticipation that she doesn't even hear Dr. Meyer asking her what Locke had to say about paternal power, even when he calls her name three times. She can't eat lunch. She picks at dinner.

"You're not dieting, are you?" Bonnie's eyes narrow. "Because if you are you should tell me. I have experience. I can make sure you're getting all your macros."

Bonnie picks a piece of raw tofu off her fork.

"I'm fine," Laura says. "Just tired. Schoolwork."

"That's St. Dunstan's for you," Freddy says darkly. "Small fish. Big pond. Get used to it." She looks pleased with herself. "Everyone has to, sooner or later."

At six forty-five, the bells ring; then Laura can no longer breathe.

She walks with Bonnie and Freddy across Devonshire Quad. She lets them muscle her into the front pew. She catches sight of Isobel and Miranda, hand in hand, in one of the back rows, but she can't bring herself to acknowledge them.

It's not like she's betrayed them or anything, she tells herself. She signed that petition. All she's done is join a choir—plus, she isn't even formally in. Even Isobel, she tells herself, never said a person couldn't join choir if they wanted to.

Bonnie waves to Brad. Brad winces a smile. Laura watches Virginia stiffen slightly, and she stiffens, too, instinctively, in case Virginia holds her responsible for Bonnie being Bonnie. But Virginia keeps her face upward, implacable, turning her chin just slightly toward the pews, the edges of her mouth curling in a smile that Laura realizes, too late, is directed at her.

By the time Laura smiles back, Virginia's gaze is already in the middle distance.

Probably, Laura decides, Isobel and Miranda are too hard on Virginia. It's simply, Laura thinks, kindling the warm glow of approval, that Virginia has high standards for people. She tries not to think about hell.

Then service begins, and Laura stops thinking altogether.

It passes so much more delicately this week. No longer overwhelmed by its sheer novelty, Laura can pay attention to all the little details: how Barry Ng finishes the prelude from the organ loft and then tiptoes under St. Peter to get to the choir stalls in time for the Magnificat, how Reverend Tipton bows his head when he says, *Thine is the day, and also the night*; the syncopated echo on the floor when everybody gets down to kneel to confess their sins; the eerie, echoing a cappella chant of the Psalms; how Brad Noise's warbling tenor carries on the Nunc Dimittis; that line from the General Thanksgiving, with the old Elizabethan language, about how *we shew forth thy praise / not only with our lips, but in our lives*, which strikes Laura as such a fittingly wonderful way to talk about being alive. It is only when they murmur, all together, the Apostles' Creed, the *I believe in God, the Father almighty*, that Laura feels a slight prickling of guilt. It makes her feel like she's lying, saying a thing like that, when she has no idea whether there even is a God, whether Isobel is right that it's ridiculous that the whole school has to say it, whether they mean it or not. She cranes her neck, trying to catch another glimpse of Isobel and Miranda. They remain sitting. Their lips don't move.

Only then the choir starts up singing again, and Laura forgets what she is worrying about, because to worry you need to be capable of conscious thought, and when Virginia and the rest of them sing, Laura can't think about anything at all.

If there *is* a God, she decides, when they at last fall silent, He must be in that harmony, too.

It ends so quickly. Suddenly it is dark outside, and Reverend Tipton is putting out the candle lights, one by one, and everyone is filing out along the nave.

"Come on." Bonnie loops her arm around Laura's. "I want you to meet Brad."

Bonnie prances up the nave before Laura can stop her.

"Brad!"

He looks up so awkwardly when he sees her.

"Bonnie?"

Virginia's face is frozen in disdain.

"You sounded great!" Bonnie's head bobs on her neck. "All of you. Gorgeous. I got *chills*!" She swivels back to Brad. "You could, like, totally go to Juilliard or something. If you wanted."

Barry Ng blushes at this. Virginia glares at him.

Brad sighs a long and heavy sigh.

"One of Bonnie's best qualities," he says slowly, catching Laura's eye, "is her tolerance for mediocrity." His mouth distends into an apologetic grin.

Bonnie just laughs.

"Don't be *shy*, Brad." Bonnie touches his shoulder.

Virginia arches an eyebrow; Laura looks at the floor.

"He's *so* shy about his talents. Anyway, this is my friend Laura." Laura recoils at *friend* and then feels guilty about it. "We're *roomies*."

"Hello, Laura." His nod is perfunctory.

"It's nice to meet you." Laura wills herself to make eye contact. "I've, uh, heard a lot about you."

Brad bites his lip. He rocks on his heels.

"Well," he says, "you're in for a disappointment." He smiles, pained, and Bonnie laughs too loud.

"Right." Reverend Tipton is making his way down the nave. "Terribly sorry. It's just—erm." He makes a fumbling gesture at his watch. "Probably good to, erm, keep to time, you know." He shuffles past them.

Bonnie swivels to him. "You were *great*, too," she says. "How do you remember all those lines every time?"

Virginia's lips contort into a sneer. "It's not a play, Bonnie," she says.

Reverend Tipton looks from Virginia to Bonnie and back again. His nose twitches. "I mean, erm, we *do* have it all written out for us. Just in case. In the Book of Common Prayer." He exhales. "Lucky, that." He waits helplessly for someone else to say something. "Ah, anyway, shall we . . ." He motions at the loft stairs.

Virginia snaps to attention. "Gentlemen! Come along," she says. "No dawdling!"

Anton bounds toward the staircase. Ralph, Barry, and Ivan trot after him.

Bonnie smiles vaguely. "Well, it was nice seeing you," she says to Brad. "We should just . . . me and Laura, I mean—we actually have dinner plans. In town. At the Wayfarer." She yanks Laura down the nave.

There is no getting out of it now.

"Actually . . ." Laura unloops her arm from Bonnie's. "I was planning to stay."

Bonnie rounds on her in confusion.

"So *you're* the new girl," Brad says at last.

Laura stares at the floor.

"You mean . . ." It takes Bonnie a second longer to work it out.

"I just auditioned," Laura says, without looking up. "That's all."

"Oh," Bonnie says, nodding a little too intensely. "Great. *Great.* Good for you. That's so—great." Her smile is pasted on. "Have a *great* night!"

Her heels echo off the rafters as she totters out.

Reverend Tipton leads them all up to the choir loft.

"Right," he says. He eyes Laura. "You weren't here last week."

"She's new," Virginia says quickly. "She auditioned for me last night."

Reverend Tipton looks from Virginia to Laura and back again. "For *you?*"

"I always run auditions," Virginia says. "Heeno—Reverend Heenan, I mean—always specially requested it." She gnaws on her lower lip. "Less trouble that way." She clears her throat. "It's worked smoothly up to now," she says.

He looks her over. "Right," he says. He looks unconvinced. "Very good."

They do scales. They practice chanting the Psalms. They do next week's Magnificat and Nunc Dimittis, which are by Hubert Parry, and Laura tries to keep up without looking desperate. She is all too conscious that her music-reading knowledge is only rudimentary—half-remembered assortments of sharps and quarter notes and flats and rests garnered from middle school recorder lessons—but she keeps close to little Ivan Dixon, who is singing alto, too, and finds she can follow along with him.

She comes to know everybody's voices: Brad's arch and elegant tenor; Anton's bombastic bass, which fills the loft so completely that Laura wonders she can hear anyone else at all. Laura comes to recognize the self-satisfied punctuation of Ralph's jovial baritone, a little too full—or so Virginia informs him after a run-through of the Magnificat—of unrestrained emotion; to recognize, too, Barry's careful, note-perfect melodies, how he can vary his register with every piece's need: on baritone in one, on tenor in the next. Laura starts to anticipate Ivan's intermittent, crystalline eruptions of sound—like little cries, Laura thinks, of joy or pain. Reverend Tipton keeps chords on the organ, and Laura marvels, with every run-through, at how the piece comes together.

Laura falls in love with each of them, a little, in turn, because of their voices.

But it's Virginia Laura can't stop watching: leaning in over the organ—just a little too close to Reverend Tipton, who has to arch his back to see the music through her dark-falling hair. Laura can't stop watching everyone else watching her.

Laura worries, at first, Virginia will look up, that Virginia will perceive her hangdog adoration and know what a fool she is, letting this affect her.

But Virginia's eyes are fixed instead on Reverend Tipton: on his hands turning the pages of the music, on his brow furrowing over the odd false note, on the veins in his neck, bulging and receding like the pipes of an organ. She blushes a little when he turns to her; she lowers her gaze and bites her lip.

She's looking at him, Laura realizes, like she cares what he thinks.

"I'm so relieved," Virginia tells him, when at last they declare the Nunc Dimittis in good enough shape to set aside, "that you're keeping up the standard of this place. I was so worried the new chaplain would want us to switch to that horrible Rite Two. But then, you know, I Googled you, and I read about all your past work."

He looks up at her, perplexed.

"As soon as I read your thesis," she goes on, "I knew we could rely on you. I always used to tell Heeno: the old language, you know, the old ways—you can really hear the voices of the Oxford martyrs in them." Her eyes blaze. "You can't expect anyone to take worship seriously if you use those silly modern liturgies, the ones that water everything down to make everything accessible. *And also with you* and all that. I'm sure you didn't use modern language at Oriel College *Oxford*." She laughs and draws out the word.

Reverend Tipton considers her. His eyebrows wriggle like insects.

"Well," he says tightly, "there are, erm, benefits, to accessibility, you know. From a pastoral perspective. One wants people to feel welcome in church."

Virginia flinches, but only slightly.

"Of course," she says. Then, with more emphasis. "Naturally. From a pastoral perspective." She clears her throat.

"No change!" Anton bellows suddenly. "That's what I always say." He thumps the organ. "If it was good enough for John Devonshire, back in 1790, then it's good enough for us now."

"Hear, hear," says Ralph.

Now Virginia smiles. "Or Sebastian Webster." She catches Laura's gaze and holds it, waiting for Laura to return her smile, before looking back at Reverend Tipton. "As far as I'm concerned"—she gets a little louder—"that's my guiding principle for life. Whenever I'm not sure what to do next"—she takes a deep breath—"I always ask myself, *What would Sebastian Webster do?*"

Reverend Tipton smiles vaguely.

"Huh," he says idly. "Never read him."

He turns back to his music.

. . .

"I was thinking," says Virginia, as she and Laura walk back to Desmond together across Devonshire Quad. "We really should band together, as a choir, to buy him a copy of *All Before Them*. If he's going to be teaching here . . ." Her voice trails off. "Of course he'll love it. He's a very serious person. He's an actual intellectual, not a neoliberal fossil like Heeno. Oriel was Newman's college, you know."

Laura doesn't, but she smiles and nods anyway. The remnants of the music scrape against the inside of her throat, like stray swallowed pieces of shell. The moon shines bright and full upon them.

"You have an amazing voice," Laura says at last.

"You don't mean that."

"I *do*."

Virginia's smile twitches. "My voice," she says matter-of-factly, without any trace of self-pity, "is average." She looks up at Laura. "Totally middle-of-the-road. That's why I have to work so hard. Sure, it's good *now*, but only because I practice as much as I do. If I had a voice like yours . . ." She falls silent for a moment. "I don't mind having to work for things. Nothing worth having ever comes easy."

She opens the Desmond door for Laura with her key card. She checks her wristwatch.

"I'll see you later," she says. "I'm going to get in a run before curfew."

She is gone before Laura can answer her.

Bonnie doesn't look up from her phone when Laura gets in. She is zooming into photographs of herself, adjusting them with her fingertips, replying to Laura's sheepish pleasantries with monosyllables.

"You know," she murmurs, when Laura gets into bed. "You could have *said*."

"It only happened last night," Laura says. "And I didn't know for *sure*. Not until rehearsal. They could have still cut me." She doesn't know if she's lying.

Bonnie keeps scrolling. She makes a show of sighing, with increasing volume, until at last she caves. "Did Brad say anything?"

"Brad?"

"Like a message for me," Bonnie says. "Or something." Her voice notches up an octave.

"I . . ." Laura doesn't mean to lie exactly. In the moment it feels like kindness. "He said to say hello," Laura says. "And that he's looking forward to seeing you soon."

Bonnie's owlish eyes glaze over with satisfaction. "Oh," she says, weighing anew the practical merits of Laura's membership in choir. "Well, *that's* nice. Tell him I'm excited to see him, too." She sits up straight. She swivels her head. "Was it amazing?" She has forgotten her anger. "I bet it was amazing."

"It was."

"Do they have, like, an initiation ritual?" Bonnie asks. "Like—something cool, in Latin? All the secret societies do cool things with Latin. I mean, obviously, you don't have to tell me. But . . ." She leans in. "Blink once if there *is* an initiation ritual; blink twice if there isn't." Laura blinks instinctively. "Was that one or two? Sorry. Sorry."

"Honestly," says Laura. "We just sang. That's all."

"That's *all*?"

"That's all," says Laura.

"Huh," says Bonnie. She wriggles under the covers.

· · ·

Laura doesn't see Virginia all weekend, although she keeps her customary morning vigil. But the following Tuesday afternoon, as Laura scurries down the corridors of Mountbatten, three minutes late on her way to Assembly, she hears someone calling her.

"Stearns!"

Virginia is standing with four of the boys on the staircase. She is wearing a black fur collar, with matching muff. Her boots are laced to her ankles.

"*Stearns!*" Ralph calls out, in compliant echo.

It takes a moment for Laura to recognize herself. Her own name has always felt so awkwardly, accurately soft: a pliant name for a pliant person. But *Stearns*—it's a boy's name, Laura thinks, like one of those names they bray across the quad in Webster—lithe and taut and hard.

"I have been reliably informed," Brad says with a soft smile, "that you should be sitting with us. Today is a momentous day." His mouth twitches. "Front-row seats to the end of history. Popcorn?"

"What?"

"Assembly." Barry winks. "He's talking about Assembly."

Ralph rolls his eyes. "Chairman Zhao's Crusade. Sounds like a children's book."

"The debate." Laura had almost forgotten. "Of course."

"Until 1968," Barry Ng informs them, "Morning Prayer was mandatory daily. And a full mass on Sundays, Eucharist and all. The choir did every service."

Virginia's smile flickers. "Anton's the contra," she says. She nods, as much to herself as to Laura. "He'll do a good job. He has vision." She pauses, for a moment, to meditate on it. "Anyway, you should sit with us."

"This is the way the world ends," Brad says. "Not with a bang but with a policy debate."

"Ignore him," Virginia says. "Gallagher's going to win. He's convincing." She addresses Laura without turning. "Brad just enjoys being melancholy."

"There's a surprise," mutters Ralph.

Brad shrugs.

Ralph tightens his bow tie.

They file into the Assembly Hall. They follow Virginia to one of the red-upholstered benches right under the old oil portrait of John Devonshire, St. Dunstan's first headmaster, his face obscured by muttonchops. Anton is already onstage pacing. His blazer's too small for him; his hair is greased with sweat. Isobel is sitting next to him. Her legs are sprawled wide, her boots kicked out; she fixes him with something between a glare and a smirk. Her hair is blue now; she has haphazardly chopped off half her bangs.

Laura catches sight of Miranda in the audience, in a leopard-print dress and somewhat ratty-looking vintage fur coat, next to a scowling Freddy Barnes. Miranda looks up at them when they enter.

Laura tries to smile at her, hoping to convey amiable, inoffensive neutrality. Miranda doesn't smile back.

"Don't even start with her." Virginia sighs as they sit. "Miranda MacKinnon is just a self-righteous, bitter little"—she chews the air, deciding—"*epigone.*" She crosses her arms. "Going around like she's some kind of revolutionary. She just likes to feel like she's doing something with her life."

"You've got to feel sorry for her, though." Ralph nods from Laura's other side. "Having to compete with you."

"What are you talking about?"

"You're the Other Woman."

Virginia stiffens. "Don't be ridiculous."

"Isobel wouldn't even be doing this," Ralph turns grandly to Laura, barely containing his voice, "if she weren't still trying to get Strauss to notice her." He pantomimes swooning. "All that pent-up, unrequited, sexual tension, nowhere to go—"

"Ervin—"

"I'm right," Ralph crows. "I'm always right. I have a sixth sense for character motivation."

Brad rounds on him. "How about you develop a sixth sense for shutting the fuck up?"

Ralph retreats into a pout. "Come on—she's not *subtle*. She's practically gagging. . . ."

"That's *enough*."

Virginia's eyes are still straight ahead. She doesn't even look at them.

The boys fall quiet.

"My problems with Isobel Zhao," Virginia says, twisting her hands in her lap, "are Ideological. That's all."

Assembly begins.

Dr. Charles, the headmaster, shuffles to the podium and makes his customary Assembly speech, muttering his way through a series of anodyne announcements about repair work being done in Carbonell on Friday and the updated hours of the weekend shuttle bus taking students into Weymouth proper. He launches into a series of prepared remarks about free speech and debate and school bylaws, and about how St. Dunstan's is all about discussion and free inquiry, and how the goal of a liberal arts education is to decide what you think about things, and how the faculty welcomes the chance to learn from the diverse voices of its promising student body before they take a private vote.

"Tradition sometimes means change," Dr. Charles drones on. "Change sometimes means tradition."

"Black means white," Ralph mutters. "Up means down. War is peace."

Onstage, Isobel rolls her eyes.

Then Dr. Charles hands over the debate to Isobel and Anton— "two of our most *passionate* young students," he says, without making eye contact with either of them.

Isobel goes first, sauntering over to the lectern, grabbing the microphone right out of Dr. Charles's hand. Miranda emits a full-throated "Iso-BEL," which about twenty people in the audience echo. A few people groan.

Isobel leans in on her elbows. She grins at her audience. She fixes her gaze—just for a moment—on Virginia. Then she looks up. "All right," she says. "We all know why we're *really* here. An extra hour of free time on Friday nights."

A bunch more people cheer.

"Also"—Isobel pauses for maximum effect—"bringing down the Man."

Isobel's good. Laura has to give her that. She is by turns irreverent and impassioned, poking fun at the arbitrary silliness of getting down on your knees on Friday night in a smoky little room, when 36 percent of people under the age of forty (she cites the studies) don't even believe in God, before launching into a tirade about the blood-soaked history of St. Dunstan's itself—the fact that it didn't admit Jews until the 1850s, or black people until the 1890s, or women until 1968. She talks about John Devonshire's sugar plantations in Jamaica and the slaves he owned, and the particular irony of a man like that, who made his money plundering the seas, wanting to make men of God out of the sons of fishermen. She talks about Webster and Franco, which makes Laura flinch.

"Just because something is pretty"—Isobel's cheeks blaze—"doesn't make it good. Just because something is old, doesn't make it good. There's plenty of old *bullshit* out there." She turns to Dr. Charles, who has gestured a pantomime warning. "Sorry." She turns back to her audience. "Whaddya say to some better traditions?"

Virginia does not move.

Laura searches her face for answers.

It's not that Laura thinks Isobel is right, exactly. It's just that she can't figure out how, exactly, Isobel is wrong. It can't be true, of course—God, how could she stand it if it were true!—if all the things Laura loves are somehow already irredeemably broken, if her love for them makes her heedless at best; at worst selfish and cruel, the way Isobel says.

It's just that when Isobel says things, Laura believes them, and when Virginia says things Laura believes them, too; it's just that Laura knows she is so soft, soft enough that anyone can shape her, and she knows enough to know this softness makes her weak.

Virginia, she thinks, has never been soft in her life. Whatever Virginia loves, Laura is sure, she loves because she has decided to, through sheer force of will, rather than surrender.

Oh, if only Virginia could explain to her!

Virginia, Laura knows, would be able to defend Webster, defend Evensong, root her passions in notions solid and firm, in a truth more substantial than the fact that every page of *All Before Them* makes Laura cry with the joy of being alive.

Virginia, Laura knows, would discount Laura's tears entirely. There's nothing *hideous*, Laura worries, about loving a book that is beautiful.

But Virginia watches Isobel, with her dark lips curling back, saying nothing.

Anton comes to the podium.

"My fellow students," he says. "I'm not here to argue that the past was perfect. Nor am I here to argue that nothing can ever change." He draws himself up to his full, impressive height.

"Rather," he bellows, "I am here to argue for *transcendence.* I am here to argue for realism. I am here to argue for love. I am here to argue that what we owe, to those who came before us, as to those who will come after, is a vision of continuity that collapses the here and the now, the future and the past. Something to carry us through."

Virginia leans close into Laura's ear. Laura can feel her breath on her neck. "Magnificent," she whispers. "Isn't he? He's really, you know, a natural man. It's all instinct, with him. Look how he projects."

"Tradition, Chesterton tells us," Anton goes on, "is the democracy of the dead. Chesterton ..."

"*Understood what it means to be a polity ...*" Virginia mouths all the words. She beams at Anton, with maternal benevolence. "*To see ourselves as part of a community in time, as well as space.*"

"You wrote it," Laura says, when at last Anton and Isobel have been duly applauded—each by half the audience—and Dr. Charles has sent them away with a sweaty look of relief. "Didn't you?"

Everyone is getting up, gathering their coats, putting on their scarves.

"Anton Gallagher is many things," Virginia says. "A thoughtful political philosopher is not one of them." She smiles. "He *should* go into politics, though. I want that for him. He has presence. He could be president one day."

"But—I don't understand. Why didn't *you* sign up for the debate? If it was your speech."

Virginia's smile tightens.

"Nobody'd listen," she says. "If it was me." Her nostrils flare a little. "I'm not likable."

Laura can't tell if she's saying it with pride, or resignation, or both.

"I think you're likable!"

Virginia's smile softens. She takes Laura's hand.

"*You*, Stearns," she says. "Aren't like other people."

She squeezes Laura's hand a little tighter. Laura's heart leaps.

"Anyway," Virginia says. "It's all moot. The debate's just smoke and mirrors, to give us a semblance of choice. It's the faculty that decides on these things. And they'll probably delay any *actual* decision with bureaucratic red tape until we're all long graduated—or dead."

They make their way toward the exit. Anton and Isobel are stepping down from the stage, studiously avoiding looking at each other.

"Miss Zhao!"

Reverend Tipton is in the front row, stepping toward them. Virginia freezes.

"Yeah?" Isobel barely looks at him.

"That was . . ." Reverend Tipton swallows. "That was an impressive speech. Very—very thoughtful."

"I mean . . ." Isobel half shrugs. "I— Thanks. No offense, though, obviously," she adds quickly.

"None taken," Reverend Tipton says. "I, personally, always do well to remember that faith and tradition aren't *quite* the same thing. A reminder we could all use, from time to time."

Virginia's nails dig into Laura's palms.

Reverend Tipton turns to Anton. "And to you, Mr. Gallagher. Quite—quite—fervent."

Anton beams. He shakes Reverend Tipton's hand a little too vigorously. "Someone," he says, "has got to stand up for what's right!"

"You've both done very well," says Reverend Tipton. He coughs. "Anyway, erm, I should ..."

He scurries out the side door.

"I *do* feel for Reverend Tipton," Virginia says, as they make their way onto the light of Devonshire Quad. "It must be difficult, you know. Balancing his *personal* sympathies with what he *has* to say to people, as an impartial representative of the administration." She swallows. "He really should read Webster, though," she adds. Then, a little louder, "I think he would find it useful." She bites her lip absentmindedly. "For his work."

In the end, Virginia is right. On Wednesday, the St. Dunstan's administration announces, via a public statement in the *St. Dunstan's Chronicler*, that it has formed a steering committee to discuss the future of Evensong for the twenty-first century. They will produce a white paper on the topic before the end of the academic year. No changes will be made until then.

"Cowards," says Virginia when she hears the news. "They should all be lined up against the walls of Mountbatten Hall and shot."

"I thought you'd be relieved."

But Virginia snorts. "Sebastian Webster fought and died for things like Evensong," she says. "And all *we* can do is have *committee meetings* about it." Her mouth twitches. "It's a *sclerotic modern world*, Stearns. Nobody dies for anything."

Friday comes, and with it Laura's first Evensong as a member of the choir. Laura can't think about anything else. She gets hopelessly muddled in Topics in European History, confusing what Rousseau said about natural man with the natural man of Hobbes, and forgets which one is supposed to be nasty, brutish, and short. She trips in Keble and spills her lunch tray everywhere. She even manages to accidentally blank Freddy Barnes at Carbonell Library, where Freddy is manning the checkout counter for work-study.

"So," Freddy says lightly, scanning out Laura's copy of *Leviathan*, "she's got you forgetting us already. You know, that's the first thing they do in cults. Make you forget about everybody else."

Freddy cuts off Laura's attempt at an apology. "Don't worry," she says, in a tone that makes it obvious Laura should. "You couldn't offend me if you tried." She slides the book across the counter and turns her face back to the screen.

But once Evensong comes, nothing else matters. From the moment the bells echo out from the chapel spires, there is nothing outside the stained glass; no sound outside the quiet and ferocious rumbling of the organ—like a sea serpent, Laura thinks—as Barry plays the prelude. There is nobody but Virginia, pulling the musty black choir robes over Laura's head; Virginia fastening the white, apron-like surplice behind Laura's neck, brushing Laura's fine, frizzy hair from her neck with the tips of her fingers.

"*There*," Virginia says, leaning back on the prie-dieu. "Now you're one of us."

Nobody exists but the seven of them, standing shoulder to shoulder in the choir stalls, as everybody else files in; nothing but Reverend Tipton's high, melodic voice, as he starts once more with the bidding prayers, the *seek him who made the Pleiades and Orion*. They start to sing; there is nothing but sound.

Their voices soar and meld together; their voices break apart. Their voices are in the fish St. Peter holds; their voices are in the light in Mary's palms; they are in the wood of the pews; they're in the pursed lips of Bonnie and Freddy and Yvette Saunders in the front row; they're in the marble of the floors; they're in Sebastian Webster's powdered bones. Maybe they are, Laura thinks, nothing but their voices, or else maybe their voices are coming from outside them entirely; maybe something great and unenumerable has broken them open, like hazelnut shells, and entered into them; maybe Laura is not Laura at all, any longer, but just the sorry, meaty thing through which that something moves.

In that moment, there is no such thing as time; there is no difference, Laura thinks, between Webster's Evensong, and this one; every Friday night that has ever happened, or will happen, on this marble, is one and the same Friday; and everyone who has ever lived or died or was buried in this chapel is present, and Sebastian Webster is present, too, only Laura does not know if Webster is the ghost, or if she is, or if they are all ghosts, together, bodiless, with nothing theirs but this voice.

They sing the Psalm, and the Magnificat, and the Nunc Dimittis. Laura can't see through her tears. But at the final rounding of *Mine eyes have seen thy salvation*, she feels the cold abruptness of Virginia's fingers, snaking through hers, tightening around her hands.

Now it is over; now everybody is leaving; now Reverend Tipton extinguishes the candles; now Barry is clapping Laura on the back and saying, "Well *done*, Stearns," because she got that high E exactly right; now Anton is stamping gleefully on the floors and making an echo, and there is a melancholy tightness in Laura's chest, all through the hour of rehearsal that follows, because they are in ordinary time, now, and ordinary time is just that little bit less pure.

After rehearsal, they break out onto Devonshire Quad. It is nine o'clock. The air is chillier than it was a week ago; the moon slices a curve in the sky. Laura's heart is still too full for her to speak.

"What is it, Stearns?" Brad's voice is low. He touches her shoulder, so lightly—almost, Laura thinks, in surprise—tenderly. "Everything all right?"

"It's just . . ." She knows how silly it sounds out loud. "I didn't want it to end."

Virginia, two paces ahead of her on the quad, stops short.

She turns back. Her eyes are glittering. Her lips are dark. "It doesn't have to," she says. She considers. She draws in breath. "Gentlemen!"

They all fall still. They are all watching her.

"I propose"—she waits for them to lean in—"an excursion." She folds her arms. "We have two hours until curfew. And—more important—we have a new recruit." She turns her face out to the direction of the sea. "Bethel Beach."

Ivan beams at being noticed.

"Bethel Beach!" Anton crows. "Hear! Hear!"

Ralph makes a half-hearted noise about having homework and another chapter of his novel to finish. Virginia just smiles at him.

"I mean . . ." He fumbles, like it has not all already been decided. "It's awfully *cold*, isn't it?"

"You afraid of a little chill, Ervin?" Virginia cocks her head at him.

Ralph looks from Virginia to the others, in fruitless hope of appeal. "I—just—I promised to call Sadie tonight." He looks at his feet. "She likes to know how I'm doing."

"Come on, Ervin." Virginia's smile spreads. "Mommy can wait. *What would Sebastian Webster do?* It'll inspire you."

He throws up his hands.

"I'd better feel pretty fucking inspired at the end of this," he says.

They all follow her across Devonshire Quad.

.   .   .

They make their way past the sports fields, into the beech woods. They come to Farnham Cliff, and Laura tries not to think about Isobel and Miranda teaching her how to smoke. They turn right, toward the down-hill slope away from town, the one leading to the weathered pebble beach. Virginia leads them in lithe, long strides, without even looking at her feet, or using her phone as a flashlight, the way Laura and the others do.

"Careful." Brad comes up next to Laura. "These cliffs will kill you—if you don't know what you're doing." He is smiling his usual pained-looking smile, and Laura wonders—not for the first time—how Bonnie could find him handsome. "Decent night, isn't it?" He nods at the water.

"Oh, it's wonderful!"

"Times like this"—Brad clears his throat, just a little too loftily—"a man could almost believe in God."

"You don't?"

Laura has assumed everyone in choir does.

Brad sighs a long, deep sigh. "I believe," he says at last, "in Virginia Strauss." He huddles a little against the wind. "Hope that suffices." He sees Laura's face. "Don't get me wrong," he says. "It sounds nice. I'm not saying I wouldn't if I could." He considers this. "It'd be reassuring, think-ing there's something, you know, out there." He nods to the water. "But it takes a particular kind of person to be able to actually take the plunge." He coughs slightly. "At least, you know, in this day and age and all."

"Someone like *her*, you mean."

Virginia is leaping from rock to rock without looking down.

Brad watches her.

"The thing about Strauss," he says, "is that she can do anything she puts her mind to. If she decides God exists then, bam, God exists." His smile tugs at his lips. "Now, normies like us, Stearns . . ." He stops himself. "Sorry. I didn't mean to assume. For all I know you could be the next Mother Teresa."

"No!" Laura is surprised by her own vehemence. "I mean—I'm not like that." She swallows. "I don't know what I believe," she admits. "I mean, there's got to be Something out there, right?" She doesn't like how cowardly it sounds in her mouth. "I mean, a particular *kind* of Something. Sorry. That sounds so dumb."

"I mean, it's fitting," says Brad, with a worldly sigh, "for *our sclerotic modern world.*"

It is so much easier to talk to him than to Virginia. He doesn't make her afraid. "Do you love Webster, too?" She isn't even self-conscious saying *love*.

Brad is quiet for a moment as they walk.

"No," he says at last. "No, I *admire* him. His language, his style. Even the martyrdom thing, a little bit. But if you're asking if I, personally, want to go off and die in wartime . . . Well, Stearns, I'm perfectly comfortable with being World-Unhistorical." His mouth crinkles. "You have to remember, I knew the O.G. Strauss."

"O.G.?"

"Pre-God."

Laura can't imagine Virginia Strauss pre-God.

"Was she always—" Laura doesn't even know what she means. "This intense?"

Virginia leaps over a mossy rock onto the dirt trail. Bethel Beach is at last visible at their feet. Anton and Ralph barrel after her, Ivan and Barry behind them. Laura can hear the water lapping at the shore.

"She was always . . ." He lets his words fade. "Dissatisfied? No—that implies you're actually seeking satisfaction. If Strauss were satisfied she wouldn't know what to do with herself." He coughs. "Anyway, we weren't as fancy as we are now," Brad says. "No choir. No pretty music or candles or Latin. Just a couple weedy social rejects, hanging around Carbonell, talking shit about our parents. Strauss and me and—" He winces again. "Well, that's ancient history."

"Isobel?"

Brad glances up. But Virginia is already at the water's edge, turning her face to the sliver of the moon.

"Thing is," his voice is soft, "Strauss has very fixed ideas." He doesn't look at Laura.

"What h—"

But Brad has made a point of moving on. "Strauss decided that what St. Dunstan's needed was a proper choir. A *real*, honest-to-God Latin-spewing choir—the kind Webster had in his day. What we actually had, of course, was a couple of rejects from the Dewey Decibel, one Barry Ng, who could actually sing, and one desiccated old man. But Strauss had a vision of what she wanted . . ." He offers Laura his arm. "And of course old Heeno was only too happy to hand the whole thing over. And so . . ." He nods at the water. "Now we're here."

They have come by now to the beach's edge. The water leaves a faint striation of foam on the sand. Seaweed carpets the pebbles. The boys are all sitting in a semicircle, looking out at the water. Virginia is on her knees, in the foam, her choir robes billowing in the wind.

"Do *they* believe in God?"

Brad shrugs. "Ivan does, I think. At least his parents do. Barry is just here for the music. Ralph? Depends on whoever he's reading that week. As for Anton—fucked if I know. I think Anton hopes we all turn ourselves into robots and colonize Mars. It's not really the point."

"So what is?"

Brad closes his eyes. He breathes in the salt air.

"All this," he says.

The water churns black. The shore continues, dark and unvarying, as far as Laura can see, broken only by the stark ruin of Jarvis Lighthouse. The smell of brine is overpowering. There are so many stars.

They get to where the rocks get steeper. Anton leaps down first, nearly tumbling into the darkness, and then Virginia lets him take her by the waist and hoist her after him.

"He likes her, doesn't he?"

"Don't we all?"

"Do you?"

Brad winces again.

"I know Strauss well enough," he says, "to know she doesn't want that kind of love."

"What do you mean?"

He snorts. "Come on. Can you picture it? Strauss, on the arm of some lovesick senior at the Mayfair dance, with, what, a corsage that matches his cummerbund? Strauss, swiping on Tinder? Strauss, worrying about whether or not to double-text?"

Virginia takes several votives from her bag. She lights each one in turn. They cast her face in shadow, illuminating only the darkness of her lips.

"Besides . . ." Brad smiles. "Who could possibly compare to *him*?" He nods back toward the coastal path, where the statue surveys the sea.

Laura smiles.

"Nobody," she says.

What a relief, she thinks, that Virginia understands this part of her.

Brad clears his throat. "We normies," he says, looking out into the distance, "make do with other normies. People capable of normie love."

"Like Bonnie?"

He grimaces. "Quite."

Laura tries to probe this further, but it is too late. Virginia is beckoning them over now, with glittering eyes.

"We did this last year," she says, "when Ivan joined. So, you see, now it's tradition." She swallows. "We do Compline twice. Once at the beginning of Michaelmas, once at the end of Trinity. Do you know what it's supposed to be for?"

"What?"

"Death."

Laura starts. Virginia smiles.

"It's called Compline. The night prayer. English monks used to do it in medieval times. A plague could get them at any moment. Or bandits. So they had to be thinking about it, all the time. It's supposed to get you ready to die." Her smile remains fixed. "I think it's the most *hideous* of all the prayers." She lingers on the word.

"Goth A.F.," says Barry.

"Nobody," Virginia murmurs, "likes to think about death." She is no longer looking at any of them, although they are all looking at her, leaning in, like they can inhale her. Laura wonders if Virginia notices. "People are so easily frightened. They're *neutered,* in a way. Killing, dying—the things the whole of human life *used* to be about, once upon a time. The things that matter. We've tried to cut them out from our consciousness. We've tried to pretend that we control everything. That *we're* all there is. So that we can lie back, live an easy life."

Laura swallows.

It unsettles her, when Virginia talks like this. It makes her so ashamed. If Virginia only knew, she thinks, how terrified she is of everything, all the time—not just mattering, existential things like killing or death, but also such mediocre, ordinary things like missing a note in rehearsal, or offending Isobel Zhao, or not being loved. She wonders if Virginia would hate her if she knew.

But Virginia just takes the final candle from the pebbles.

"Gentlemen," Virginia says. "Let's begin." Her voice is like ice.

"*The Lord Almighty*," she says, "*grant us a peaceful night—and a perfect end*."

The boys all murmur at once, "*Amen*."

They confess their sins. They recite a Psalm—the one that goes *You shall not be afraid of any terror by night / nor for the arrow that flieth by day*. Virginia says the first half of each verse, with the rest echoing after her. They all know how it goes.

Laura mouths the words she doesn't recognize. She watches them: their shining eyes, the candles flickering in the coast wind; the shadows flickering on their faces, as they all watch Virginia, as they all sing that droning, eerie hymn that goes *Before the ending of the day*, their voices jagged against the blowing of wind. She marvels at the understanding that passes between them, like the light from the candles; that beatific smile that spreads from Virginia outward to the rest of them, that gives them all that same complicit sense: that they are all in this together. She remembers what Brad said, about few of them believing it, and for a moment fear passes over her, that they shouldn't be doing this if they don't mean it the way Virginia does.

But then she sees Virginia's face—the terrible, certain way Virginia pronounces *Because your adversary the devil like a roaring lion walketh about, seeking whom to devour*—and then her fear curdles into a surprising pleasure: the thrilling prickle of being just the tiniest bit afraid.

Whatever this is, whatever they believe in, whether it's God or Sebastian Webster or being World-Historical, or whether it's just Virginia Strauss's illuminated face, she wants to be part of it. She wants to give herself up to it. She wants it to strike her down.

When it is over, Virginia goes to the water's edge. She places her candle on the waves. Then, one by one, they follow her.

They sit, in silence, on the beach, watching the little lights bob in the darkness.

Ivan Dixon is crying noisily.

"I'm sorry." He's shaking. "It's just so . . ."

Ralph Ervin hands Ivan a monogrammed handkerchief.

"And to think," Barry says, to Stearns, with a smile, "you thought we were cool."

Ralph looks offended.

"It's . . ." Laura is just so relieved not to be the only one crying. "It's wonderful."

They sing so many songs that night, on the waterfront. They sing the Magnificat they've practiced in rehearsal, and some of the Tallis Barry loves; they sing the old navy hymn "Eternal Father, Strong to Save," and "Jesus Calls Us Oe'er the Tumult," and all the other hymns Virginia and Barry know about sailors drowning, but for the grace of God, which St. Dunstan's has been using since the days it primarily made clergymen out of fishermen's sons; they sing "The Mary Ellen Carter," even though it isn't even a hymn at all, because it's about shipwrecks, too, and also everybody knows it, and when they sing their voices lattice together; Laura sings with them; now Laura is tentative, afraid of forgetting the words; now she is a little louder, after Ivan Dixon squeezes her hand; now she is letting Barry conduct; now she is full-throated, on that *rise again, rise again*, almost as loud as Anton; now they have stopped singing, because now Barry is telling everyone how before he got into sacred choral music, he was really into musical theater, and so the first time he was asked to play "Salve Regina" at a church he played the opening number from *Evita* instead.

Virginia watches them, wordless, with a strange, triumphant smile.

Then Brad's phone buzzes.

Nobody says anything at first. But it buzzes a second time, and a third.

"Go on then," Virginia snaps. "Check it."

Brad hesitates.

"She won't stop," Virginia says this without blinking, "until you do."

Brad unlocks the phone.

"It's nothing," he says after glancing quickly at the screen. "Really."

"Hand it over."

She holds out her hand without looking at him.

"Look, Strauss . . . ," Brad says softly.

She keeps her palms outstretched.

He gives it to her.

Virginia holds it there, for a moment, nonplussed, like she's never seen a phone before. Then, she opens the text.

"Look," she says, with treacly disdain. "She's sent you a video."

"Strauss, wait. . . ."

Virginia has already pressed Play.

"*I just wanted you to know . . .*" Bonnie's voice echoes, tinny, from the speakers. "*How much I've been missing you, lately.*"

It takes Virginia until the first moan to realize what it is. She doesn't move.

She just sits there, frozen, with the phone in the folds of her robes, letting it play, as her mouth falls open, as her eyes widen, as Bonnie moans a second time.

"Strauss, please!"

Her head snaps up. She slams the phone facedown on the sand. Bonnie's moans muffle in the dirt.

Virginia's face is white. Laura's stomach lurches.

"So," she says. "*This* is what you do in your free time. Fridays you come sing with us, then the rest of the time . . ." Her voice lacerates.

The others are all looking at the ground.

"It's disgusting, you know." She bites her lip so hard it turns purple. "Sending videos of herself like that. God, it's even worse than *actual* sex. It's all for show. It's everything wrong with . . ."

"Disgusting!" Anton echoes onto the wind.

"Don't tell me you're in *love* with her?"

Brad's face is like bone.

"I'm not," he says. "I'm not. It's just—"

"Sex?" Her voice notches higher. "Is *that* it?"

Brad is silent for a long while.

"Yes," he says at last. "It's just sex."

"Christ," Virginia says. "How boring." She sits up straighter. "There's nothing," she announces—to all of them, now; she is no longer looking at Brad—"more boring than sex. It makes even *serious* people into petty, self-indulgent morons. I don't know why everyone's so obsessed with it."

Brad keeps his eyes on the sand.

"I'm ending it," he says.

"You'd better."

"Soon."

"Tonight."

He looks up at her in surprise.

"Tonight?"

"You know this is unworthy of you," Virginia says coolly. Then, with more tenderness: "I mean, *she's* unworthy of you."

"She's not . . . ," Brad begins, and then stops trying.

"Plus, it's not like it's fair to her, either. If you're only with her for sex." She considers him. "It's unethical. It's taking advantage."

Brad doesn't say anything.

"Tonight," he says at last.

Then the bells start to chime, faint but unmistakable, from the chapel tower.

"Curfew," says Virginia, leaping to her feet. "Let's go."

"You probably think I'm a prude," Virginia says to Laura, when they are alone on Devonshire Quad. She searches Laura's face. "Maybe I am. I don't know."

Laura considers her vast absence of experience.

Virginia huddles against the wind. "It's just—everyone today's so obsessed with sex. It's so—so . . ." She sighs. "Petty."

"Petty?"

"Like, everyone's telling us it's supposed to be this big, important, all-encompassing thing, that if you don't have it, or if you don't have it *enough*, or the right kind of it, or in the right position, that your life isn't even worth living. And then everything, you know, I mean everything else: like love, and sacrifice, and—and—fighting, and dying, and causes. It's all just reduced to . . . God, I don't know, bodies. And sweat. And being . . . ugh, *horny.*" The word doesn't fit her. "It doesn't make any sense. It's like—it's like if someone told you that the whole human condition was defined by how we defecate. Though I suppose Freud thought that." Her laugh is dark.

"Besides," Virginia says, as they scan their key cards, "it's not like he's in love with her or anything. You heard him. It's just sex."

She folds her arms.

"I don't see how anyone could be in love with a person like that," she says.

She sighs as they make their way up the stairs. Then she turns back toward Laura. She leans, for a moment, on the banister, searching Laura's face.

"*Do* you think I'm a prude?"

"Maybe," Laura admits.

Virginia's face falls just slightly.

"But if you are—then so am I! I mean—I've never even kissed anyone."

Virginia peers at her with interest.

"Have you ever wanted to?"

"No," Laura admits. She thinks of the kind of beauty she has loved: the vague, shadowy beauty of notions without flesh. "At least, not in real life."

Virginia nods. "Exactly," she says. "Real life is boring."

She checks her wristwatch.

"I should go," she says. "I have to be up early tomorrow."

"Running?"

"How did you know?"

"I mean—" Laura blushes. "I see you, sometimes. On the quad. When I'm awake, I mean," she adds, too quickly. "I get insomnia, sometimes. So I'm already up."

Virginia's expression doesn't change.

"You should come with me."

Laura's heart leaps. "You want me to . . ."

"If you're up. It's good for you. Running that early. It boosts your metabolism. It helps you think more clearly. Only if you want to, of course."

Laura hasn't run on purpose since seventh-grade PE.

"I'd love to," she says.

"Then it's settled. Tomorrow. Meet in the common room at four fifty-nine sharp. I won't wait for you if you're late. Just so you know."

"I wouldn't want you to," says Laura.

Virginia reaches out and touches Laura's shoulder—a stilted, awkward gesture—before turning on her heel and heading across the corridor. It takes Laura until Virginia vanishes into her room to realize this is Virginia trying to be kind.

Laura unlocks the door. Bonnie is already there, waiting by the window, looking out over the quad. She starts when Laura enters.

"Oh—hi!"

"Hi."

Laura tries not to think of the sound of Bonnie's moans.

"You were out late."

"We were just hanging out," Laura says. "That's all."

"Where did you go? Anywhere fun?"

"Just the woods."

"Was Brad there?"

"Yes."

"Did he say anything?"

Laura flinches. "We just talked about choir," she says. "Mostly."

"Did he say anything about me?"

"No."

"What *did* he say? Just asking. I mean, obviously, you don't have to tell me, if it's, like, secret-society stuff." She winks. "Obviously, if it's secret-society stuff, that's *sacred*."

"Christ, Bonnie, there's no secret-society stuff!"

Laura feels a sudden, raging irritation with Bonnie, one that eclipses even her pity. It's just like Bonnie, she thinks, to reduce the wonder of Evensong, the awful, chilling *perfect end* of Compline, to *secret-society stuff*, something to be stored neatly in Bonnie's mental closet between Bonnie's rowing blazer and Bonnie's tweed and Bonnie's tacky lingerie.

No wonder, Laura thinks, Virginia despises her.

"It's just choir," Laura snaps. "That's all."

"Right," Bonnie says. "Okay." She turns back toward the window.

Laura turns off the light.

Bonnie keeps staring out the window, scrolling through her phone. It glows like an ember in the darkness.

"Could you not?" Laura says, conscious of her rudeness, unwilling to stop it. "I have to be up early."

"Fine," Bonnie says. She lowers the phone's brightness. Laura can see it, even through the covers.

The spirit of the age, she reminds herself, nursing her own irritation, as she puts a pillow over her head and turns, at last, to sleep.

4

Virginia is already waiting for her. She looks even more severe than usual. Her hair is in a bun, pulled so taut that it has stretched the skin of her forehead. She is hopping a little, first on one foot, and then the other, as if she can't stand to stay still.

"You made it." Like this was ever a question.

She leads Laura onto Devonshire Quad. It is a cold day, even for late September, and her breath hangs stagnant in the morning air. Laura shivers. Virginia doesn't notice.

"I usually go all the way to town," Virginia says. "At minimum. Four miles there, four miles back. There's a diner there that's open twenty-four/seven. The Grinning Griddle." She looks pleased with herself. "It mostly caters to fishermen."

Laura tries to calculate how long it will take to run eight miles.

"Unless . . ." Virginia considers her. "That's too much?"

"No," Laura says. "Definitely not." She takes a deep breath.

Virginia is gone by the time she exhales.

Laura watches her, for a moment, darting indefatigable between Latimer and Cranmer Halls. She wills her body to keep pace. She follows her.

It's as miserable as she'd feared. Within a quarter mile, Laura is huffing hopelessly, wheezing up phlegm as she tries to keep up, not with

93

Virginia herself—that hope is fruitless—but with the tiny image of Virginia at the edge of her field of vision. Her muscles wrench from the bone. Her breath is like a knife inside her.

She doesn't stop. She can't. If she stops, she knows, Virginia will notice; Virginia will see how weak she is, and how feeble; how feminine and frail. Virginia will know what a mistake it was, asking someone like her on an adventure like this. Virginia will regret choosing her: regret setting her apart from the Bonnies and the Freddys of the world for reasons Laura still fears are mistakes. Maybe, Laura thinks, her knees will pop loose from her shins, maybe her hips will break out of her body; every breath she takes makes her hack up frost, but she forces herself to keep going anyway, chasing that elusive figure whose shadow she can barely see.

They run through the beech woods, to Farnham Cliff, and then turn left—away from Bethel Beach, past the Webster statue, then past the bounds of campus itself. The road is rock-strewn, and narrow; more than once Laura feels sure she will slip and tumble over into the frothy water below, but Virginia jumps dauntless over stray branches and fallen trunks, and Laura knows that, as terrible as this is, not doing it would be so much worse.

Finally Weymouth comes in view—the docks, the bobbing fishing boats, the few streetlamps illuminated at this hour, the old Wayfarer Hotel with its Victorian display china visible through the great glass windows, the ponderous blue curtains drawn apart.

Virginia slows to a stop. She pivots back to Laura, her cheeks pink.

"There," she says. "Was that so bad?"

Laura's pain has dissolved already into hazy joy.

"You do that *every* morning?" Laura breathes, when she can speak again.

"Sometimes farther. When I have time. It helps me think." She bites her lip. "I like having a routine. Otherwise I'd never accomplish anything." She smiles, so nonchalantly that Laura wonders for an unnerving moment if Virginia is making fun of her. Then she turns back to the water. "I like it here, at this hour," she says. "I don't like coming into town at daytime—it's all awful tourists wanting to buy seashell art and gawp at leaves."

Dawn cracks open the horizon. A small pink light has appeared at the end of the dock, refracted across the sky into kaleidoscopic slivers.

"I never take anyone else here," Virginia goes on. "Not even the boys. I thought about taking Anton, once—*he* runs, too, you know." Pride steeps her voice. "But I couldn't. He'd enjoy it, of course. Maybe even love it. But he wouldn't *get* it." She slips her hand into Laura's. "You get it."

Laura watches the sunrise. It feels so thrillingly unreal, as if somehow the two of them had made a wrong turn in the woods and ended up in an alternate Weymouth in some alternate world: just a little more enchanted than theirs.

"It feels like we've earned it, somehow," she says.

"Exactly," Virginia says. "Exactly." She exhales. "Come on. Let's get waffles."

Virginia leads Laura to the Grinning Griddle. She greets the gray-bearded man who runs it and settles into the window table, under a neon string of Christmas lights. The diner is empty, except for an old man half asleep at the counter.

"They're year-round," Virginia says, as Laura tries to disentangle them from her hair. "I find them reassuring. Got a pen?"

Laura hands her one.

Virginia takes a little black notebook out of her jacket pocket. She starts writing numbers.

"What are you doing?"

"Hold on!" Virginia murmurs a few more operations to herself. Then she looks up. "Three hundred fifty-six," she says. "Each way, assuming we keep time on the way back."

"What?"

"The number of calories we've burned. You have to adjust for your weight." Her eyes travel over Laura's body. "You're—what? One forty-five? Forty-six?"

"I don't know." Laura flushes, although this is a lie. "Around that?" Laura is exactly that.

"Let's say seven fifty. What looks good?"

Virginia traces her fingers on the menu.

"I'm—I'm not that hungry," Laura lies about this, too.

"Don't be ridiculous. You're running eight miles. You need to keep your strength up. There—you should have the Call Me Fish-Pail. It's got smoked salmon and haddock on top. That's high in protein. I always get the Lime of the Ancient Mariner—that one's key lime and meringue, obviously."

Virginia orders both before Laura can stop her.

"It's like you said," Virginia says, when the plates come. "We've earned it. Anyway, it's *fuel.*" She measures out a careful tablespoon of chocolate sauce and adds this to her key lime. She marks it down in her little notebook. She slams it shut and puts it away.

"You think I'm nuts."

Laura starts. Virginia is looking at her so calmly across the table, unblinking.

"I don't think you're nuts."

"Dragging you out here at five o'clock in the morning."

"I don't mind," says Laura. "Really." She laughs a little. "It's not like I had anything better to do."

"But that's the thing!" Virginia's eyes light up. "That's exactly it."

She stops herself. "What I mean is—there *isn't* anything better to do. Not really. I mean—in ordinary life. We could be sleeping in, right? Or watching Netflix. Or doing whatever the hell it is Bonnie does at this hour. Filming ourselves sleeping." She smiles at herself. "I mean … we'd probably be more comfortable. We'd certainly be warmer. But there's got to be more to life than being comfortable and warm. There's got to be something *real*, right?" She scans Laura's face. "I mean, people don't get to be World-Historical by being warm and comfortable. Not in a boring, history-textbook way, obviously. I mean World-Historical in the Websterian sense. . . ."

"I know."

"Of course you get it," Virginia says so quickly. "You get Webster."

"I mean—I think I do," Laura says. "Living a life that really matters."

"Living a life that means people can't forget you." Virginia shovels a forkful of whipped cream in her mouth. "Doing something that pushes you beyond your limits—the limits of what an ordinary human being can be. Like—like Napoleon! Or Joan of Arc. Or Webster, obviously."

"Obviously," Laura echoes.

"I mean—haven't you ever wanted that for yourself? To be . . . World-Historical?"

Laura considers.

"Not really." Laura lets herself smile a little.

She is less afraid of Virginia than she was earlier this morning. There is something about the strangeness of the hour, the odd light refracting off the pools of water in the docks, the emptiness of the diner, that makes her feel safe talking about the things she has always wanted to say. She wonders if this is how people feel in confessionals.

"I think," she says at last, "I've always wanted to be the least interesting person in any room."

Virginia looks at her in surprise, whipped cream suspended on her fork. "But—why?"

"It means a room is full of interesting people," Laura says. "I think—that's what I want. Just to be part of it. I think it would be a little lonely, wouldn't it? Being World-Historical."

Virginia's eyes are shining.

"It is!" she says. "Or at least"—correcting herself—"I feel it must be. Webster must have been *so* lonely. Up there in Desmond, scribbling away, having his visions—you know I have his old room, right? I came top of the housing ballot. You should come see it. I like to think that he's there haunting me. Reminding me to be World-Historical."

"Do you want that?"

But Virginia is already onto her next sentence. "When it's midnight, and I haven't finished my history essay, or I haven't arranged all the pieces for chapel, and I'm feeling sorry for myself, and I just want to go to bed and sleep and be comfortable and warm, I think—*what would Sebastian Webster do? What would any World-Historical person do at this moment?* And then I'm too ashamed to let myself go to bed until I'm done." She takes another forkful. "It's why I could never be a nun."

"A nun?"

"Nuns don't do anything. They just sit there and pray."

"Don't they do, like, charity and stuff?"

Virginia licks the chocolate syrup off her fork. "I mean, they don't do World-Historical things. Things that matter on the macro level."

"Like what?"

Virginia searches for words. "Like—conquer countries, or discover radium. Or start ideological revolutions." She smiles to herself. "I think I'd like to start an ideological revolution," she says. "I told you. Madness. Right?"

Laura knows it's madness. Laura doesn't care.

"What's the ideology?"

"Moral realism, mostly. That there's such a thing as Good and Evil." Virginia leans in on her elbows. "Most people nowadays are total moral relativists—basically anything goes, as long as it makes them feel good on the inside. It makes people self-indulgent—*whatever makes you feel good is okay.* Sex. Adultery. Cowardice. It's all fine and dandy. *You do you.*" She throws up her hands, letting her fork clatter on her plate. "Because nothing matters, right? So you can do whatever! Whereas, you know, if things do matter, if things do mean things, then suddenly you can't trust your gut. Your happiness isn't the only thing that counts. Anyway, I want to make people realize the importance of moral vigor as a counterpoint to our moral lassitude. I want to make people serious again."

"Like Webster?"

"Exactly!" Virginia bangs the table so loud she wakes the man dozing at the counter. "Now, there was a serious person! Literally bayoneted men, right in the guts!" She closes her eyes for a moment, as if she is picturing the battlefields. "Anyway, the problem is, you can't start an ideological revolution until you have a platform, and you can't have a platform until you have a substantial body of work. So I'm going to go into law, first—Harvard, ideally, but I'm not picky—with a sideline in political journalism I can parlay into something broader once I've got a solid practice going. I've got an internship at the American Institute for Civic Virtue this summer. You know, in DC. My parents are horrified—because of the whole Kissinger connection. They're pretty stereotypical, you know, that way: Democrats, upper-middle-class Jewish, *definitely* relativists ..."

"You're Jewish?"

"Only technically." Virginia shrugs. "You should have seen their faces when I told them I was getting baptized."

"So you're doing it."

"I want Lloyd Tipton to do it." A soft, girlish smile crosses Virginia's face. "I'm planning to write him a letter, asking. I think it's more solemn, doing it by a proper, handwritten letter, than in an email or something." She leans her head on her palms. "I just want to do the whole thing right. I want to take it seriously."

"But do you—I mean—do you really believe it?"

Virginia snorts. "That's not the right framework," she says. "Believing is all about *feeling*," she says at last. "Affirming is about *deciding*. There's a difference. It's all there in Webster. In his letters."

Laura has read all those letters. She has never fully understood them.

"Well, *he* converted. For the same reason. He didn't want to just go on believing comfortable, modern bromides about progress or science. He wanted to believe in *hideous* things! Things that break open your brain. Like, that God *actually* became man, and that that man *actually* came back from the dead, things you can't compromise on. The way people compromise every day. On—on moral seriousness, or capitalism, or sexual immorality, or . . ."

A shadow of memory passes through Laura.

"Is that why—?" she lets herself ask. "You and Isobel. You used to be roommates."

Virginia's smile dies.

"Oh," she says. "That."

"Was it because she was—? And you—?"

Virginia shakes her head. "No," she says. "I mean—not the way you think. I mean, I never had a problem with *her* . . ." She doesn't meet Laura's gaze. "As far as I was concerned, she could do whatever she liked, with whomever she liked. Only—" Virginia sighs. "She liked me." She says it so simply.

Laura tries to ascertain how Virginia feels about this. But Virginia's features betray nothing.

"Oh," Laura says, not knowing quite what to say. "I'm sorry. That's—awkward."

"She had a whole story in her head about it. That I was *repressed*..." She scoffs. "That if I hadn't converted, we would have ... you know."

"But you're not, I mean—" Laura's mouth is dry. "I mean, you don't like girls...."

"I don't like anybody." Virginia's mouth twitches. "Not like that. I find sex profoundly boring. When I think about sex, you know, all I can ever think about is Natasha getting fat."

"Who's Natasha?"

"*War and Peace*. You've read it." This isn't a question.

"Years ago. Why?"

"Well, don't you remember the ending?"

Laura doesn't.

"Give me your phone." Virginia stretches out her hand across the table. "A thousand pages of bloodshed and hallucinations and World-Historical events, and Andrei dies and Pierre tries to shoot Napoleon and what does Natasha get? Fat." She takes Laura's phone. She types into it furiously.

"She marries Pierre, and then—here it is: *She had grown stouter and broader, so that it was difficult to recognize in this robust, motherly woman the slim, lively Natasha of former days.* Not subtle, is it? And it gets worse: *Natasha didn't follow the golden rule advocated by clever folk, especially by the French*—the French!—*that a girl should not let herself go when she marries*—I'm cutting a bit—*but Natasha on the contrary had at once abandoned all her witchery, of which her singing had been an unusually powerful part.*"

"She gives up *singing*?" Laura had remembered Natasha happy.

"That's what happens. You get content. You get complacent. You get, you know, *soft*." Laura bristles and tries to hide it. "I just don't want that to happen to me." Virginia turns to the window. She breathes, a little, on the frosted pane. She traces her initials into the fog left by her breath. "I want to do too much." She turns back to Laura. "You understand that, don't you?"

Her voice trembles only a little.

"Yes," Laura says.

They run back along the coastal road to campus. It is an easier run than the outward journey. The sky is pink; the air is warm. But it's Laura's joy that carries her.

Virginia trusts her, she thinks, with quiet pride; more importantly, she *understands* her. Virginia talks, at last, at last, about real things, mattering things; she talks with such ferocious certainty, giving words and frames to all the notions Laura has only ever had the vaguest idea of: her hunger for meaning; her revulsion for sex. Laura feels her muscles tighten; she imagines that her body is hardening, the way Napoleon's must have, or Joan of Arc's, or Alexander the Great's; she imagines that she is purifying herself, burning away the soft tissue of her ordinariness, revealing her World-Historical core.

They pass the statue; they pass Farnham Cliff; they turn inland into the woods, and then when the beeches recede they see Devonshire Quad before them, the red brick and pale stone rosy alike in the morning light; the grass carpeted with leaves.

"You know," Virginia says. "You really should come to my room, sometime. 301. I can show you Webster's desk and everything. Plus, you can get away from Bonnie. I don't know how you stand it," she says. She bites her lip. "After my revolution," she says at last, "they'll make pornography illegal."

Laura can't tell if Virginia is joking.

Virginia leans against the last of the beech trees. Virginia keeps talking. "Her whole life is pornography. It's vile. I don't know why she does it."

"Maybe she just wants to be loved," says Laura. It is easier to feel sorry for Bonnie when Bonnie isn't right in front of her.

Virginia snorts. "That's the problem," she says, "with wanting people to love you." She zips up her jacket. "Anyway, they're done now. Brad said he broke up with her last night." She puts her hands in her pockets. "So she's not our problem any longer."

Laura lingers on the *our*.

"Come on," Virginia says. "Let's go."

Laura and Virginia keep running.

They run every morning, on the same coastal path, which gets starker and colder with each passing day; they go each morning to the Grinning Griddle, and Laura listens, rapt, as Virginia talks about World-History and Webster and revolution; every day hurts less. Laura drinks it all down, delirious.

She has no doubt that Virginia *is* World-Historical, or at least will be, in some sense. The notion thrills her. She has never been close to a World-Historical person before, at least not a World-Historical person you can reach out and touch across the table, whose hair tumbles over their collarbones and onto your plate.

It doesn't bother Laura that she is not, herself, World-Historical. For every Samuel Johnson, she thinks, there is a Boswell; every Don Quixote needs a Sancho Panza; every Robert Lawrence needs a Gus Parnell, attending meticulously to the meaningful facts of their life, setting them all down. Laura has a role to play, however small, in World-History. In the biography they will write of Virginia, she thinks, Laura will be a footnote.

A whole footnote, she thinks, just for her.

Laura gets so much stronger. She runs so much faster. She knows the words to use—*realism, relativism, revolution*—to talk about the things she loves.

Laura and Virginia keep singing. Every Friday Evensong Laura's heart breaks open anew with the glory of it. They keep rehearsing with the boys, and Laura comes to know them, and love them, not merely as a wonderful but undelineated mass—the Lost Boys to Virginia's peremptory Wendy—but as creatures in themselves. She loves Anton for his energy, for the brutal certainty he brings even to the most mundane questions, for his obsession with alchemizing his life into perfection, even if it means drinking raw garlic in the morning, or doing a hundred push-ups on Devonshire Quad after lunch. She loves Ralph Ervin for the novel he is writing—longhand, he insists, in a little Moleskine notebook he carries around with him everywhere—which is called *The Year of Plenty* and which Ralph admits, and sometimes rages to Laura after rehearsals, is meant to be kind of like a modern *All Before Them*. (She loves him for how he lets Laura read it. It isn't good, exactly, but he uses the word *sclerotic* every other page, and every time Laura sees it she feels soft fondness for him)—and for how he always refers to his mother, with a combination of fondness and disdain, by her first name. She loves Barry Ng for how deeply he gets lost in the music; how he forgets the candles and the prayers and the stained glass; focusing, so intently, on the precise calculation of a single note; how he talks with not just knowledge but feeling about the differences between the Mixolydian mode and the Phrygian, and how different modes are like different colors you can use to paint, a distinct palette for sounds. She loves Ivan Dixon's blubbering innocence, the way he, too, cries at everything.

Laura even comes to love Brad, although he unsettles her. She does not understand the embarrassment he seems to feel in just living, the way he winces every time Laura asks him how he's doing, as if she's walked in on him watching porn. He never mentions Bonnie straight-out, Laura notes, but he makes a nervous point of avoiding Laura's gaze, as if he's afraid he will see there Bonnie's bright, unblinking eyes.

But what Laura loves most in all of them is Virginia. She loves their love for her; the shared joy they take in singing whatever she proposes, in following her to the choir loft or to Bethel Beach; the way they take up words or ideas of hers, like motifs, even when she is absent. She recognizes Virginia in Ralph's book—thinly disguised as the prim but impassioned teacher Victoria Berg; she recognizes her, too, in Anton's thunderous jeremiads against CAME ("Moralistic therapeutic deism!" he pronounces, once, over fish and chips at Keble); she recognizes her in Barry's growing interest in cataloging the different Anglican prayer books and his speculation on whether the 1549 or 1662 edition captures more of the wild piety of the early modern age.

The only person who doesn't love Virginia, Laura realizes, is Reverend Tipton.

The knowledge dawns on Laura slowly. At first, she chalks it up to Reverend Tipton's twitchy British exasperation, which renders him harassed by human beings in general. But, as September drags into October, and October into November, Laura starts to notice how Reverend Tipton's eyelids twitch, slightly, when Virginia breaks into a joyful tangent about the Prayer of Humble Access; how he hurriedly turns the pages of his music whenever she tries to engage him about his thesis on the Pelagian heresy, cutting her off to suggest they run through the Magnificat a few more times.

What is more surprising is that Virginia doesn't seem to notice. The more Reverend Tipton tries to avoid her, the more Virginia tries to get his attention: bringing him an antique copy of *All Before Them* she bought at Manifest Books, in town; interrupting rehearsal to fusillade the same questions about his time in Oxford and all the different august and magisterial theologians he must have met there; reminding him of obscure collects and fragments of medieval prayer she thinks belong in that week's Evensong.

"I do appreciate the thought, Miss Strauss," Reverend Tipton stammers back, "but, erm, you see, Evensong, it's really meant to be, rather, a unified occasion; you know, for the whole school; one wouldn't want anyone to feel that it has become too narrow."

"Of course," Virginia says, putting her hand on Reverend Tipton's arm. "You couldn't get away with doing something really elevated like that. Not under this administration, isn't that right?"

It is the only respect, Laura thinks, in which Virginia ever seems vulnerable.

It is the only respect—although this part Laura would never admit, not even to herself—in which Virginia reminds her, a little bit, of Bonnie.

Bonnie, for her part, has taken to treating Laura with strained nonchalance. She makes a show of not caring about Brad, or what has passed between them: asking Laura perfunctory questions about rehearsal, only to leave a punctuating pause in her sentences, as if to underscore all the ways she *might* change the topic of conversation to Brad, if she were any less dignified, or any less mature.

Laura welcomes the silence. In any case, she's rarely around. She spends mornings running with Virginia in Weymouth; evenings with Virginia in her room, tracing their fingers over what they like to imagine is Sebastian Webster's desk—although deep down Laura suspects it was constructed in the 1970s—or else with the whole choir, lingering in the choir loft, or on Devonshire Quad, or on Bethel Beach until the chapel spires ring out the curfew bell.

The days flow into one another. Laura's life outside of choir—the ordinary St. Dunstan's life of classes and homework; afternoon sports and evening meals—is little more than an impressionistic blur. Classes matter only insofar as Laura can glean something of use for her early-morning conversations with Virginia: she devours political philosophy, in case it is somehow useful for their ideological revolution; she pays extra attention in Latin to the orations of Cicero; she listens keenly during Topics in European History for any mention of moral realists.

Her grades improve—with the exception of math, which Laura has judged useless to the revolution—but this success feels coincidental, irrelevant to her greater transformation. When Laura runs, when Laura studies, when Laura muscles through her nighttime exhaustion and the morning frost, she tells herself, she isn't doing so for such quotidian things as grades, or slender thighs. She is transforming herself into someone worthy of the challenge of World-History.

By the week before Thanksgiving break, Laura can make it all the way to Weymouth and back without stopping.

"You're a natural," Virginia says, as they crunch the frost of Devonshire Quad beneath their feet. "I knew it—the first time I looked at you."

It is seven thirty in the morning. It is still dark.

"I finally wrote to Tipton," Virginia says, "asking him to baptize me. I want to do it before I go home for Christmas." She turns to Laura. "My parents are going to have a heart attack."

Her smile curls like burnt paper.

"What did he say?"

"Nothing yet. But he'll do it. Obviously," Virginia says. "Priests have to. If you ask. They're not allowed to deny you sacraments." She considers. "I wonder if he's read his Webster yet." She stops short in front of Desmond. "I need to take a shower. I'm disgusting. Meet you at Keble in fifteen?"

She unlocks the door and bounds up the stairs. Laura trots up after her, tiptoeing across the third-floor corridor, lest she wake Bonnie. She places her key, so delicately, in the lock. She sidles in.

"*Shit!*"

Brad is sitting straight up, shirtless and sweat-slick, in Bonnie's bed.

"Oh!" Laura almost drops her keys. "I'm—"

"*Laura!*"

Bonnie bounds up from under the covers. She blinks rapidly. "I thought you were running," she says at last. She fixes her gaze on Laura. "You're *always* out running."

"I am. I mean, I was."

She looks from Brad to Bonnie and back again.

Brad sighs a long and exhausted sigh.

"Well," he says, "this is fun."

He puts his arm around Bonnie. He rubs her back. His smile is weak. Bonnie closes her eyes.

"Look, Stearns. What do you say we keep this need-to-know?" His voice wavers. "You know Strauss—it'll just upset her."

Laura takes a step back toward the door.

"You want me to lie to her."

"Not lie. Just—omit." His arm is so gentle around Bonnie's shoulder. "For a good cause. Young love?"

The word stops Laura short.

"Stearns"—it's the first time Laura has ever seen Brad look serious about anything—"I'd—I'd owe you one, okay?" He swallows. "Please?" His voice wavers.

He's looking at her, Laura thinks, like he's afraid of her. She doesn't like it.

"She'll find out eventually," Laura says.

Brad exhales. "I know, I know," he says. He swings his legs out of bed. "But, you know, *gather ye rosebuds*, et cetera, et cetera." Laura averts her eyes as he grabs his trousers, his shirt, his bow tie. He ties it in Bonnie's mirror. He pulls it taut, before turning back toward the two of them, his smile jagged once again. Bonnie is beaming up at him, flushed with joy, her hair tumbling long and loose over her naked breasts. It is the first time, Laura realizes, that she has seen Bonnie without makeup on.

Bonnie, she realizes, is beautiful.

Brad bends to kiss Bonnie's forehead; he lingers there. He clears his throat. "I should go," he says, making for the door. He stops with his hand on the handle, turning back to Laura.

"Actually—" he says. He grabs his phone out of his jacket pocket and opens it, handing it to Laura. "Would you? Just for us?"

It takes Laura a moment to realize what he's asking.

"You know what they say," Brad says. "If you must sin—*sin boldly.*" He holds Laura's gaze a little too long.

Laura takes a photograph of the two of them on Bonnie's bed, Bonnie's pink duvet pulled all the way up to her collarbones, Bonnie's cheek leaning on Brad's chest. His arms encircle her. His chin brushes the top of her hair.

They look, Laura thinks, happy.

Brad takes back his phone.

"I'm in your debt, young Stearns," he says. He bows to her—a stilted, awkward gesture—and then tiptoes out.

"I'm sorry I didn't tell you," Bonnie says, once he's gone. "It's just—Brad wanted to keep it quiet. Because, you know, *her.*" She swallows. She scampers to the edge of the bed, letting the coverlet fall. "Promise you won't tell, Laura," she whispers.

"I promise," Laura says, and immediately regrets it.

Laura spends the rest of the week worrying. The thought of lying to Virginia, even by omission, terrifies her. *Moral relativism*, Virginia would call it: evidence of selfish laxity, or else of cowardice. A sign of the *sclerotic modern world*: the three of them conspiring, together, to allow Brad to keep having sex, worse, to keep receiving *pornography*.

The sign of three profoundly unserious people.

Only, Laura can't stop thinking about how tenderly Brad nestled his arm around Bonnie's shoulder, how he'd rested his lips against her forehead, how he'd said the word *love*. Surely, whatever is passing between them has to be about more than sex; surely *sex*—dull, boring, sclerotic sex—can't explain how Brad looked at Bonnie, in that photograph, like he was afraid of ever forgetting her.

Not, Laura thinks, ruefully, that she would know.

Laura tries to weasel her way out of the situation altogether. She changes the topic whenever Virginia makes an idle comment about Bonnie's Instagram; she avoids Brad's grateful eyes during Evensong, keeping her gaze fixed firmly on the stained glass St. Peter. Still, she is distracted: her mind wanders in Friday rehearsal, and she misses so many notes that Barry Ng throws his entire sheaf of music across the organ loft in despair, sending reams of pages scattering to the floor, and making Ivan Dixon yelp.

Luckily, Virginia is too preoccupied with Reverend Tipton to notice. She spends the whole rehearsal trying to catch his eye; standing when he stands; sitting when he sits; anticipating everything he says with solicitous quickness.

At last, when they have finished running through the Nunc Dimittis for the fifth time, Virginia can stand it no longer.

She comes up behind Reverend Tipton, standing so close he nearly trips on the folds of her robes.

"I left a letter in your pigeonhole," she says. "Did you get it?"

Laura catches a glimpse of his irritation before he arranges his face into a mask of complacency.

"I did," he says. "Thank you."

"And?"

Virginia taps her foot just slightly on the wooden floor.

Reverend Tipton takes a deep breath. "I'm . . . delighted . . ." He forces out the words. "To see someone take such an interest in the Christian life."

Virginia's face lights up.

"We should certainly have a meeting about it," he says. "After Thanksgiving break. We'll set up a time."

"How about the first Friday, then? The thirtieth?"

"I don't have my diary on me," he says. "Send me an email?"

Virginia's face freezes.

"Of course," she says.

As Thanksgiving draws nearer, Laura's dread intensifies. It is only a week away from St. Dunstan's, she knows, but the thought of talking to her parents about Evensong and Webster and Virginia, of reducing everything to a few anodyne sentences ("I've made friends. I've joined a club") seems like a violation. Virginia, too, is increasingly fractious, though whether it's because of Tipton or the impending break, Laura isn't sure. She starts extending their morning runs: leading them an extra two miles each way toward Howlham; she stops eating, staying at the Grinning Griddle only long enough to order them black coffees then charging back to campus before the first bell. On the last full day before break, Virginia announces that she needs the evening to herself to study for their chemistry final.

"I can't stand any distractions," she says. "Not even you."

Laura can't bring herself to face Bonnie. She trudges instead to Carbonell. She checks out a copy of Hegel's *Phenomenology of Spirit*— half for her Topics in European History term paper; half at Virginia's recommendation—doing her best to ignore Freddy's brittle smirk at the checkout counter, before heading to the carrels upstairs.

She tries, at first, to work on the second floor, plodding her way along Hegel's sentences, but Yvette Saunders and Gabe Meltzer are loudly debating Dr. Charles's sexual orientation at the next carrels over, and Laura can't seem to get all the way to a verb without Yvette's hysterical laughter, and so in desperation Laura makes her way to the dusty silence of the rare-book room.

Isobel Zhao is already there.

She looks up when Laura enters. Her hair, Laura notes with surprise, has been dyed back to its natural black. Isobel has grown out the sides.

"Shit," she says. She looks Laura over. "Hey, no offense, but I've got a date in a hot minute. You'd better clear out." She snorts. "The missus and I have been barred from entering each other's rooms, you see. Noise complaints." She waits for Laura to look scandalized.

Laura feels a vague sense of shame, as she always does whenever she sees Isobel. She tries to remind herself that she's done nothing wrong.

"I'm just trying to work," she says. "That's all."

Isobel's eyes land on the book Laura is carrying.

"*Phenomenology of Spirit*," she says. "Heavy stuff. That for Dr. Meyers? Or one of *hers*?"

The possessive way she says it makes Laura bristle.

"As it happens," Laura says, trying to keep her voice cool, "Virginia recommended it."

"Of course she did. Bet she's got you on a whole syllabus, too. Let me guess: she's got you praying together, too?"

Laura's face burns. "I don't know," she says, with great effort, "what your problem is."

"My problem," Isobel says, "is that Virginia Strauss isn't some kind of saint. And she should stop trying to be one."

"It's not like that! She's just—serious." Laura tries to remember where she's heard that excuse before.

Isobel snorts. "Right. So very serious. So very special."

It sounds so much worse when Isobel says it.

"God forbid," Isobel goes on, "Virginia Strauss ever let herself be a normal person."

"She's not a normal person!"

"Face it," says Isobel. "We're all normal people. Maybe you should tell your cadre that. Or are they too busy polishing their jackboots?"

"They're not . . ." Laura doesn't even know what that's supposed to mean.

"Right," Isobel says. "Right, sorry, they just—what? *Love the language?* Christ, Laura, that's like reading *Playboy* for the articles."

Shame floods Laura's face; she curdles it into fury.

Isobel is just jealous, she tells herself; she is petty; she is angry; she takes delight in tearing things down for the sake of it; she takes delight in profanation, because she desperately hopes it will one day prove Virginia wrong.

She can't believe she ever let Isobel make her feel ashamed.

"It's not their fault," she says, in a high, cold voice she does not recognize. "That Virginia doesn't love you back."

This lands.

Isobel's mouth falls open. She flinches, quickly, and then tries to pretend she hasn't.

Laura immediately regrets it. She opens her mouth to apologize, to try to take it back, to explain, only Isobel cuts her off before she can speak.

"God, you're such an idiot." Her laugh is hollow. "I almost feel sorry for you." She wipes her eyes with the back of her hand. "Don't tell me I didn't warn you," she says. "Come on, Miranda. Room's occupied."

Laura wheels around toward the doorway, where Miranda is standing, glaring. Isobel loops her arm into Miranda's, and then the two of them are gone, leaving Laura: hot-faced, dry-mouthed, alone.

Isobel, Laura reminds herself, lacks transcendence. She can't quite bring herself to believe it.

Laura spends the week of Thanksgiving riddled with anxiety. She is short and snappish with her parents; she is bored and fractious when alone. She can't even take pleasure in the places she used to love. The world seems so empty without Virginia in it.

To make matters worse, Virginia herself vanishes for the whole of Thanksgiving break. She ignores Laura's emails; she leaves her texts on Read. Laura even tries to call, once, though she knows how needy it is to want to talk to someone on the phone in this day and age, but the call goes straight to *this voicemail box hasn't been set up.* She wonders whether Virginia has somehow found out about Bonnie and Brad, whether she knows Laura has kept it from her, whether she has decided that Laura is some sort of pornographic panderer, willing to betray all her World-Historical ideals for the sake of getting Bonnie di Angelis laid.

Laura spends her whole flight to Boston in agony. She spends the train to Portland tapping so wildly on the dinner tray that her companion gets up and moves to another seat. By the time the bus gets to Weymouth, Laura is in tears.

But when Laura arrives, at last, back at Desmond Hall, for the final weeks of Michaelmas term, Virginia is waiting, in room 301, like nothing has happened.

Laura almost doesn't recognize her.

Her face is gaunt. Her cheeks are hollow. Her body is like a bird's. Her lips are the same desiccated color as her skin. The window is open. The room is freezing.

"Stearns." Even her voice is weaker.

Laura forgets every worry she has spent the past week nursing.

"Jesus—are you okay?"

Virginia shrugs.

"A week with Dr. and Mrs. Strauss," she says. "That's all."

Her eyes are red. Laura feels a sudden, wild protectiveness toward her.

"I tried to call."

"I turned off my phone."

"What happened?"

"Nothing. The usual. Just bullshit." Virginia tries to smile. "I told you. They're moral relativists."

"How?" Laura can't imagine Virginia being a disappointment to anybody's parents.

She nods toward the closet. "Go on—look at what Dr. Strauss got me."

Laura goes to the closet. Hanging there, among Virginia's long black skirts, and high black necklines, is a tiny white-sequined body-con dress.

"Apparently it's what all the children are wearing these days," Virginia says. "Of course, it's a size too small." She forces her smile another centimeter. "No doubt his mistress picked it out." She takes a deep breath.

Laura fingers the sequins. She can't imagine anything less suitable for Virginia.

"Anyway," Virginia says. "I got my revenge. I told them about my baptism." She closes her eyes at the memory. "God, you should have seen their faces. My father, shouting about all the cousins we lost in the Holocaust. My mother, worrying whether her lunch friends will think her daughter's a zealot." She snorts. "Anyway"—she takes Laura's hand—"it doesn't matter, now. We're *home.*"

She presses it to her lips. She stays there, for a moment, with her eyes closed; her frozen mouth on Laura's skin, breathing in and out into Laura's palm, like Laura gives her breath.

"Yes," Laura says, when she can speak again. "We're home."

Laura corners Brad after their next rehearsal.

"You have to tell her," she says, as he walks with her between Cranmer and Latimer Halls. "Or I will." Her boots crunch the snow.

Brad keeps his hands in his pockets. He sighs.

"I know," he says. "I will. Eventually. It's just—"

"Just tell her the truth," Laura says. "Just tell her you actually like her . . ." Her voice trails off. "Do you?"

Brad is silent for a long time.

"It's complicated," he says at last. "Bonnie—she's sweet; she's *fun*. . . . She's so easy to be with." His breath frosts the air. "She likes me the way I am." He swallows. "Problem is: I don't *want* to be liked the way I am. *I* don't like me the way I am. Why should I trust anyone else who does? Whereas Strauss—"

"She makes you want to be better."

Brad nods. "It's getting to be a habit with me, you know. Disappointing her."

"She cares about you, that's all. She wants you to be happy."

"She wants me to be World-Historical," Brad says. "She doesn't care if I'm happy." He looks up at Laura. "It's one of her best qualities." He sighs. "Look, I'll tell her. Just—give me the weekend, okay? I'll tell her Monday. We'll have dinner. Promise."

He puts his hand to his chest. "On the bones of Sebastian Webster," he says.

"Monday," Laura says.

They shake hands.

In the end, Brad doesn't have to say anything.

Monday morning, Bonnie posts a photograph on Instagram.

It is the one Laura took: Bonnie's cheek against Brad's chest, Brad's chin against Bonnie's hair.

She has captioned it with the words of the Compline hymn.

> *Before the ending of the day / Creator of the world we pray*
> *that with thy wonted favour / thou wouldst be our guard and keeper now.*

She has added a heart emoji to the very end.

"You see," Bonnie says, when Laura looks up at her in horror. "Now he *has* to tell her."

•   •   •

"It's a profanation!" Virginia rages as she paces the length of her room. "She *knows* what those words mean. And you just know she was naked under that duvet."

Laura makes a vague and sympathetic noise.

"And him!" Virginia keeps pacing. "Is there nobody in this godforsaken school who isn't inordinately horny all the time?"

"Maybe he likes her?"

"Impossible!" Virginia throws up her hands. "No, no, Brad's just— he's going through some sort of horrible spiritual crisis, something that makes him want to debase himself, utterly, just because he can, just because he wants to see what it's like. It's like Augustine and the pears. I bet he takes pleasure in the very act of defiling himself, in the sense of total degradation, the artificial . . ." She sees Laura's face. "Did you know about this?"

Laura hesitates. "He said he was going to tell you."

Virginia's nostrils flare. "You—"

"I wanted"—Laura is so glad she rehearsed this part—"to give him the chance to do the honorable thing. Before I told you myself, of course." She puts the emphasis on *honorable*.

Virginia's face softens. "He owed it to me," she says quietly. "To let me know."

"I wanted him to tell you directly," Laura presses further. "He promised he was going to. Tonight."

Virginia goes to the window. She looks out across the snow-driven quad.

"You think he really likes her?" Her voice trembles, just a little.

"He said she was easy to be with."

"They always are, aren't they?" Virginia swallows. She looks back at Laura. "I just don't understand," she says at last, "why everybody's always so obsessed with sex."

At first Virginia doesn't acknowledge her discovery. At Evensong, and at rehearsal afterward, she treats Brad with impeccable, if efficient politeness: handing him his sheet music, turning his pages. It is only when Brad misses a high A on the Tallis Magnificat that she finally looks up at him.

"Disappointing, Noise," she says, cutting off Reverend Tipton's gentle correction mid-sentence. "Have you even practiced this at all?"

Brad doesn't say anything.

"I mean," Virginia goes on. "Aren't you embarrassed? Turning up to Evensong—without even knowing the music. You know, you were off by a quarter beat the whole Nunc Dimittis."

Brad keeps staring at the floor.

"Virginia, *please*," Reverend Tipton tries.

Virginia is undeterred. "I just think it's sickening," she says. "You're meant to be the vice president of this choir, and it's obvious you haven't even bothered to look at the music. This isn't the Dewey Decibel System, you know—or were you just looking for an extracurricular to look good on your Yale applications, is that it?"

"Strauss, please," Brad murmurs.

"Because, if that's what you want, you shouldn't bother to *show up*, just take a picture for the yearbook, or for Instagram, and—"

"*Virginia!*" Reverend Tipton slams the organ cover shut. The sound echoes to the altar.

Virginia stands motionless, looking from Reverend Tipton to Brad and back again.

"Withdrawn," she says.

She keeps her gaze on Reverend Tipton a little longer, watching him watching her.

At last she lowers her eyes.

"Once more," Reverend Tipton says. "From the top."

The end of Michaelmas approaches so quickly. There are instrumental Christmas carols in the corridors of Mountbatten Hall, strings of lights around all the trees in Devonshire Quad. The campus is thick with snow; there is hot apple cider in Keble, and plates of gingerbread cookies on the dessert table. Dr. Meyers teaches a whole lesson on the Franco-Prussian War while wearing a Santa hat. Choir spends the final Friday Evensong of term singing Christmas carols instead of the usual canticles—"O Come, All Ye Faithful," and "O Come, O Come, Emmanuel," Virginia's favorite, and "We Three Kings," with Ivan Dixon's warbling high notes, his voice halfway to castrato on *Myrrh is mine / Its bitter perfume / Breathes a life of gathering gloom / Sorrowing, sighing, bleeding, dying / Sealed in the stone-cold tomb.* It makes Laura shiver, hearing him.

There is no rehearsal that night, and so, after Evensong they all disperse into the frost and the cold, except for Virginia.

"I've got to go to Latimer," she says, lingering on the chapel doorstep, slipping her hands into a black fur muff. She has braided her hair with special attention, wrapping it across the crown of her head like a Renaissance princess or—Laura thinks, a moment later—a saint. "My meeting with Reverend Tipton. Remember?"

"Yes." Virginia has been reminding her all week. "Of course."

"I wish he hadn't left it so late. We've only got a few days of Michaelmas left. . . . I want to take my First Communion at Christmas." She glances back toward the chapel doors. "I wonder," she says, "if he'll want to test me or anything. Sometimes they want to make sure you know your catechism. I've been studying the BCP, just in case. I've even gone back and reread his doctoral thesis—"

"I'm sure you'll do great," says Laura.

"I'm just glad"—Virginia exhales frost—"that I didn't settle for Heeno."

Laura goes back to Desmond. Bonnie is already there, wearing a red velour jumpsuit with faux-fur trim and a little elfin hat, holding an enormous tray of gingerbread cookies, posing with them against the window while Freddy photographs. They look up when Laura comes in.

"Merry Christmas, Laura!" Bonnie hands Laura a cookie. "Have as many as you want; the company sent me tons."

"Merry Christmas, Bonnie. Freddy."

Freddy scowls from behind her camera.

"It's a *gorgeous* night," Bonnie chirps. "Isn't it? The snow on the ground—what did we say, in the video, Freddy? *The ermine virgin carpeting of snow?*"

"*Virgin ermine.*"

"Yes." Bonnie breathes in the acorn-scented candle. "Virgin ermine. That was *good*, Freddy. Freddy and I made snow angels, today, didn't we, Freddy?"

"I saw," says Laura. Bonnie has already posted it. Two thousand five hundred people have already Liked it.

"It's a gorgeous day," Bonnie says again. She smiles beatifically into the middle distance. "You know—I *told* him. I told him! All you have to do is be honest with her, and everything will work out all right. He always said she's nice, deep down."

"I'm happy for you," says Laura. "Really."

She nestles into the window seat, watching glimmers of people across the quad.

"I *knew* she wasn't as scary as everyone says," Bonnie says. "She's just a Sagittarius, that's all."

Laura keeps watching out the window. Bonnie and Freddy keep taking pictures. A blizzard has started up now, and shards of snow sear sideways across the quadrangle; the wind wrenches branches from the trees, whipping up the water in the distance. Laura does not know how she can bear three whole weeks away from this place.

At last, at eleven, the curfew bell rings.

Laura closes her eyes. She drinks in the sound, trying to hold on to it, to form a perfect memory of each distinct note.

Then the door slams open. Virginia is standing in the doorway.

Her eyes are red. She is shaking. Her face is striated with tears.

"My room," she says. "Now."

"He's a bastard." Virginia slams her fists against her bedroom wall. "He's a cretin. He's—he's a *heretic*!" Tears are flooding her face, pooling in her collarbones.

"Who?"

"Who do you think?"

"Tipton?"

"*Serious reservations*, he said! About my, my—*insistence on haste.*"

"He wouldn't do it?"

"Oh, he'd do it," Virginia spits. "Technically, they can't refuse you. I checked. But—oh, you just know he wanted to! I could see it in his face."

"What did he say?"

A quick, sharp intake of breath.

"*Now, Virginia,*" she does his accent so well. "*You know that baptism is a serious undertaking*—as if I didn't know it was the only serious thing in the whole world! *I'd hate to rush into such an important sac-rament without ensuring you had a*—what was it?—a *robust grasp of the fundamentals of the faith.* Maybe by the end of Trinity, he said. In time for summer break." She blows her nose in her black lace sleeve. "At first, you know, I thought—I thought it was just that he wanted to talk theology with me. Weekly meetings. Maybe he wanted to talk about the Pelagians, or something. But, *no,* no, *he's* too busy, he wanted me to enroll in some fucking adult education *class,* over at St. Mary's in Howlham."

"Oh. I mean—that's not so bad, is it?"

"Not too bad?" Virginia's ears are pink. "Are you joking?"

"I mean, the bus is—"

"It's his way of telling me to go fuck myself! Telling me I'm sup-posed to spend my Sunday nights sitting through some bullshit *Christianity 101* class with a bunch of pimply teenagers and bored housewives who've probably never even heard of Augustine. As if I hadn't done more of the reading than *he* ever has."

"I'm sorry," Laura says. "I didn't realize."

"I told him," Virginia goes on. "I told him! I've done the reading. I know the creeds—I know the whole liturgy. I don't need to go to a class to teach me what I already know. And you know what he said?" She doesn't wait for Laura to find out. "Some bullshit about *pastoral life.* He said it would be good for me—to go to a normal class. Good for me *spiritually.*" She swallows. "And you know what the worst part is?" She closes her eyes. "He enjoyed it."

Laura can't imagine Reverend Tipton enjoying anything.

"God, he took such pleasure in it. In humiliating me. In making me feel—that he'd seen right through me, that I was some kind of fraud, that, God, I was faking it. You could see it in his eyes. *Look, it's that irritating Virginia Strauss, with her stupid furs, and her stupid gloves, who doesn't know when to stop talking, who only wants to convert to shock people.* You think I don't know he hates me? That he gets off on humiliating me—"

Her tears fall faster now.

"I'm sure he doesn't think that," Laura tries. She takes Virginia's hand; Virginia yanks it away.

"Maybe he's right." Virginia can barely get the words out. "Maybe I'm nothing but a—"

"You're *not*."

"It *is* real." Virginia buries her face in her hands. "It *is*."

"I know."

Virginia sits straight up.

"Reverend Tipton," Virginia says at last, "would never die for any cause." She snorts. "God, no, he'd just sit around, stuttering about his cheap conception of grace, how it doesn't matter, because God is some sort of a fucking all-you-can-eat buffet, *just show up; don't bother doing anything hard; just ask for forgiveness; make sure to say please, though; God loves you anyway; just do you.* That's not *my* God." She swallows. "I wouldn't even fucking accept grace like that. I'd send it back! I bet he never even read the Webster."

Laura strokes Virginia's hair. Laura wipes Virginia's tears with the back of her hand.

She knows nothing about grace, or sin, or sacraments; she doesn't pretend to. All she knows is that Virginia is shaking, with rapid sobs that convulse her body, that threaten to break her bones apart, and that Reverend Tipton has made Virginia feel this way. She hates him more than she's ever hated anybody.

"I'm sorry," Laura says. "He's awful." In this moment she feels sure it is true. "I bet—I bet he doesn't believe in the Resurrection, either."

This finally makes Virginia smile.

"No," she says. "I bet he doesn't. Oxford degree or no. I bet if he'd baptized me, God wouldn't even notice!" She bites her lip. "He's a profoundly unserious person. He's just better than most at hiding it." She takes a deep breath. "Come on," she says. "We're going out."

"But it's past curfew!"

Virginia smiles through her tears.

"What?" Her voice is hollow. "Scared?"

"No. No!"

"What can those bastards do to us?" Virginia wipes her tears with the back of her hand. "Sebastian Webster ran off to Spain in the middle of the night to get himself killed—and you're afraid of, what, early curfew?"

Laura is no longer afraid. Where Virginia goes, she will go, too.

"Text the boys," Virginia says. "Tell them to meet us in front of chapel."

They wait by Virginia's window, watching. They wait until everyone, even Mrs. Mesrin on the second floor, turns out their lights, one by one. Then Virginia puts a finger to her lips.

"Come," she whispers.

They creep along the corridors. They tiptoe down the stairs. They cross the common room, and then Virginia goes to the front window, its wood warped with cold.

"We did this last Trinity," she whispers. "When we snuck out for Compline." She closes her eyes at the memory. "It was a farewell. Ed Mandelbaum's last Evensong."

Virginia slips a credit card between the wood frames. She sidles it in, digging deeper and deeper until the wood groans, and then yanks it upward, until there is a small sliver of space.

"Now," she says.

She slips so easily through. She lands, catlike, on the balls of her feet.

Laura follows her—struggling to fit herself through the space, squeezing herself out at last until she belly-flops into the snow.

"Around the back," Virginia whispers. "Security prowls the quad."

They go around the back of Desmond, to the little rear parking lot earmarked for the few off-site teachers, and harried parents on move-in day, past fetid trash cans and discarded pizza boxes.

The boys are already waiting there, shivering.

"Hello, Strauss," says Brad. He doesn't meet her gaze.

"Gentlemen." Virginia fingers the key around her neck. "We're going to go pay our respects."

They slip into the chapel.

Laura has never seen the chapel dark. It unnerves her. A faint, sweet smell hangs in the air; dust mingling with shadows; the blizzard wind howling up the nave. In the darkness, the stained glass merges with the night sky so that all Laura can see is the lighthouse Madonna: a single pink shard of her face rendered visible by the moon.

They make their way down the altar. Their shoes echo on the marble. Anton takes out his phone and turns on his flashlight, sending a single beam of light along the nave.

"Turn it off," Virginia whispers. "It's better like this."

Ivan whimpers; Ralph shoves him.

"Don't be cringe, Dixon."

Virginia crosses the altar. She goes to the grille door, taking the key from her neck, unlocking it in one smooth and single motion.

She turns back toward them.

A slow, sure smile spreads across Virginia's face. Then she vanishes into the stairwell.

They follow her down into the crypt, down the rickety wooden stairs that creak and splinter with every step, feeling their way along the rough, moss-moist stone until, at last, Laura feels solid ground.

A rushing sound; then a flicker of flame. Virginia stands in front of the candle. The lacelike shadows render her face paler. She traces her fingers on the crypt walls.

"Nineteen," she murmurs to herself. "Nineteen."

Anton touches the stone. His breath is visible.

"He understood." Virginia closes her eyes, pressing her cheek to the stone. "When he had his vision, he didn't go to some idiotic adult education class in Howlham. He didn't ask for permission. He didn't do *class prep*. He got on a boat—no warning, no waiting, not even a letter home. He just did it." She taps against the crypt walls. "*Come, shipwreck my soul.* That's more like it!"

Laura feels that familiar prickling at the back of her neck, that formless fear that comes over her whenever Virginia goes somewhere Laura cannot follow. She is grateful for Brad at her shoulder.

"How many of you," she whispers, "would *actually* die for something that mattered? When it came down to it?"

"I would!" Anton is so quick. "We all would!"

"Would you? I mean, would you *actually*?"

Virginia scans them all, one by one.

Her face is jaundiced in the candlelight. Laura steps back, instinctively, right into Brad. Virginia's smile flickers.

"Would you swear to it?"

Laura feels Brad stiffen at her shoulder.

"Of course," Anton cries.

Ralph is nodding, too, and Ivan is squeaking assent.

Barry is still leaning against the crypt wall. "Why not?" he says.

Virginia's smile widens. "Gallagher, give me your pocketknife."

He scrambles for it. He places it into her palm.

Virginia watches them, for a long while, watching her.

"For *him*," she says.

She slides the blade across her palm. At first nothing happens. Then a thin, bubbling line appears between her forefinger and thumb.

"Repeat after me," she whispers. "I solemnly swear . . ."

"I solemnly swear," Anton echoes.

Brad and Laura look at each other.

Laura's chest is tight. She knows, of course, that this isn't a thing people do anymore; that you can't swear a blood oath, in a crypt—only you can, if you're Virginia, if you're like Virginia, if you're with Virginia, if you only want it badly enough; only, Virginia is smiling; only, all of them are smiling, even though they know, already, how impossible a thing this is; only, all Laura has ever wanted is for this world to be Sebastian Webster's; maybe Virginia is right, Laura thinks, and all you have to do is decide.

"I solemnly swear," Laura whispers.

Brad, at her side, echoes her.

Virginia's face is flushed. Her teeth are chattering. She trips over her words.

"To face the . . . *sclerotic modern world* with courage, with"—she gets her stride—"vigor! With strength!"

"To face the *sclerotic modern world* with courage, with vigor, with strength."

"To reject cowardice! Artifice!" She thinks for a moment. "Mediocrity!"

"To reject cowardice, artifice, mediocrity."

"To become World-Historical." Virginia is almost shouting.

"To become World-Historical."

"Even"—Virginia's smile widens—"should it mean my death."

Virginia presses her palm to Sebastian Webster's name.

"Even . . ." They fade into syncopation. "Should it mean my death."

Anton takes the knife from Virginia. He jabs it into the meat underneath his thumb and presses the blood below the imprint Virginia has left. Ralph goes next, a light, quick slice, and then Barry, who mops up his blood with a handkerchief; then Ivan, yelping when the blade goes in.

At last Laura takes it. It is thin and cold and so much heavier than she expected in her hand; her tongue is metal, too.

Hideous, she thinks suddenly, joyfully. *Hideous.*

She slices into the crease. She watches, transfixed, as the blood appears. She presses her hand, still trembling, to the wall; she imagines the stone sucking it in, with the moss and the mildew; she imagines it traveling, through the rock and the earth, straight into Sebastian Webster's bones.

Laura turns back to Brad.

He is standing there, so still against the wall, his lips quivering. He looks like he is going to be sick.

She hesitates for a moment. But then Brad holds out his hand; he takes the knife.

He cuts himself in a quick, sharp line, as if he can't stand to draw it out. Then, he presses his hand beside the others.

They stand there, for a while, looking at the seven red smears against the stone.

"*And the rocks and the harbor are one,*" Virginia whispers into the silence.

"There," Virginia says. "It's a covenant." She turns back to them. "Now we're a real family."

"Cringe," Ralph says, "complete cringe." Only he's smiling when he says it.

Brad doesn't say anything.

Virginia takes his hand. She wipes the last of the blood with the sleeve of her shirt. She lingers there.

"You know," she says, "what you have to do."

He nods.

They climb up the stairwell without another word. Virginia locks the door.

Laura and Virginia cross behind Desmond in silence.

Virginia keeps her eyes straight ahead.

"I want so much more for him," she says, "than an easy life."

They slip back in through the window.

Laura tiptoes along the corridor. She turns the doorknob so quietly of room 312.

The light is already on.

Bonnie doesn't even register her when she comes in.

She just lies there, in Freddy Barnes's lap, rasps wrenching her shoulders, muffling her sobs in the crevice between the bed and the wall.

Part II

CANDLEMAS

5

CANDLEMAS STARTS IN LATE JANUARY.

The trees are bare. The rocks are black. The air is blisteringly cold.

Laura hadn't minded the cold so much, last term. Then, there were fairy lights on branches; then, even the coldest classroom was warm with festive holiday glow. The snow that carpeted Devonshire had been welcome, even picturesque. But the frost cuts more bitterly now, the wind has a deeper chill; there's such starkness to the black and dessicated trees.

Virginia loves it.

"Candlemas," she says, as they run one bone-shattering morning along the slippery coastal road, by Farnham Cliff, "might just be my favorite term."

"It's the ocean," Virginia decides, staring out the window of the Grinning Griddle, a slice of the Lime of the Ancient Mariner on her fork, while Laura tries to warm her hands over the steam of her coffee. "That's what it is. The rest of the year—there are so many distractions. The leaves in the fall. The flowers in Trinity. But now . . ." She leans her cheek against the glass. "You really notice it, don't you?"

Laura watches the waves batter the dock. Flecks of foam fly into the air, mingling with intermittent snow. Jarvis Lighthouse cuts darkness into the dawn.

"It's wonderful," she says.

Laura never knew it was possible to miss a place so much. She'd spent the three weeks of Christmas break listless, waiting to return. She'd known better than to try to reach out to Virginia—although this time, at least, she'd had the solace of knowing it wasn't anything to do with her. She'd tried, at the apex of her loneliness, to bring St. Dunstan's closer: to read Webster again, or go for a run along the boxy suburban roads. But she'd never made it more than a couple of blocks. Without Virginia, without Virginia's flushed face and quick breath and insistent shouts of *faster, don't stop now*, the act of running felt perfunctory: something you'd do to improve your heart rate, or lose a couple of pounds, no different from the classes at Planet Fitness. Only with Virginia do the wild frozen mornings, the splintering in Laura's shins, the ache she savors the morning after, mean anything.

"I'm working on a white paper," Virginia says. She keeps her eyes on the fishing boats.

"A white paper?"

"You can read it. When I'm done. It's about the absence of a genuine conception of virtue in the modern world. It's ripped off from MacIntyre, obviously. But still."

"Obviously," says Laura, like she knows who MacIntyre is.

"I want somebody at the American Institute for Civic Virtue to publish it. They publish interns sometimes. I checked. I mean, just on the website, obviously, but it's still a byline. It's important to develop a byline early—that way people can track your intellectual growth over time."

Virginia smooths her hair behind her shoulders.

Then she smiles, as she always smiles when she realizes she is being ridiculous: a knowing flicker of a grin that is—for Virginia, at least—almost warm. "God," she says. "I'm so boring. Aren't you bored of me, yet?"

"I could never!"

Virginia scoffs. "It will surprise you little to learn," she says, "that Dr. and Mrs. Strauss *strenuously* object to any daughter of theirs publishing a white paper with the American Institute for Civic Virtue." She lifts her chin. "My mother used to use Bill Buckley's books as toilet paper in college. She brags about it at parties."

Virginia has said little about her family since their return to campus. The white-sequined dress still hangs, untouched, in Virginia's closet. She has not brought up the crypt.

Virginia's gaze softens. She considers the water.

"I just want to leave something of myself behind," she says. "Before I'm nineteen."

They run the four miles back in thirty minutes flat.

Laura gets dressed in Virginia's room. Since the beginning of term, she's spent more and more time there: leaving her schoolbooks on Virginia's desk, leaving her running clothes in Virginia's drawer; falling asleep more often than not at the edge of Virginia's bed, curled up cat-like against Virginia's feet, or else with her hair twisting with Virginia's on the pillow, and Virginia's arm flung over her side. She has grown so used to this, to falling asleep to the sound of Virginia's heartbeat, that the few nights she spends in her own bed, alone, she feels a phantom absence, like a limb removed. She is used to Virginia's smell.

Bonnie doesn't say anything about it. She doesn't acknowledge, in any way, that Laura might know more than she does about her breakup with Brad. Instead, she treats Laura with a brittle chipperness that, somehow, feels worse.

"You don't have to worry about me," Bonnie announced, their first day back, before Laura could bring herself to ask. "I know it's for the best. He had commitment issues. I mean, so would *I* if my mother had left my father for my therapist. A *female* therapist. I didn't tell you that."

"He told me."

"Oh." A note of disappointment. "Well, I imagine he's got a lot of work to do, you know, on himself, before he's fit for a relationship with *anyone*. And besides—I'm focusing on *me* this term. Schoolwork. The Dewey Decibel System. And, of course, my *art*—Freddy's got access to all the AV materials through the library, so we're going to do this, like, concept-art thing—it's, like, me, but as a mermaid, on all the different rocks near Farnham—"

Bonnie has already recorded several videos of herself living her best, post-breakup life. There is one—with three thousand likes— where she's singing with Yvette Saunders and the rest of the Dewey Decibel System under Langford Gate, and another of her sitting on the table of the rare-book room in Carbonell, wearing a tartan miniskirt and red Mary Janes, her socks up to her knees and her legs just slightly spread.

"Thank God"—Virginia shrugs, scrolling through Bonnie's feed— "we don't have to ever think about her again."

Brad, meanwhile, has rededicated himself to the pursuit of being World-Historical. He talks loudly about his plan to spend the summer as a research assistant with this Harvard Middle East Studies profes- sor his mother knows; the Intensive Greek class he's signed up for. He'll be applying early to Yale this fall. Laura returns a draft of his Common App essay with two pages of handwritten comments.

"Strauss," Brad tells Laura, "thinks I should become an ambassa- dor. God knows why," he says.

"You're good with people?"

He shrugs. "Who knows?" he says. "Maybe I'll stop one of Strauss's wars."

But it is in rehearsal that Brad is most attentive. He is early to Evensong; he stays at rehearsal late. He sings with bell-like clarity, his high notes curlicuing with the incense smoke. He never misses a note.

In fact, Laura notices, a few weeks into term, all of them are so much better than they were. She doesn't know if it is Brad's newfound fervor, or the oath they swore in the crypt, or simply that in the cold of winter none of them has anything else to do, but they have become so naturally, so instinctively accustomed to one another's sounds. Laura can anticipate Barry's measured breaths; she knows, before Ralph does, when he is about to pop some lusty chest note like a cork. She no longer needs to stand next to Ivan to follow with the music. She can shape the notes now, put herself more into the phrases, decide how she wants them to sound. She no longer feels like a vessel, wide-open, letting something unthinking pass through. What she sings now is hers.

"Really, Laura," Reverend Tipton tells her one day after rehearsal. "You're getting quite good."

"Oh?" Laura avoids his smile.

"You haven't considered—which is to say," he starts stammering again, "pursuing this, have you? I mean, at the collegiate level. Or, erm, further?"

"Oh. Oh! No." Laura can't imagine singing anywhere but choir.

"You might want to consider it. If—if it ever occurred to you to spread your wings, that is." Laura bristles.

Any compliment he gives her, she knows, is theft; a violation of the attention Virginia is due.

"I don't want to spread my wings," she says coolly. "Thank you."

"If you do change your mind . . ."

"I won't."

"Little weasel," Virginia says when Laura tells her. "He's up to something. I know it. He's trying to trick you by buttering you up. Turning us against each other. Don't fall for it."

"Don't worry," says Laura. "I saw through the whole thing. I knew he didn't mean a word."

The thought of this makes Laura a little sadder a little longer than she'd expected.

Tipton aside, however, the first weeks of Candlemas are some of the happiest Laura has ever spent. The constant nervous terror of Michaelmas has abated; in its place is a newly settled joy. She lets Anton prepare one of his garlic shakes for her and pretends to enjoy it. She and Barry go to the choir loft to practice Italian art songs he digs up from the Carbonell music archives; she reads the completed first draft of Ralph's novel ("Sadie says I could be the next Pynchon. But, I mean, she might be a little biased. She dated him once"), avoiding his eager, desperate gaze as he watches her turn the pages from across their Keble table. She and Ivan go shopping at Manifest Books the week before it closes down because nobody else ever shops there, and then go to Donut-ism for dessert, and Ivan asks her if it's normal that he's never kissed anybody before, and whether he should ask out Freddy Barnes, who always scowls at him whenever he tries to flirt.

He asks Laura what she thinks. "Haven't *you* ever had a crush on someone?"

Laura hesitates.

The idea of a *crush* still perplexes her. She's read enough to know what it's supposed to feel like—the breathlessness, the blushing, the battering of the heart; none of the boys she knows has ever made her feel like that. She's aware, theoretically, that Anton is good-looking, but she has never once woken, breathless, imagining what his body would feel like on top of hers.

She has never thought of anyone's body against hers, except maybe Virginia's body, some mornings, only that's different. She knows already how good that feels. But, of course, she tells herself, that isn't the same thing at all. Sure, it makes her breath catch sometimes, but it isn't *sex*. It's too sacred, she thinks, for sex.

She shakes her head.

"I like things the way they are," she says.

"I've got a good feeling about this term," Virginia says the day they make it all ten miles to Howlham Point and back before the morning bell. "Everything's finally as it should be."

For the first few weeks of Candlemas, everything is.

Then comes the day the heat in Desmond goes out, and so Laura has to go to Carbonell to study, curled up underneath one of the carrells until the curfew warning bell rings.

She takes her copy of MacIntyre's *After Virtue* to the front desk.

"Name?"

"It's me, Freddy."

Freddy doesn't even look up.

"Name?"

"Stearns."

Freddy keeps her eyes on the screen. Laura can see its reflection in her glasses. She is editing one of Bonnie's photos.

"*Laura* Stearns," Laura says, relishing the pettiness of it.

Freddy's lips curl upward. She takes the book. She scans it.

"It's amazing," Freddy says suddenly, "that you have *any* time to read for pleasure. What with choir and all." Her smirk is unnerving.

"I don't know," says Laura vaguely. "I make it work."

Now Freddy looks up. She considers Laura.

"It must be hard," she says. "Just the two of you, doing all the female parts." She allows a significant pause to elapse. "Must be a lot of pressure."

"It's fine," Laura says. "Ivan sings alto, too."

"No other sopranos, though."

"No," Laura says. "We don't need one."

"Tough job. Arranging *and* singing."

"She can handle it."

"Well." Freddy's smile curdles. "I hope you're able to set aside time"—she slides the book across the counter—"for, you know, self-care."

Laura takes the book. "I don't need time for self-care."

"It's important," Freddy says. "For your mental health and all . . ." Her voice trails off. "Maybe soon." She turns back to her screen.

"Ignore it," Virginia says, when Laura mentions the conversation. "Barnes is a professional troll."

But Laura can't stop turning the exchange over in her mind. She has an uncomfortable feeling that Freddy knows something she doesn't.

On Friday, after Evensong, Laura learns what it is.

The service itself is uneventful. They do Stanford canticles, which always fill Laura with particular joy. Brad does a solo one of the Psalms; Isobel falls asleep on Miranda's shoulder and starts to audibly snore.

Yvette Saunders and Gabe Meltzer from Laura's Calculus class hold hands underneath their coats. Reverend Tipton gives a sermon about winter and melancholy and mindfulness in times of despair, which Virginia snorts her way through.

"*Mindfulness*. Really," Virginia scoffs into Laura's ear, as everybody files out. "Why doesn't he put a yoga studio in the crypt while he's at it?" Then: "What's she still doing here?"

Bonnie is still sitting in the front row.

Her honey-colored hair is braided into a bun. She is wearing all black, with a turtleneck that skims her chin. She is wearing gloves.

She rises when they approach.

"Vir-*gin*-ia!"

She crosses the nave so quickly. She flings open her arms.

Laura realizes too late what she is about to do.

Bonnie thrusts herself at Virginia. She kisses her on the cheek. She squeezes her rib cage.

Virginia just stands there, gaping, as Bonnie lurches at her other cheek.

"Sorry," Bonnie says, as Virginia recoils. "I always do it the French way! Force of habit, I guess!"

"I—"

"I'm just so *excited*," Bonnie says. She rubs her hands along Virginia's shoulders. "To be working with you."

Virginia blinks.

"What are you talking about, Bonnie?"

"Oh—Rev didn't tell you?"

Virginia blinks a second time. "Rev?" she says, with great effort.

"I *thought* he'd have told you. Maybe he forgot. I know he's been *so* busy lately, you know, with the CAME committee stuff, and obviously planning music for the term." Her smile glitters. "Or maybe he just wanted to surprise you."

"Bonnie?" Brad has come up behind them with the others. He keeps his voice low. "What are you talking about?"

Bonnie's grin broadens. "*Choir*, of course!"

She stampedes to Brad. She presents him with her hand.

Brad gapes for a moment, looking from Bonnie to Virginia and back again.

Bonnie's hand is still suspended, like a baton in the air.

Slowly, tentatively, Brad shakes it.

"Dude, what?" Ralph says from behind them.

"I just ...," Bonnie enunciates each word so deliberately, "think it's *so great* that we can be adults about this."

Brad's smile is pasted on.

"After all," Bonnie continues, "what's important is that we be professional." She drinks in their faces as the truth sinks in. "As colleagues."

"You ..." Now he gets it. "Choir."

"Of *course*, silly!" She punches his arm. "I auditioned last week. For Rev."

Ivan and Ralph exchange wary glances. Barry looks at the floor.

All the color drains from Virginia's face. She stands there for a moment, motionless. Her eyes are vacant. "That's impossible," she says. "The chaplain never holds auditions." She swivels around to find Reverend Tipton, who is still putting out the candles on the altar.

In a moment she is gone, marching all the way up to the altar.

Reverend Tipton looks up. "Virginia?"

"Is this true?" Her laugh is nervous and high. "I mean, it can't be *true*, right?"

"Is what true?"

"Her. Choir. *Her!*"

Reverend Tipton allows himself the smallest hint of a smile.

"I was going to announce it at the start of rehearsal. She came to me last week, expressing interest in arranging an audition, and—"

Virginia's smile is stretched thin. "Why wasn't I consulted?" Her lips barely move.

"Virginia—"

"I hold auditions," Virginia says. Her mouth doesn't even move. "I *always* hold auditions."

Reverend Tipton takes a deep breath.

"I think you'll find," he says, "that it's the chaplain who determines the membership of choir." His mouth twitches. "It's in the bylaws."

"*Fuck* the bylaws!"

"Virginia, please!" Bonnie's eyes travel upward, toward the lighthouse Madonna. "We're in a house of God!" Her smile is triumphant.

She knows, Laura thinks, exactly what she's doing.

It makes her respect Bonnie a little bit more.

"I think it's healthy," Reverend Tipton says, sauntering down from the altar. "A bit of fresh blood. Change, you know, can be invigorating."

He leaves Virginia gaping in the nave.

The worst part? Bonnie's good.

Her soprano, trilling and light, is as delicate as whipped cream. She reads music expertly; she hits every note exactly; she keeps the melody easily, even with the rest of them all singing different parts in her ear, never once letting them steer her off course.

She is almost—Laura hates to admit this—as good as Virginia.

Where Virginia is careful and precise, hitting every note like she's aimed a shotgun at it, Bonnie is extravagant, even operatic, pouring her entire soul into every phrase. Tipton compliments her, repeatedly, on her *depth of feeling,* and although Laura knows he is enjoying this so much more than he should, she knows, too, that he isn't exactly wrong.

It wouldn't be so bad, Laura thinks, if it were only Tipton who noticed it. But the boys all notice, too. Ivan Dixon is shuffling uncomfortably. Anton is glowering. Ralph is checking out Bonnie's breasts. And Barry—who knows the music better than anyone—is swelling with professional pride Laura hasn't seen since they did Wood in D Major last Michaelmas.

Virginia notices, too.

Her voice gets tight. Her vowels grow uncertain. Halfway through the Nunc Dimittis she goes sharp and then flushes into silence, her cheeks burning, as the bad note echoes down the rafters. It is the first time Laura has ever heard her miss a note.

"Well done, Bonnie," Reverend Tipton says when they've finished. "You have a real talent for this sort of music."

Bonnie beams.

"It's just that it's my passion," she breathes.

She is looking straight at Virginia.

Virginia rages all the way across Devonshire Quad.

"It's an outrage!" she fumes. "A travesty. A conspiracy!"

She kicks a cube of snow into the air.

"She's only doing it to annoy me." She crosses and then uncrosses her arms. "And—him! Everyone—everyone—knows I'm always the one who holds auditions."

"It's a coup," Anton says. "That's what it is." He gazes out toward the woods. "No respect for custom. No respect for tradition!" He coughs into his fist. "No respect for student self-governance!" He mops the sweat from his forehead. "It's—it's communism."

"The nanny state," Ralph Ervin says sagely. "There's no telling what they'll do."

"The next thing you know," Anton bellows, "they'll be teaming up with Chairman Zhao to ban Evensong completely!" He harrumphs, horselike. "I bet Sebastian Webster is turning in his grave."

Brad says nothing.

"But you have to admit," Barry sighs. "She *can* sing."

Virginia rounds on him.

"Bonnie di Angelis," Virginia says, "sings like she's expecting people to hurl bunches of roses from the front row. All she needs is a good death scene."

She storms ahead alone.

"Maybe she'll get bored." Laura turns to the others. "After a couple of weeks—I'm sure she'll feel like she's made her point and move on to something else."

Anton snorts. "Once she's done posting about it."

"No." Brad shakes his head. "Bonnie's stubborn. Once she's got something in her head she'll never let it go." He strains out a smile.

"Never let it be said," he murmurs, half to himself, "that I don't have a type."

"Didn't I tell you?" says Bonnie, so lightly, when Laura at last makes her way back to Desmond 312. "I could have sworn I told you." She doesn't look up from her phone.

"You didn't," Laura says.

"Oh," Bonnie says. "Whoops."

She swipes idly.

"*Anyway*," Bonnie says, "I've been so busy lately. With all my projects. Things just keep slipping my mind!" She finally looks up at Laura. Her jaw is steel.

"Look, Bonnie—"

"Rev's so happy about it," Bonnie goes on, undeterred. "It's a priority for him, you know, making Evensong *accessible*. None of that exclusionary Skull and Bones vibe. We've been having lunch, sometimes." She watches Laura's face. "He's really quite insightful, really. People don't get that about him. He's a visionary, if you ask me."

"Bonnie, *please*."

Bonnie considers Laura with wide, unblinking eyes.

"What?"

"You can't do this."

Bonnie's face is a burlesque of innocence. "Why not?"

"You know why."

"The only thing ever stopping me from joining was Brad." Bonnie sniffs. "He said it would make it awkward, us spending so much *extracurricular* time together." She shrugs. "But now that we're not together ..."

"Bonnie, please."

Bonnie trills out a laugh. "God, Laura, I don't know what you're getting so worked up about," she says. "It's just choir."

Her smile curls. "It's not like it's a secret society or anything."

Laura spends more and more nights in Virginia's room.

"Exiled from your own bed!" Virginia fumes. "Is *nowhere* safe?"

She flops back on her bed. "The whole *sclerotic modern world*," she mutters.

She puts a pillow over her head and screams.

• • •

Bonnie treats Virginia—and the rest of choir—with ostentatious civility. She greets them when she sees them in the corridors of Mountbatten Hall, or on the snowbanked Devonshire Quad. She waves to Brad in Assembly; she stops Barry Ng in the lobby of Carbonell to ask him, fluttering and wide-eyed, to explain to her the difference between keys and modes.

"There's nothing we can do," Brad says, one Wednesday evening, over Keble dinner.

"You could apologize to her," Ralph suggests between mouthfuls of kielbasa. "Fall on your sword."

Anton chokes on his sauerkraut. "Or she could fall on *yours*!"

"Don't be disgusting," Virginia snaps. She slams down her tray at the head of the table. "If you think Noise is going to prostitute himself to that . . . that . . ." She stops herself.

Bonnie is striding toward them, tottering under her tray.

Laura stiffens. Brad drops his fork. Ivan lets out a high-pitched yelp.

"Bonnie."

"*Hi*, guys! And gals, of course." Her voice undulates.

Bonnie sets her tray down on the table. She slides Barry's aside, making a little place between him and Ivan.

"How are we all *doing*?"

They all stay silent. They look wildly at one another, at Virginia, waiting for instructions. But Virginia just sits there: her cheeks pulled so tight in a smile Laura fears she'll tear the skin from her ears.

Bonnie trills on. "Did everyone have a good week?"

Ivan is the first to break.

"Fine, thanks," he squeaks, avoiding Virginia's glare.

"Oh my God, *Barry.*" Bonnie swivels to him. "I was just thinking about you! I just *have* to send you this article I found in the *New York Times,* all about this, like, adorable Renaissance music group they have in New York, in the Village—it's been going for, like, *forty* years—they do these open-air concerts on Christopher Street, like, the sweetest old queens, there's a bunch of videos on YouTube; anyway, you'd love it." She taps the table. "I'll text it to you. I have your number, right?" She cocks her head at him. "*Do* I have your number?"

Barry looks helplessly at Virginia.

"Oh," he says. "Uh, no. I don't—think so."

Bonnie's smile widens. She takes out her phone. She hands it to him. Her eyes are on Virginia the whole time.

"That's okay," she says. "You can just type it in."

Barry does.

Bonnie takes down her ponytail. She shakes out her hair, pursing her lips halfway, as if she is deciding whether to blow a kiss.

"Oh, and Brad?"

Brad inhales.

"Yes, Bonnie?" he says with great effort.

"You don't mind if I hold on to that copy of *All Before Them* you lent me, right?" She rests her chin on her hands. "I figure, you know, now would be a good time to reread it. You know, because, I'm, like, *in* it, now." She trills a little bit.

"Sure, Bonnie," Brad says.

Virginia still says nothing.

"Amazing, right? That there were people like us—just like us—a hundred years ago. I just find that so inspiring, don't—"

A loud bang thunders across the table, followed by the clattering of silverware. Anton has already stormed out.

Bonnie considers his absence. "What's wrong with him?"

Nobody says anything.

Then, at last, Bonnie turns to Virginia. "Are you okay?"

"Fine," Virginia slices into the word. "Thank you."

"Because you're not eating."

Virginia's nostrils flare.

"It's really good."

"I'm fine."

"You're not on a diet or something?"

"I'm not hungry."

Bonnie leans in just a little closer. Her eyes gleam.

"Because you're really skinny. You really shouldn't feel like you have to diet—if you're that skinny. My cousin, you know, *she* was that skinny, and *she* tried to diet, and she ended up in inpatient for, like, six months. They had to feed her sugar in an IV."

Now everybody is staring at Virginia.

The silence takes hours.

Virginia slowly picks up her fork, gripping it so tightly it trembles. She stabs a piece of kielbasa straight through. She chews it into pulp. She swallows.

Virginia throws up the entire meal in the Desmond third-floor bathroom. Laura holds back her hair.

"How dare she," Virginia gasps between retches, "make me eat with her."

She wipes the bile with the back of her hand.

She exhales. Her eyes are red. Her cheeks are hollow. Her lips are jaundiced, and her hair is tangled with sweat and spit.

"I'm sorry," Laura says. "She shouldn't have done that."

"I wonder why she bothered to sit with us at all," Virginia goes on. "Given her numerous lunches with Lloyd Tipton. Rev. Ugh. God! God—we ate at her table."

She turns back to the toilet. She convulses a final, acrid time.

Laura massages Virginia's back. Her spine prickles at the smell.

"You really don't have to do this," Laura tries. "It's only food."

Her stomach growls uneasily. She, too, ate at Bonnie's table.

"It isn't only food," Virginia says, her throat hoarse. "It's the principle. You don't break bread with an enemy!" Laura takes a piece of toilet paper and dabs the vomit on Virginia's collar. "You know—in the old days, breaking bread with someone—it was a sacred bond. A covenant. It bonded you."

Laura's gorge rises.

It's not that Laura doesn't know that Virginia is being ridiculous. People don't go around throwing up their food just because they're sitting with a person they don't like. (Not in this *sclerotic modern world*, Laura thinks, without meaning to.)

But Virginia isn't people.

Virginia runs ten miles without stopping. Virginia doesn't need sleep. Virginia takes things seriously. The rules for Virginia must be different, somehow; Virginia's life must be purer, more carefully constrained. You couldn't ask Virginia to just *get over something*. That would be going against Virginia's nature. It would, Laura thinks, be like asking Isobel to turn straight.

Laura brings Virginia a cold, wet cloth. She presses it to Virginia's forehead.

"She's just trying to get Brad's attention," Laura says. "And annoy you because she's jealous. That's all." She sighs. "She's just—she's just sad, and lonely, and heartbroken, and she wants to feel like she matters somewhere."

She pulls Virginia's hair from her neck. "It's not worth getting angry with her," Laura whispers. "Just feel sorry for her."

"Feel sorry for her?" Virginia pulls herself up against the bathroom wall.

"She's just—"

"You know what your problem is, Stearns?" Virginia's eyes are burning. "You're always going around feeling sorry for everybody." She spits out the last of her bile. "Some people don't deserve pity."

"She just wants to be like you. That's all."

Virginia coughs out a scoff. "Like me?" She snorts. "Don't be ridiculous. Why the hell would she want that?"

Laura looks up at her in surprise.

"I mean, you're . . ." She fumbles. "You?"

"Please." Virginia laughs weakly. "Bonnie has everything she could ever want already. She's beautiful; she's thin; she's talented, apparently; people like her; she's got, what, fifty thousand followers Liking her breasts on Instagram?"

"Something like that," Laura says.

"Plus"—Virginia's gaze is somewhere in the distance, somewhere beyond the bathroom-stall door—"she's *easy to be with*." She scoffs. "The only reason she cares about choir is because it's the only thing she can't have."

She holds her knees to her chest.

"Why," Virginia says, holding Laura's hand a little more tightly, "can't there be one thing she doesn't have?"

Things only get worse.

Isobel and Miranda put out a new petition.

This time it's CREWS (Campaign to REmove the Webster Statue). Miranda and Isobel cite a half-dozen instances, both in *All Before Them* and in Webster's personal letters home, where he expresses not just an affinity for the reactionary side of the Catholic Church—troubling enough—but for Franco himself. It gets fifty signatures in a matter of weeks, and Ralph ends up debating Miranda on the Assembly stage about whether Sebastian Webster was a fascist or a genius.

Miranda makes mincemeat of him.

For starters, Ralph isn't nearly as good a debater as Anton. As flamboyant as he is in real life, onstage he stammers; he stumbles over words. His airy allusions—which seem so natural when he lobs them off after Evensong—come across stilted and forced. He coughs, and misremembers lines from Webster, and insists in an increasingly high-pitched voice that it doesn't matter who Webster ended up dying for, because all mortal causes are irredeemable, at least all causes in the twentieth century, what matters is that he died fighting for a foreign cause, on a foreign shore, hundreds of miles from home, because he wanted to defend the Catholic Church from all the Republicans who were going to ban it like they did in Mexico, and it's not like General Franco was Hitler, or anything like that, only once you've said *at least he's not Hitler* you've already lost. Miranda barely needs to say anything at all.

Virginia watches the whole thing with pursed lips.

She watches Miranda bound offstage; she watches Isobel take her into her arms; the two of them do a little joyful fist bump that seems even more intimate, somehow, than a kiss.

"You know she used to love that book," Virginia says suddenly.

"Miranda?"

"Isobel," Virginia says. Her lips get thinner. "We read it together. She likes to pretend she doesn't remember."

Laura looks up at Virginia in surprise. Virginia speaks so rarely of their time as roommates.

"I thought—"

But Virginia is already halfway across Assembly Hall. She marches right up to Ralph, who is scurrying down from the stage.

"*He's not Hitler*? Are you kidding me?"

"Look, Strauss, I—"

"Is there nobody in this whole fucking school," Virginia rages, "with any sense? Webster would be ashamed of all of you!"

She storms out before Ralph can answer her.

The Webster petition goes to the faculty board. The faculty say they'll vote on it before the end of term.

Laura and Virginia have more imminent problems. Any hope they might have had that Bonnie would quickly bore of choir life is quickly extinguished. As Candlemas wears on, Bonnie becomes increasingly enmeshed in Evensong. She befriends Barry, wheedling him into spending weekdays practicing with her in the choir loft; she flirts shamelessly with Ralph, who blushes and splutters every time she appears, in all black and high heels, leaning ostentatiously over the organ, jutting out her hips. ("He salivates over her like she's a *New Yorker* byline," Virginia snaps.)

But it is Reverend Tipton who is Bonnie's most reliable protector. He compliments Bonnie's singing; he overrules Virginia's objections to Bonnie's rare melodic mistakes. Within a few weeks, Virginia's resistance has dwindled to a persistent glower and a consistent refusal to hand Bonnie her choir robes at the start of Evensong when asked.

Laura knows Virginia will never accept Bonnie's presence. She holds out hope that Virginia will learn to ignore it: learn to close her eyes, the way Laura does, when they sing the Nunc Dimittis and the Magnificat, to focus only on the light, cherubic trill of Bonnie's voice—to love the music in spite of whom it passes through. When Bonnie inevitably comes up in conversation, Laura tries to turn the topic to one of Virginia's other, less fraught favorites—running, say, or their revolution. She is unsuccessful.

They remain in this stalemate until late February, until the Friday, thirty minutes before Evensong begins, that Reverend Tipton replaces Virginia with Bonnie as first soprano during the run-through of that week's Magnificat.

"The thing is"—his gaze lingers on her as she splutters—"you've had so many opportunities already. And this one"—he breathes in—"requires a certain *robustness* of tone." He wrinkles his nose. "It still doesn't sound quite right."

The first soprano part has several solo lines, and an astonishing high C Virginia has been rehearsing all week.

"The second soprano line's lovely," pipes in Barry.

"It really is," Bonnie echoes. "And the top line *needs* support."

Laura watches Reverend Tipton twitch with satisfaction.

Yes, she decides. He's enjoying this.

They sing Evensong together. Bonnie stretches her neck like a flamingo. She sings the solo, with such extravagant joy.

"For he hath scattered the proud ..."

Virginia's whole body jerks up.

Laura follows her gaze to the pews.

Freddy Barnes is filming the whole thing from the front row.

Virginia digs her nails into Laura's palm so hard Laura gasps.

But Bonnie remains, implacable, her hands pressed to her heart, her face toward the camera, her golden hair glinting in the Madonna's refracted light.

"Don't worry," Freddy says to Virginia, as she files out, "I can always crop you out."

Bonnie posts a picture before the end of rehearsal.

In it, her face is turned upward, her lips pursed, her hands clasped in prayer. She looks, Laura thinks, like Joan of Arc.

Virginia spends ten minutes reading the caption, over and over, in increasing horror, in the common room of Cranmer Hall.

"*And, in the shadow of her red-drenched homecoming, Shrimpy's voice still echoing in his ears, Robert felt his soul at last drawn under . . .* How *dare* she?"

"It's tacky," Ralph sighs. "*Everybody* quotes the ending."

"Please. You're one to talk. Why don't you print these out and put them on your bedroom wall? You'd be less obvious that way."

Ralph looks down and says nothing.

Virginia sniffs. "God, she's even got a picture of Tipton on here—preening in his collar; it's disgusting." She shows them all the photograph, for emphasis. "He's worse than di Angelis. *She's* an idiot, but he's—I mean, he's a full-on fraud. Claiming to be all *morally serious* when all he actually wants is to stare at Bonnie's tits like the rest of you."

"I thought he was gay," Ivan says.

"He's not gay," Barry says. "Just British."

"Come on," Anton says. "He's totally gay."

"He's not," Laura says.

"How do you know?"

"He's on Tinder."

Virginia rounds on her. "What do you mean, he's on Tinder?"

"It was just a dumb joke. Isobel"—it makes her so ashamed to think of Isobel—"told me, once. She keeps this Tinder account to see what teachers are on it. He's probably not even still on there."

Virginia's face lights up.

"Hold on a second."

"Aw, come on, Strauss." Ralph rolls his eyes. "We're not going to—"

"I just want to see!"

She downloads the app.

"Christ, they want you to set up an account and everything." Her fingers move so quickly. Her eyes are shining. "Fine, fine, good, what's my name?" She points her chin at Ralph. "Give me a good name. Something literary."

"Viola?"

"Too obvious. What else?"

"Rosalind?"

"That's good. There we go. Rosalind, 21—no, even *he's* not that stupid—25. God, they want a picture." She starts searching for one on Google Images. "Location? Weymouth's too close—he might suspect something. Let's say . . . Howlham?"

She starts swiping furiously.

"Nope, nope, nope—*ugh*, the Grinning Griddle guy!"

"The Grinning Griddle guy?" Ivan grimaces. "Gross."

"No; no; Christ, Dr. Meyer, I always knew he was a pervert—he must be fifty!—Ted, no; Nate, no, Jasper no; sorry, Alvin." She stops, suddenly. An exultant smile spreads across her face. "Hello, Lloyd."

A younger, less harried-looking Reverend Tipton stares back at them.

"Thirty-one?" Virginia snorts. "*Please.*"

She flips through his photographs. "*Looking for a poetically minded young lady for seaside walks, candlelit dinners, and claret. Must love Keats.* Ugh, it *would* be Keats."

Laura takes a quiet pleasure in no longer being impressed by Keats.

"Claret?" Ralph blows out his lips. "What kind of pretentious asshole calls it *claret?*"

"Actually," Barry says, "that's what British people call—"

"*Seaside walks,*" Virginia scoffs. "We're in Weymouth, all the walks are seaside!" She looks up at them. The edges of her mouth twitch. She takes a deep breath. "Wish me luck."

"Wait!" Ivan tries. But she has already swiped right.

"You didn't!" Ralph is purple.

"He probably doesn't even check it," Virginia says. "He's probably too busy thinking up new and noxious ways to ruin choir." She sets down the phone. "I think it's telling," she announces, "that he doesn't even mention being a priest. I always said he wasn't a serious person."

Brad watches her from across the sofa. He arches his eyebrows.

"I never thought," he says, "I'd see you missing Heeno."

"At least Heeno knew not to interfere!"

"God, remember his *cigars?*" Ralph closes his eyes.

Barry turns to Laura. "You know he set the chapel on fire once? Fell asleep in one of the pews with a fat Cuban in his mouth—the whole place almost went up in smoke."

"You'd think St. Dunstan's could afford fire doors," says Anton.

"It's a conservation site," Barry says. "You can't change anything in a conservation site. John Devonshire built it in—"

Virginia's phone buzzes.

They all exchange glances. They wait, together, for Virginia.

She leans in so slowly. She slides the phone over, leaving it face down. She watches them, for a moment, watching her. Then she picks it up and opens the home screen.

"Lloyd," she savors the word, "Likes Rosalind."

They all groan at once.

"I mean, she *is* called Rosalind," Ralph says, with more than a little pride.

"And what," Virginia says, "does Rosalind have to say to Lloyd?"

"Strauss, don't!" Ivan collapses into giggles.

"Why not?" Virginia arches her neck. "Surely, the good students of St. Dunstan's have a right to know how our esteemed priest"—she pronounces it *esteemèd*—"conducts himself in the wider world." She licks her lips. "Whether he's falsely representing himself as an ordinary member of the public."

"Can they even date?" Anton snorts. "I thought they were supposed to be celibate."

Brad rolls his eyes. "He's Protestant, Gallagher. You know this!"

Anton looks confused. "It's still weird, though."

Laura's stomach knots.

"Are you sure we should—"

"Come on, Stearns. Where's your *mettle*?" Virginia looks up at her. "Are you afraid?"

"No—of course not!"

"Then give me a Keats poem."

"'Ode on a Grecian Urn'?" Ralph bounds over before Laura can say anything. "'Ozymandias'? 'Lamia'?"

"Christ, Ervin, that's not even—wait, no, good. How's this? *I've been told I'm something of a Lamia, myself....*"

"Say something about the claret!" Anton cuts in.

"*But apparently I improve after a few glasses of claret*? Ugh, gag me."

Virginia catches Brad's eye across the coffee table. She lets her smile spread across her face, cocking her head at him, just slightly, as if she is waiting for him to stop her. She presses Send.

Tipton's reply is immediate. *I like difficult women. Especially after claret.*

"Lies," Virginia mutters. "You can't stand them."

Ralph and Barry roll their eyes.

"Cringe," Ralph says. "Total cringe." He looks up at Laura. "You know, Stearns, there's no greater sin than being *cringe.*"

"Quick, Ng." Virginia looks up. "Tell me something useful about claret."

But it is too late. The curfew bells have already started to ring.

Virginia puts down the phone.

"Just as well," she says. "I don't know anything about claret."

"You're not going to keep messaging him, are you?" Laura asks, as they make their way across Devonshire Quad.

"I might." Virginia shrugs. "I haven't decided yet."

"You *can't!*"

"Why not?" Virginia turns to her. "Doesn't he deserve it?" Snow studs her hair.

Laura fumbles to explain the tightness in her chest. "I mean, he *does*, obviously, but—"

"And how often"—Virginia draws out the words—"in this world, do people actually get what they deserve?"

Laura has no answer for her.

"And to think," Virginia says, looking out across the vast blankness of the quadrangle. "I almost let him baptize me."

She swipes her key card. She goes inside.

6

ROSALIND KEEPS MESSAGING LLOYD.

She messages him about Keats. She messages him about Byron.
She messages him about the wild, gasping loneliness that comes from
being someone who hungers, really *hungers*, for all those glorious, vanished things of the world, which in this desiccated day and age have all
puttered, like a stopped engine, into mediocrity and decay. She messages him about the black water at the Howlham shoreline, just a few
miles north of Weymouth, and how she loves it, in a savagely possessive
way, even though she knows that Maine is the last place in the world
she wants to ever live (she has so many dreams; Paris is one of them),
because when she gets up at five every morning, to take her morning
walks along the shoreline, she exults in the knowledge that she has
been initiated, by the cold, by the dawn, to a higher and more esoteric
plane of life.

"We're naturals," Virginia says, as she and Laura huddle over her
phone at the Grinning Griddle. "We've got him right where we want
him."

I, too, Lloyd Tipton writes, *enjoy those cloistered moments. It is a
strange feeling, don't you think, to ache for further loneliness, even though
I suffer such loneliness already, being a stranger in a strange land? Perhaps we are all strangers to each other.*

"He still hasn't mentioned being a priest," Virginia considers. "All
he's said is that he's a teacher at the school. It's like he's ashamed of it
or something. I don't see why."

"Maybe he's waiting for the first date."

"If I were a priest," Virginia decides, "it'd be the first thing I told people. It'd be the most important thing about me."

After all, Rosalind has already told Lloyd so much about herself. She grew up in Howlham but spent her college years in St. Louis, before returning to take care of an elderly relative and work on her first novel. She was in one serious long-term relationship before, with the graduate student TA in her World Lit class ("It's important," Virginia determines, "that he know she has a type"), but it ended when he slept with their professor.

I can't imagine, Lloyd Tipton writes, *anyone who has you on his arm ever so much as looking at anyone else.*

Laura takes the phone.

In the two weeks that Lloyd and Rosalind have been corresponding, Laura has discovered a knack for romance. She enjoys, she finds, the breathless anticipation whenever Virginia's phone buzzes; the nervous glee that comes over her when Lloyd suggests taking Rosalind down to Boston some weekend, so that he can expose her to her very first live opera.

"Men always want to be women's first." Virginia snorts. "It's disgusting!"

It's not that Laura doesn't feel guilty. When Reverend Tipton first tells Rosalind about his ex-wife's affair, when he says, *You don't know how lonely it is, at a school like this, full of unhappy children who expect you to fix them,* Laura has to slam down the phone, convinced he can somehow see her, through the darkness of the screen, convinced he now knows how cruel she can be.

Only then it's rehearsal, and Reverend Tipton nods so approvingly at Bonnie, complimenting her *vigor* and *force of will* and telling her she reminds him of that Botticelli Madonna where she's all in pink. He makes such a point of flagging Virginia's musical mistakes—increasing, even Laura has to admit, by the week—of avoiding her gaze, or else of saying *Virginia, please* in that warning tone. In those moments, Laura's uncertainty kindles into conviction.

In those moments, Laura feels sure Virginia is right. It's so rare, in this world, that justice gets done; so rare a person gets exactly what he deserves.

And Lloyd Tipton, Laura knows, for all his British bluster, his pointed stammering and his fake-posh accent ("*Nobody* from Huddersfield talks like that," Virginia sniffs, like she's ever been to Huddersfield), is nothing but a petty tyrant: relishing the trappings of bylaws to allow him to torment teenage girls.

"It's to get back at his ex-wife," Virginia decides. "I'm sure of it. How petty."

Also, he never baptized Virginia.

In those moments, Laura takes such delight in their plan. When she and Virginia stand shoulder to shoulder in the chapel stalls, Virginia dutifully singing second soprano as Reverend Tipton punctuates the air with his fingers, Laura glows with the knowledge that, just that morning, Lloyd Tipton admitted to Rosalind he thinks his students are *the precise kind of coddled, intellectually pretentious, Adderall-popping know-it-alls one feels with a sickening sense are going to be running the world one day.*

In those moments, Virginia's fingers twining hers, Laura glows with the exultancy of righteousness. They are not schoolgirls, then, but angels. It may not be World-Historical, but at least it feels like practice.

Their shared knowledge makes the indignities of Candlemas easier. When Bonnie posts caption after Webster-quoting caption, hitting her twenty thousandth follower with a post about how choir makes her feel like God exists; when Isobel and Miranda put up signs all over campus with NO WAY NO S.O.W.!—with a picture of the statue and a red line straight through it—when Reverend Tipton tells Virginia *jeal-ousy is unbecoming* after he puts Bonnie on first soprano for the third time in a row, Laura can glance at Virginia across the choir loft, and catch her eye, and know that there is one corner of the world, however small, in which justice gets done.

"I told you," Ralph says, scrolling through the messages—from which Virginia has just done a dramatic reading—in the Cranmer common room. "Cringe." He looks up. "His prose style's atrocious. He's barely thirty, and he writes like a dirty old man."

"And he likes all the most basic operas." Barry cranes his neck.

"You know," Brad says softly, "I wish I *had* been coddled, at least once."

Anton grabs the phone and scans. "I don't *fucking* use Adderall!" He slams down the phone in fury. "Just nootropics."

Even Bonnie seems more bearable.

She still treats Laura with the same brittle cheerfulness; she still hums too loudly, while folding her laundry, or making her bed; she still has Freddy rearrange all the dorm room furniture in order to do a photoshoot of herself, swaddled like the Christ child in her choir robes, with a single black bra strap sticking out.

But the sense of knowing something Bonnie doesn't insulates Laura from these exchanges: once more, Laura thinks, they have erected that necessary border between Bonnie's world and their own.

If Bonnie registers that the rest of choir is keeping a secret from her, she doesn't show it. She continues to monologue so brightly—to Barry in the choir loft, to Ralph on the chapel steps, to Laura in their room—about the goals she's been ticking off her vision board. She doesn't have time for the Dewey Decibel System any longer, what with choir and all, but she and Freddy are still working on her art project (she's expanded the mermaid; now it's a Madonna/whore display with side-by-side pictures of her in choir and her naked, except for seaweed, on Farnham Cliff). She's moved on, romantically. She's started talking to this guy from Portsmouth who slid into her Instagram DMs the other week to tell her how much he admires her work: a proper *intellectual*—more mature than these high school boys—someone who reads actual books and poems written by actual people who didn't go to St. Dunstan's, someone who's actually seen something of the world.

"I feel *sorry* for Brad, really," she trills, tacking photos into foam board. "High school boys aren't even human yet."

Rosalind and Lloyd keep messaging until late in Candlemas term. Rosalind always has excuses for why she can't meet: her great-aunt is sick; she's working a double shift. *Soon*, she says, *and it will be all the sweeter when we do.*

Not through a screen darkly, she says—Virginia comes up with that part—*but face-to-face.*

It is only in early March that Reverend Tipton grows impatient.

"Look at this!" Virginia shoves her phone in Laura's face. They are sitting on Virginia's bed.

Is it wrong . . . he uses so many ellipses . . . that I've started to dream about you?

"He's still typing."

About what I'd do to you, if you were here with me?

Virginia's cheeks are pink, her forehead slick with sweat. She bites her lower lip.

"I told you." She breathes in and out, slowly. "Pornography. That's all anybody wants these days."

She takes the phone. She looks up at Laura. She starts typing.

If it's wrong, then we're both doomed.

What have you been thinking about?

"Stop! You can't."

"Why not? If he's idiotic enough to be on Tinder, under his real name . . ."

She leans in over the phone. She grabs Laura's hand. She waits.

The reply comes in:

I'd start, Lloyd Tipton says, *by caressing the back of your neck, the crescent-curved line I ached to kiss from the moment I first saw your photograph.*

I would trace the tips of my fingers along your collarbones—learning, for the first time (but I hope not the last), precisely which configuration of pressure and place make you shudder, which make you gasp, which make you moan.

You know, I've always had a thing for blondes.

Laura is suddenly horribly conscious of her heartbeat.

She is so afraid Virginia will notice.

Virginia will think Laura's turned on.

It's not that she's turned on, of course; at least, not exactly; certainly, she isn't turned on by Lloyd. All his prose does is embarrass her: it is purple, desperate, sweaty and sick. It reminds her of men she's seen masturbating, late at night, under the streetlights on the South Strip.

Only, Virginia is right there.

Not that Virginia is turned on, either, of course—Laura can't even imagine what Virginia *turned on* would look like, or sound like, or feel like—only, Virginia is flushed, breathless, beside her; only, Laura feels the fine stray sweeps of her hair, breeze-blown against Laura's cheek;

only, Laura likes that feeling, which is neither purple, nor sweaty, nor sick; only, it is not not any of those things, either.

They stare together at the screen.

"Quick," Virginia whispers. "We've got to write back."

"But what do we say?"

"I—I don't know. Make it up!" Virginia shakes her hair loose. "Something like—I don't know— *I* … *I* … *I've been thinking about* … no, *dreaming about, opening myself up to you. No, not opening myself up.* I mean, write *that*."

"Not—opening—myself—up?"

"*But being opened by you.*"

Virginia keeps her eyes on the screen, keeps nodding. She is speaking so much more quickly now.

"*I dream of you discovering all those places in me that I could never bear*—no, say *stand*, *bear*'s too affected—*to show you.*"

Laura tries to keep her hands still as she types.

Virginia parts her lips. "*I dream* …" She closes her eyes. "*Of your fingers, of your lips, of your eyes: taking possession of all the parts of me I have tried to keep hidden, knowing without words what I want, what I need. Start with my collarbones; slide down between my breasts; keep your eyes on mine.*"

It sounds so different when it's Virginia saying it.

When it's Reverend Tipton, it's cringe. Laura can laugh, when it's Reverend Tipton, because the idea that Reverend Tipton feels desire at all is laughable, because desire itself is so laughable, when it's something belonging to the Bonnies and the Reverend Tiptons of the world.

But when Virginia says it, in the same low, urgent voice she uses for Compline prayers, it sounds like something a serious person can feel.

Not, of course, that Laura feels it.

To feel it, Laura knows, would be the most cringe thing in the whole world. It would be to become ordinary and pornographic: salivating after dull bodies, carved into sclerotic words.

Virginia would be so disappointed in her.

"Don't stop. Look at me. Keep going. Look at me."

Laura keeps her eyes fixed determinately down, hoping Virginia does not notice the beating of her heart, nor the heat in her cheeks, nor her humiliating breathlessness.

Maybe, she thinks, she is no better than Reverend Tipton after all.

"There," Virginia says at last. "Send it. Give me the phone."

She looks up. Her face is inscrutable. Her dark lips twitch at the edges.

Laura hands the phone back to her.

Virginia types the words: *Next Wednesday. The bar at the Wayfarer Hotel. 8 pm. The booth under the chandelier. Book a room. Carry a copy of Keats. I'll bring one, too. We can read poetry together.*

She sucks in her lips.

I'll carry mine.

She puts the phone in her desk drawer.

"Pornography," she says, and slams it shut.

"I've got the whole thing planned," Virginia announces to the choir, over breakfast at Keble the next day. "Rosalind will Unmatch him, right at eight on the dot. He'll spend weeks wondering what he did wrong."

Isobel and Miranda break up that weekend.

Laura watches it happen.

One minute, they are sitting together, holding hands at one of the window tables at Keble, their foreheads bent, talking low. The next minute, Miranda gets up so violently she knocks over her chair. She stands there, a moment longer, as if waiting for Isobel to stop her. There are tears on her cheeks.

Everybody watches them and pretends not to.

Then Miranda storms out into the frost. The oak doors swing a few seconds longer.

"Told you she was mediocre," Virginia whispers in Laura's ear.

Laura can't help feeling sorry for them. For all that she knows, logically, that they are in an enemy camp—*ideologically speaking*—she knows, too, that they have always seemed happy; she can't deny they have always been kind. Laura always found it reassuring seeing them together, somehow. The continuity of their happiness was something she could rely on, among the shifting configurations of handholding in the Evensong pews.

Laura spends the following Sunday morning alone in the choir loft, practicing that week's piece on the rickety electric keyboard next to the organ proper. Reverend Tipton has given her an alto solo, and although she bristled guiltily at accepting it, the haunting softness of the phrases have been echoing all weekend in her ears. She works out the notes, playing the other parts on her phone, trying fruitlessly to shape them, on her lips, to the shattering harmony in her head.

Then she hears a sound.

At first Laura thinks it is the heater, or else a leaky pipe, but then she hears it again: a soft, kittenish whimper.

"Hello?"

She makes her way down the stairs.

"Is anyone down there?"

Isobel is sitting, alone, in the back row.

Her eyes are red. Her head is completely shaved. Her mascara runs all the way down her face.

She blows the snot from her nose.

"What do *you* want?"

"I'm sorry. I heard a noise—"

"Great, now you can report back to *her*." Isobel scoffs. "Poor, sad, lonely Isobel Zhao with her shitty sad posters and her shitty sad drama." She keeps her eyes straight ahead.

"I don't think that," Laura says. "I promise."

Isobel snorts.

"*She* does. Let me guess—she's going around gloating about how I'm going to die alone, with cats eating my face."

"She's *not*," says Laura, although this isn't entirely true. Then, with more conviction: "*I'm* not."

She takes a seat at Isobel's side.

"I really am sorry," she says. "You guys seemed happy."

"We *were* happy." A glimmer of the old smirk comes out. "Until I fucked it up. Typical, right?"

"I mean—you could fix it, right? I mean, talk it out, or something? I mean, if you really love each other—"

"What do *you* care?"

"I just think you two made a good couple, that's all."

"Between destroying the school, you mean?"

"I don't think that," Laura says, although this is not fully true, either. "I mean—this has nothing to do with that."

"Doesn't it?"

Laura tries to smile. "We just disagree," she says. "That's all. It doesn't mean we can't . . ."

"You think she doesn't mind? That you're Switzerland?"

Laura doesn't answer her.

"You're too nice," Isobel says. Laura knows it's not a compliment.

Isobel turns her eyes back toward the altar.

"What happened?" Laura says.

Isobel's mouth twists. She is silent for a moment.

"She'll be delighted to know," she says at last, "it was all about *her*." The lighthouse Madonna casts shadows toward them. "Turns out—the *missus* was suspicious. *Why, Izzy, can't we have a single project that's not about . . .*" Her voice trails off. "We could have done a lot, you know, for this school. Arms divestments. Meatless Mondays. Mandatory volunteer work in Howlham. Hell, we could have done a GoFundMe, saved Manifest Books from closing down." She sighs. "But those lacked a certain *frisson* for me, you see. MacKinnon noticed. Thought there might be a reason."

"Is it true?"

"Who knows? Maybe." She exhales. "I mean—that's what everyone does, right? We all work out our own dumb personal shit, through petitions and flyers and—" She coughs. "Want a button?"

She holds one up to the light. There's a picture of the Webster statue with an *X* through it, and *NO WAY NO S.O.W.* in small letters. "Figured it's catchier than *die, fascist scum*." Isobel flips the button back into her pocket. "She's good at that, isn't she? Making things seem like they matter more than they do."

She is looking at Laura now with wide, glassy eyes.

"Yes," Laura says. "She has that."

"One minute you're reading some dumb book, the next—" She laughs, a little, weakly.

"She said you used to love it. When you read it."

Isobel's smile fades.

"What did she say?"

"Not much. Just that you used to love it."

"I don't remember. Maybe." Isobel swallows. "It had an *effect*, that's all."

"An effect?"

"Got us up to Farnham in the middle of January, cliff-diving like a couple of psychotic mermaids. I thought Brad was going to freeze his balls off." She gazes, for a long time, up at the altar. "Hey, I didn't say it was a good effect."

"You jumped?" The lowest cliff is easily fifteen feet up.

"It was a joke," Isobel says. She is unconvincing. "That's all. It was just a dare. Just dumb kids being dumb kids together. She told us to jump, and we did. It wasn't a thing."

She crosses and uncrosses her arms. "I mean—it wasn't about the book. You get that."

"Get what?"

"Come on," Isobel says. "Don't pretend you're not in love with her."

"I'm—" The idea burns. "I'm *not*."

"Come on," Isobel says. "You think she never took *me* running?"

"I'm not! I'm not even . . ." Laura has never thought of herself as anything. Sex, for Laura, is arbitrary; it is so distinct from all the things she wants. It is blow jobs in the rare-book room and fingering in the back pews during Evensong; it is Ralph Ervin gaping at Bonnie's breasts and Anton Gallagher telling everyone about that time he caught Ivan Dixon masturbating to Freddy Barnes's Facebook page. It is Bonnie di Angelis, masturbating on camera.

It is so removed from the things that matter, all the old, real things: from Webster, from music, from mornings shivering at the cold.

Only, she can't escape thinking about it: how they were at the foot of Virginia's bed, typing: *Look at me; look at me.*

"I'm not gay."

"Well, you're not straight." Isobel says it with such certainty.

"That's not any of your business." Laura stiffens.

"God knows *she's* not."

Laura's stomach plummets. "What?"

"Come on—you're not that dumb. *I'm too good, too pure, too perfect for this cruel world?* Yeah. Okay. Sure."

Laura's throat is too tight to speak.

"She's just not interested in . . ."

"Not interested? Please. She's dying for it! She's just decided God will strike her down the moment she admits it."

"That's not true."

It's just, Laura thinks, that sex isn't good enough for Virginia.

"You know what's ironic?" Isobel goes on. "Her parents are bougie as shit. I know their type. They'd probably be *thrilled* if she brought a girl home for Thanksgiving—they'd brag to all their other bougie friends, *a girl's fine, as long as she's not a Republican.*" Isobel snorts. "And she still has to come up with some bullshit for Daddy to punish her if she misbehaves."

"It's not like—"

"Meanwhile, the rest of us have to wipe our phones before we go home for Christmas break."

"I . . ." Laura tries haltingly. "I'm sorry."

"You know what?" Isobel throws up her hands. "I don't care anymore. You want to fuck her, then just *fuck* her already. But don't—God—don't *insult* everyone around you by pretending you're on some holy crusade."

Hot tears have come to the corners of Laura's eyes. "I don't know why"—she forces out the words through gritted teeth—"everyone's so obsessed with *sex* all of a sudden."

She leaves Isobel sitting, smirking, in the back row.

• • •

Isobel is wrong, Laura tells herself. Isobel has to be wrong. Isobel's just jealous; Isobel has no sense of transcendence; Isobel reduces everything to the basest facts: to *good* and *bad* and *just wants to fuck.*

Whatever Laura feels for Virginia, she tells herself, it has nothing to do with *sex,* at least not the sex that other people seem to have. She can't picture her mouth on Virginia's mouth, her hand between Virginia's legs, like she's a figure in an explanatory diagram. She can't picture Virginia's body—her small breasts, her narrow waist, her birdlike shoulders—except as a kind of funhouse mirror reflection of her own: to be understood only through a series of comparative adjectives—thinner, taller, better-looking. What she wants from Virginia, for Virginia, *with* Virginia, has nothing to do with bodies.

Only—Rosalind's messages to Lloyd—

It's just as well, Laura thinks, that Virginia's plan is almost complete. She can't handle much more of this.

On Wednesday, Virginia announces that they will go into Weymouth to watch her plan unfold.

"Just Brad and Anton and us," she says. "You know, the *inner sanctum.*" She presses Laura's palm, where a faint scar still gleams beneath her fingers, and Laura tries not to think—as she has tried, all week, not to think—of Isobel's words.

The boys meet them at Farnham Cliff.

"He's practically salivating," Virginia says, as she leads them along the coastal road. "He's been texting her all day, telling her how he woke up smelling her—the *pervert.* I wouldn't be surprised if he sends her a picture of his cock before we get there."

Anton bounds at Virginia's side, half jogging, hopping from one foot to the other.

"It's going to be *epic*," he exclaims. "Poetic justice. Divine retribution. Some real Dante shit."

Brad follows behind at Laura's side.

"All well, young Stearns?"

Laura has been watching the water break against Farnham Cliff, worrying once more about Isobel and Virginia, thinking once more about *look at me*.

"I'm fine," she says. "Just tired." She looks up at him. His cheeks are hollower than usual, and there are bags under his eyes. "You?"

"Fine, fine." He stretches out his arms. "We should probably say our goodbyes." He nods toward the Webster statue, hagridden over the horizon. "He's not much longer for this world, you know." He hops over a rock. "Then again—neither are we."

"What are you talking about?"

Brad smiles.

"We've got us a couple more years at most. The barbarians are at the gates, young Stearns. The donors are dying. And once their money's gone . . ." He shrugs.

"That doesn't bother you?"

"I don't like to get bothered about things."

"You know," Laura says, "you could really care about something, once in a while." She tells herself she's only teasing him.

"I accept what can't change," Brad says. "I'd make a great alcoholic." He coughs.

"Not a very good revolutionary, though."

"Aye," he says. "There's the rub."

They continue the rest of the way in silence.

·   ·   ·

They arrive in Weymouth at seven-thirty. Virginia leads them into the Grinning Griddle for coffee. They huddle against the frosted window, scanning Main Street, blowing on their palms.

"There!" she crows at seven forty-five. "Look!"

Reverend Tipton is walking from his car. It is the first time Laura has seen him without his collar on. He is wearing a tweed blazer and a bright purple bow tie. He is carrying an ostentatious volume of Keats's poems. He searches the road once and then makes his way to the Wayfarer porch.

"Perfect." Virginia's eyes glitter.

She rounds on them. "Come on," she says. "Let's go."

"But we can't—" Laura tries.

"Don't worry. I have a plan."

Virginia leads them along Main Street.

"There's a reason," she announces, as they file duck-like behind her, "that I specified which table. I called to check—he even made a *reservation*, the sap."

She stops in front of the Wayfarer. She turns back toward them, her face shining. "Through the bushes," she says, gesturing toward the two high, boxy hedges that stand on either side of the Wayfarer porch.

Before they can respond she tears into one, slipping between the branches and the wood siding, thrusting aside the leaves with her arms. She takes another step, then a few paces more. Then she stops short, right before a half-curtained window. She crouches down.

"We'll be able to see everything from here. Get low."

Laura kneels next to her, shielded from view by the heavy damask curtains. If she tilts her head she can make out Reverend Tipton, sitting in a high-backed booth against the back wall of the bar, underneath a garish seashell chandelier.

He is checking his wristwatch, then rechecking the high wooden clock along the far side wall. He is rubbing his glasses. His copy of Keats is standing, face-outward, on the table, along with two glasses of red wine.

"Seven fifty-six," Virginia whispers.

Reverend Tipton takes out a mirror and checks his reflection.

"Bastard doesn't even have a collar on," Virginia says, satisfied. "Here, Gallagher, take my phone, Unmatch him, I want to watch—"

Laura can hear Virginia's heartbeat; hear, too, the meticulous ticking of her watch, that sounds out again, that echo: *Look at me; look at me.*

"Seven fifty-nine."

The wall clock chimes eight. A chartreuse cuckoo emerges and does a little jerky dance. Reverend Tipton swallows, checks his phone, checks his watch, checks—uselessly—the clock, then turns his face to the door.

"I can't watch this," says Brad. "It's too pathetic. Come on, Strauss, we've had our fun, let's go before he sees us."

"*Wait*," Virginia hisses. She leans in closer to the window. "This is the best part." She takes a deep breath.

"What are you talking about, Strauss?"

"*Wait.*"

The bar door swings open. A young woman appears, facing away from them, bounding forward, carrying something in her arms. Her long blond hair cascades all the way to her waist. She turns, just slightly, toward the window.

It's Bonnie.

She is carrying a copy of Keats.

"*There*," Virginia breathes. "*There* it is."

Bonnie totters forward, wheeling her head around, beaming, looking from person to person in appeal.

She and Reverend Tipton catch sight of each other at the exact same time.

All the color drains from Reverend Tipton's face. He leaps up so violently he spills both glasses of claret all over the table.

Bonnie's smile vanishes.

"Holy *shit*!" Anton is laughing so hard he can't breathe. "Strauss, you *didn't*!"

"Shut up—I'm trying to read their lips!"

Reverend Tipton is hurriedly, furiously, mopping the wine from his lap, from his sweater, from his book. His ears are violet; his eyes are terrified.

Bonnie claps her hand over her mouth.

Laura feels Brad tense up beside her.

"Jesus *Christ*, Strauss," he whispers.

Virginia keeps her eyes on the window. "What? Two birds—one stone."

Tears are gushing, now, down both of Bonnie's cheeks. Reverend Tipton says something—Laura doesn't know what—his face desperate, his lips opening uselessly, like a fish's, and then closing again.

Bonnie runs back out through the door.

They can hear her footsteps running all the way down Main Street, toward the taxi stand with its single idling cab. The slamming of a car door. The whirring of wheels.

Reverend Tipton just stands there—motionless, gazing around as uselessly as he had that first Evensong, Ozzy Osbourne bellowing from the rafters.

He staggers over to the bar. He steadies himself against it.

"Come on," Virginia whispers. "Before he starts looking around—let's go!"

She shoves past them, crossing Main Street, to where the sidewalk veers to the coastal trail; she is already running.

They have no choice but to follow her.

"That was epic!" Anton finally says, when they at last make their way to the coastal trail. "Jesus, Strauss!"

"They deserve each other," Virginia is crowing. "God, did you see their faces? The two most—most—unserious, hypocritical . . ." She takes a seat on one of the rocks. "Come eat. I brought sandwiches."

She grabs one from her bag. She munches into it cheerfully.

The stone in Laura's throat gets bigger. Her stomach feels like someone has turned it inside out.

"You didn't tell me . . ." She finally gets out the words. "You didn't tell me."

"God, wasn't it *magnificent*?" Virginia is exultant. "Really, Noise, I don't know what you ever saw in that idiotic, jejune little—"

"Strauss, *please*!" Brad looks like he's going to be sick.

Virginia considers him, briefly, with a faint, mocking smile.

"Anyway," Virginia says at last, turning back to the others. "No harm done. They'll just feel a little sheepish for a few days, and then they'll get over it. Sandwich?"

"I'm not hungry," Brad says.

"Suit yourself." Virginia hands one to Anton, who tears into it. "Of course, it'll be so awkward, having to see each other now. I'd be shocked if she stayed in choir, after all this." She arches an eyebrow. "He ought to resign anyway, on principle. A faculty chaplain should be above suspicion."

She sees Laura's face.

"Come on, Stearns," she says. "Eat something. It's past dinnertime."

"We shouldn't have done that."

Virginia throws up her hands.

"Christ—both of you! Where's your mettle?"

They don't say anything.

"It had to be done. And it's a victimless crime, really—unless you count spilled wine. If either of them has any sense of self-respect they'll just pretend it never happened and get on with life. Now, are you hungry or not?"

She holds out the sandwich.

Laura takes it.

It's late by the time they make their way back past the Webster statue. Virginia leads them all the way back, Anton trotting at her side.

Brad and Laura follow her in silence.

"Come on! We'll be late for curfew if you two don't pick up the pace!"

Virginia stops short.

"What's that?"

The light is blue and red on the water.

It takes Laura a moment to follow the glare to the ambulance: parked between Farnham Cliff and Bethel Beach.

"Christ, what are they doing here?" Anton rolls his eyes. "Did some freshman puke again?"

They come a little closer. Two men are carrying a stretcher up from Bethel Beach. A foot of waterlogged white gauze sticks out from underneath the cover.

A small, dark figure is standing by the edge of the cliff.

They come a little closer.

It is Freddy Barnes. She is looking up at them.

She rounds on them. Her face is slick with tears. "You . . ." It is almost a growl. "You!" They are loading the stretcher into the ambulance. "You *murderers!*"

The men slam shut the ambulance doors. The engine revs up, and then the car lurches, groaning, back up the hill, carrying the pale, soaked figure of Bonnie di Angelis all the way back along the coastal road to the Weymouth docks.

7

THE VIDEO OF BONNIE FALLING OFF FARNHAM CLIFF GOES VIRAL.

Part of it's the aesthetic. Bonnie is wearing a long diaphanous nightgown, tied together with a pink ribbon, banded right underneath her breasts, which are just visible in the few spots the evening mist has moistened. Her hair is tangled; her makeup is smeared; the smudge of her lipstick blends with the flush in her cheeks. She is holding a bottle of Martini & Rossi.

Sometimes, she slurs her words, *you . . . just . . . have . . . to . . . express . . . your . . . pain.*

She is standing on the edge of one of the lower cliffs, teetering over the water.

All these traditions—she gulps—*all this beauty, everything you think you love about this place: it's all a lie.*

Freddy Barnes zooms in close on her face.

This place—she hiccups, straight to the camera—*is rotting from the inside out.*

Like a cancer, she says. Like a termite-infested log. It's like maggots wriggling inside the carcass of a deer.

She tries to swig again from the bottle, but it is empty. She shakes it, a few times, in frustration.

Fuck it, she says, and lifts her arm to throw it over the side of the cliff.

That's when she goes over.

• • •

"You have to admit," Ralph says, watching it for the tenth time, "it's pretty funny."

Ivan gapes at him in horror.

"It's not like she died or anything. It's just her leg!"

It was fractured in two places. Bonnie has gone back to Tarrytown to recover.

"Cringe," says Ralph, pausing the video right at the moment Bonnie falls. "Complete cringe."

Rumors flood campus. Bonnie di Angelis got drunk and tried to kill herself. No, Bonnie di Angelis got drunk, tried to make a shitty video, and tripped. No, Bonnie di Angelis was having a secret affair with Lloyd Tipton, which is why she tried to kill herself. No, Bonnie di Angelis tried to kill herself over Brad Noise. No, Bonnie di Angelis just slipped, and fell, having gotten shitfaced on a bottle of her mother's Martini & Rossi, which is somehow the most embarrassing detail in the whole story, because if you're going to get drunk and try to kill yourself—not that Bonnie di Angelis necessarily tried to kill herself—there's nothing more cringe than doing it with sweet vermouth while shooting a shitty video for your Instagram story, and then posting it anyway.

Yvette Saunders tells Gabe Meltzer, who tells Barry, who tells the rest of choir, that she saw Bonnie tearfully get out of a cab at the campus edge, an hour before it happened. Freddy Barnes was already waiting in the parking lot with a tripod and a duffel bag. Tamara Lynd tells Matt Azibuike, who tells Ivan, that Reverend Tipton showed up that night on campus, an hour after curfew, with Scotch on his breath, but everybody knows that Tamara Lynd likes to embellish things.

In the end, Bonnie di Angelis gets ten thousand new Instagram followers and medical clearance to stay home until Michaelmas, and then everyone stops talking about it.

Except Laura.

She spends the night Bonnie is taken to the hospital sitting by the window of their shared room, huddled against the radiator, the door locked. She can't bring herself to talk to Virginia; she can't even imagine looking at her. Guilt lacerates her lungs.

We have done this, she thinks, her throat tightening around the certainty. *We have done this to her.*

She should have known, she thinks—all Bonnie's talk about that mysterious fan who'd been DMing her on Instagram; her giggling intimation it was someone *mature*, someone *worldly*, someone so unlike all these piddling high school boys.

She can't even bring herself to say anything to Bonnie's parents, who come the next morning to clear out her room, packing away the scented candles and rowing blazers and ostentatious pink-and-green bedspread into a series of identical cardboard boxes.

When they leave, Laura goes to the Desmond bathroom and throws up. She doesn't eat for the rest of the day.

The thought of Virginia, of her life with Virginia, of their morning runs and their evenings spent composing messages, of their Friday nights, with their voices melding into each other, the colored light from the stained glass transmogrifying their faces, appalls her.

She can't even imagine going to Evensong again, looking Reverend Tipton in the eye, considering that awful absence where Bonnie's whipped soprano once had been, singing prayers they will never live up to, with Bonnie's sobs echoing in their ears.

. . .

Thursday night, Virginia knocks on Laura's door.

"Come on, Stearns," she says. "I know you're in there."

Laura doesn't answer it.

"Just talk to me," Virginia calls, a little louder. "Please. Please."

Laura hesitates.

"I'm not going away until you talk to me!"

At last Laura opens the door.

"Finally." Virginia marches in.

"I was worried," Virginia says. "I thought you were never going to come out."

Her face is as pale and placid as ever. She, Laura thinks bitterly, doesn't look like she spent the morning vomiting on the bathroom floor.

"I wasn't feeling well," says Laura. She keeps her eyes on the floor.

"Are you mad at me?"

"No, I—" Laura doesn't even know what she feels.

"You're mad at me. I can tell."

Virginia steps toward her.

"We shouldn't have done it," Laura says. She swallows. "Not to Tipton, not to Bonnie, not *any* of it."

"Christ, Stearns—"

"She could have died!"

"It was an accident! How were we supposed to know she'd go and chug a bottle of vermouth?"

"You should have told me."

"You'd have stopped me."

"Of course I'd have stopped you!" Laura has to believe this. "God, Virginia—I know she was annoying, but she didn't deserve—"

THE WORLD CANNOT GIVE

"She did, actually."

Laura looks up at her.

For a moment, she thinks Virginia is joking. But Virginia's voice is tight with fury. "Come on, Stearns." Virginia's laugh is hollow. "She wasn't some naive little idiot, some lost little lamb who wandered into choir by mistake and couldn't find the exit." Her face is white. "That act might have worked on Noise—not on me. Christ, Stearns, Bonnie di Angelis wanted *revenge* on us because her boyfriend didn't want her and it blew up in her face. That's all. That's justice."

Laura gapes at her.

"That can't be justice."

"What, because it isn't nice?" Virginia rounds on her. "Because it isn't *polite*?" Her nostrils flare. "She's a bad person, Stearns. You have to realize that. Just because she's nice, and friendly, and little birds come down from the heavens and sit on her shoulders when she sings, doesn't mean she's not a bad person." She seizes hold of both of Laura's wrists. "I thought you understood that."

"I don't care if she's a bad person, Virginia—there are some things you just don't *do* to people!"

It is the first time she has ever raised her voice at Virginia.

Virginia stands there for a moment, astounded.

"Aren't we supposed to, I don't know, turn the other cheek? Isn't that the whole point?"

Virginia freezes. The color has drained from her face. She is looking at Laura, flabbergasted, her dark lips half-parted.

It is the first time Laura has ever seen Virginia afraid of her.

Virginia holds Laura's gaze a moment longer.

"You're right," she says at last. "We shouldn't have done it." She swallows. "I shouldn't have done it." She sits down on Bonnie's empty bed, still holding Laura's wrists, so that her eyes are level with Laura's collarbones.

Laura remains standing. She has never seen Virginia cave before, not like this; her power unnerves her.

"God," Virginia says. "I don't know why I did it."

She closes her eyes. "I never know why I do things," she says.

Her voice wavers, then gathers strength. "I was just so angry, you know, at both of them—and, God, choir!" She swallows again; it is more difficult this time. "I was so afraid, Stearns, that they'd destroy it, choir, our little family, everything we've worked so hard for, everything that finally, actually, matters. I didn't want to lose *us.*"

She takes another deep breath. She puts her head in her hands.

"I thought—I don't know what I thought. I thought I could fix everything. I thought, I don't know, how perfect it would be, the two of them, running into each other like that: how perfect a punishment it would be for their pride, the sniveling way they use each other. I had it all planned out—I made up this whole backstory, this stupid boy from Portsmouth who wanted to draw graphic novels—not that she ever even asked for his backstory. All she cared about was that he liked her. I didn't think she'd— It's not like you can fall in love with someone from a couple DMs. It wasn't supposed to hurt her." She bites her lip. "Maybe it was. I don't know." She takes Laura's hand. She pulls it to her cheek. "Do you hate me now?"

Laura wants to hate Virginia. She can't.

"If I could do it all over I wouldn't have done it. Any of it. I'd have just, I don't know, tried to tough it out. Tried to make it matter less." Her eyes search Laura's. "But I couldn't, Laura—not when it mattered so much—"

"I know," says Laura.

Whatever resistance she'd planned wavers. She had expected Virginia cruel, Virginia righteous, Virginia exultant and terrible, her face as hideously triumphant as it had been in those few, horrible moments outside the Wayfarer.

"This is why I need you."

"Me?"

"God, you're so good, Stearns." Virginia's voice breaks. "You're sweet, and you're kind, and you just love people, even when they don't deserve it, and you stop me from being—God—whatever I am." She closes her eyes. She nods. "Yes, you'd have stopped me. I know you'd have stopped me. I'd have *let* you stop me."

Laura tells herself this is true.

They need each other, she thinks. That's how they work. Virginia helps her be World-Historical. She helps Virginia be kinder to the people who aren't.

Virginia looks so frail, sitting there before her, shivering into her cape.

"You didn't know what would happen," Laura hears herself saying.

Virginia nods. "It's just . . . ," she says, staring across the room at Laura's wall. "I can't stand the thought of losing them."

Laura thinks of the jaundiced look on Brad's face. "You won't."

"Don't let them hate me, Stearns. Please. I couldn't stand it if they hated me."

She holds Laura's hand so tightly. She pulls Laura down to the bed. Then she leans in and kisses Laura on the cheek.

Then Virginia curls up on Laura's lap, her hair falling over Laura's knees. She lies there, for a moment, motionless.

"Can I stay here tonight?" she asks in a small voice.

Laura hesitates. Her horror is still there, a steady, distant echo, like the drip of water from a neglected tap.

Only, Virginia is looking up at her, with such tenderness and fear; Virginia's eyes are glassy with tears.

"Of course," Laura says.

•   •   •

Laura lies awake all night, watching Virginia sleep on Bonnie's bed, watching Virginia's small chest rise and fall, watching the quickness of her breaths.

Virginia couldn't have known how badly Bonnie would take it. Virginia, she thinks, would never have responded like that to humiliation; she'd never be, Laura thinks, that vulnerable to another person to begin with, especially not someone she'd never met.

It's just that Virginia cares too much about things, that she loves choir with a wild and idolatrous love, that she belongs to the world of Sebastian Webster, where these are the kinds of things people do.

Virginia needs me, Laura thinks, watching Virginia's lips move wordlessly. She needs someone to stroke the hair from her face when she's in one of her rages; she needs someone to hold on to her when the fury overtakes her once more, that the world isn't the place it should be, that they live in the sclerotic present and not when warriors could dispense justice some more honorable way.

Laura can't expect Virginia to understand the kind of weak, ordinary human vulnerability that sent Bonnie di Angelis careening over a cliffside with a bottle of vermouth in her hand. The things Virginia feels so deeply are the high, divine things most people don't think about at all; she does not feel the ordinary, kitchen-warming things Laura does.

Laura is almost jealous.

None of the boys, though, seems as conflicted as she feels. Anton is, predictably, exultant; Ralph is smug. Ivan, Laura knows, is content to do whatever the rest of them decide, squeaking out guilty laughs whenever Anton and Ralph rewatch the video. Even Barry, who liked Bonnie more than any of them, seems resigned.

"I'm not saying I agree with what Strauss did," he tells Laura, as they practice in the organ loft. "But what are we supposed to do about it now? Quit choir? Go join the Dewey Decibel System? As far as I'm concerned, the best thing to do is keep calm and carry on."

Brad doesn't say anything about it at all. He sits, wordless, at meals, at Virginia's side, staring out the Keble windows until she snaps him back to attention.

That week's Evensong is a somber, awkward affair.

Reverend Tipton shuffles in late, about a quarter to seven. He doesn't make eye contact with anybody. He looks like he hasn't slept in weeks.

"Right," he says. "Let's get on with it, shall we?" He motions over to Virginia. "You'll be wanting to do first soprano, then?" He speaks so sharply even Virginia flinches.

"If you'd like," she says, looking at her lap.

"Put the boy," Reverend Tipton doesn't even look at Ivan, "on second."

They sing briskly, nervously. Ivan misses one of his cues entirely, and shakes all through the Nunc Dimittis. Even Barry drops his pages.

When it is over, they all pack up their robes and music quickly, their faces glum in defeat.

Laura is zipping up her coat to leave when she hears Reverend Tipton say her name.

"Do you have a moment?"

"Actually—"

"A cup of tea, perhaps?"

Laura watches, frozen, as the others exit out onto Devonshire Quad.

"S-sure. Yeah. Of course."

• • •

Laura follows Reverend Tipton to his apartment in Latimer Hall, past the perplexed glances of the rest of choir, standing in a huddle outside Cranmer.

He leads her up the stairs, down the hallway. He makes a show of propping the door wide open so that the whole of his living room is visible from the corridor, scooting the armchair forward so that this, too, is in plain view.

He makes tea in silence. She sees, on the edge of his bookshelf, his wine-drenched copy of Keats.

He sets the mug down before her without asking how she takes it. He doesn't make one for himself.

"I was just hoping," he says at last, "we could check in." He draws out the phrase.

"Sure," Laura says, too brightly. "Sure. Yeah. Of course."

"To see how you're finding the term. Workload not too demanding, I hope?"

"It's okay," Laura says, hiding her face behind the mug. "Not too bad."

He peers at her.

"And choir?"

He lets this linger.

"Choir's fine, too!" Laura chirps. "I mean—more than fine. I mean—it's *great*. Great."

"Nothing you want to tell me? Or discuss?"

He leans back into his armchair. A cool gaze flickers over his face—a slight, cruel twitch of his mouth—that makes Laura think of *the crescent-curved line I ached to kiss*. She takes another gulp of tea and burns her mouth.

"No, I don't think so."

"Because—if you did . . ." He drinks the silence in. "I hold it as point of principle that no student of mine should ever be punished for telling the truth."

Laura understands.

Her embarrassment kindles, at once, into anger. So, Laura thinks, he thinks she's the weak link—the most likely to turn. However guilty she might feel, deep down, over Bonnie, she has enough self-regard to know she'd never *narc*.

"I'm sorry," she says. "I don't know what you're talking about."

He searches her face.

"It's a real pity," he says slowly, "what happened to her."

"Awful," Laura agrees. "I'm glad she's okay."

"It's interesting to me," he goes on, "that she didn't say anything to the administration, about what precipitated her . . ." He does not blink. "Crisis."

Laura shrugs. "Guess we'll never know."

"She could have, of course. If she'd chosen to."

Laura knows she is supposed to find this admirable. But all it does is calcify her stubbornness. If even Bonnie di Angelis wouldn't narc, then Laura can't either.

After all, she thinks, in some distant part of herself, Reverend Tipton really did deserve it.

She faces Reverend Tipton so coolly it astonishes her.

"Maybe she had nothing to say."

"You know, don't you, Laura"—Reverend Tipton's voice is low—"that you're a very talented singer. That you have a real—shall we even say, God-given?—gift."

Laura twists her fingers in her lap.

"It would be a terrible shame," he says, "to waste it."

"Waste it?" Laura cries before she can stop herself. As if choir weren't the only thing she ever wants to do; as if she didn't feel, each week, such overflowing joy. "How could I waste it?"

"Subordinating it to . . ." He raises his eyebrows. "A dedication to something else. Or someone else."

"What's wrong with being dedicated to something else?"

"Nothing," Reverend Tipton says. "In moderation."

"Is that what you are?" Laura says before she can stop herself. "Dedicated to God—*in moderation?*"

No wonder, she thinks, that he didn't tell Rosalind that he was a priest. Virginia is right, she concludes. Virginia was always right. He's nothing but a fraud with a collar on.

Reverend Tipton doesn't say anything. Neither does Laura.

"Things will be back to normal soon," Virginia tells Laura that night in Desmond. "I can feel it. No more Bonnie. Tipton defanged at last. The boys still feel a bit nervous. But they'll get over it. They're just panicked—they don't understand the *moral* element at all." She swallows. "Remember the night we went to the crypt?" She touches Laura's shoulder. "Wasn't that wonderful?"

"It was."

Everything had felt so easy then. Everything had felt so suffused with enchantment. Laura had even believed in God.

"It'll be like that again now," Virginia says. "I can feel it." She swallows. "It *has* to. We've earned it, you see."

Virginia's triumph is short-lived.

For starters, Isobel and Miranda get back together. Laura doesn't know when, or how, but one day, in the second week of March, she crosses Devonshire Quad to find the two of them standing underneath the still-curled blossoms of the cherry tree outside Keble Hall, holding hands.

Within a few days they've revived their poster campaign. The *NO WAY NO S.O.W.* posters blanket the walls of Keble and Mountbatten Hall, along with every single common room. Isobel and Miranda pass out buttons on Devonshire Quad.

So many people have started to wear them. Freddy Barnes wears one, which Laura supposes is only to be expected, and so does Isobel and Miranda's friend Pavel Gorinsky, along with the rest of the theater kids, but so do people she only vaguely knows, from class or from Desmond, people she can't imagine caring about the moral status of Sebastian Webster.

Yvette Saunders wears one, along with the rest of the Dewey Decibel System; Gabe Meltzer wears one, and so do all the boys in Morris Hall. Matt Azibuike from Calculus class wears one, and so does Ursula Thale from Topics in European History, pinning it into her customary brown. Jasper Piedra, who always used to let Laura use his Latin notes, wears one, too; so does Tamara Lynd.

"It's personal," Virginia rages. "They don't even *care* about Webster; they've never even *read* Webster—you know that. It's a referendum on *us*."

That just makes it worse.

It's not that Laura doesn't know what people say about choir. She has always been dimly aware that there are people who aren't Isobel or Miranda who think that choir is insular and snobbish, that Virginia is insufferable, that Anton is a bellowing brute, and that Ralph is pretentious, and that Brad is an overprivileged, out-of-touch asshole who's never had to face a consequence in his life. It has just never mattered before.

The wider St. Dunstan's has always only ever glimmered on the periphery of Laura's vision, a perfunctory network of classmates and hallmates to be encountered on her way to her real life, which is her life with Virginia. She has always assumed the choir operated, for others, the same way: something people might roll their eyes at half-heartedly, but that they otherwise ignored.

Only then Bonnie di Angelis made that video.

It's not that people particularly liked Bonnie. The opinion that everything Bonnie di Angelis does is a little bit cringe is the only view that Virginia and Isobel have ever shared; there is no one at St. Dunstan's, except maybe Freddy, who didn't slink out of frame when Bonnie was making one of her videos, or wince when Bonnie draped her arms around one of their shoulders to take a selfie. Even Yvette Saunders, who was president of the Dewey Decibel System and sang with Bonnie almost every week, would shuffle to the bathroom whenever Freddy showed up with her camera under Langford Gate. Bonnie's videos, Bonnie's rowing blazers, Bonnie's gingerbread cookies and brand-gifted tweed skirts, Bonnie's fundamental *Bonnie*-ness, was a source of collective embarrassment, the sepia-tinged St. Dunstan's she displayed to her thousands of followers as removed from their own shared experience as the Las Vegas Venetian was from the real thing.

But then Bonnie slipped on a piece of seaweed while sobbing and fell into the waves.

This place, she said, *is rotting from the inside out*. Everybody has watched it so many times. Now they believe it.

Laura doesn't know if she believes it.

She clutches Virginia's hand whenever they cross Devonshire Quad, willing her not to see the stream of *NO WAY NO S.O.W.* buttons, not to see the glares. She uses her old platitudes: everyone's just jealous, Isobel's just bitter; everyone just *wishes* they could sing like Virginia can; people in this *sclerotic modern world* just don't understand what it means to want a shipwreck of the soul.

Laura cannot doubt her.

Sebastian Webster fought and died for the mystic vision that came over him one fog-ridden night in the St. Dunstan's chapel, for the face of the lighthouse Madonna, for the Catholic Church, and also for transcendence more generally. He was a genius; he was a visionary; he was World-Historical in the truest way, the Virginia way: elevated from the mediocre ranks of ordinary men. Laura doesn't know how to understand transcendence any way but through him.

She clings to this, all through the rest of Candlemas. *What would Sebastian Webster do?*

She clings to this, even at that Evensong, late in March, when the choir stands to sing, and begin Psalm 51, in their low-drowning chant, the Evensong that half the students in the pews do not rise as they always do for the confession of sin but rather remain motionless, in protest, in their seats, their arms crossed across their chests, their buttons glimmering in the candlelight.

Isobel's face is set in stony satisfaction. Miranda's arm laces around Isobel's waist.

They are sitting, Laura notes with surprise, in the front row.

Then Isobel stands, right in the middle of the Magnificat, when they're all meant to be seated reverently. Miranda stands with her.

Isobel is staring right at Virginia.

Virginia keeps singing.

Isobel turns her back to the altar. Miranda follows her.

Another fifty students rise. Fifty pairs of shoes echo on the marble floor.

They all turn back toward the wall.

Laura can feel Virginia stiffen beside her.

For a moment, everyone hesitates. Even Reverend Tipton looks to Virginia in appeal.

"Keep singing," Virginia hisses. "Don't you dare stop."

They look at each other, and then out into the pews.

"Don't you fucking dare."

It is Laura who breaks the silence, forcing through her tightening throat *He hath exalted the humble and meek; he hath filled the hungry with good things.*

Then Ivan breaks in, too, on *the rich he hath sent empty away*: now all of them are singing it.

They sing the whole Magnificat to people's backs.

We're bound together now, Laura thinks, as she hears Brad and Anton sing on either side of her, as she watches Virginia turn her face to the light; Virginia, who does not care that people hate her; Virginia, who relishes it; Virginia, who is so much stronger than she is.

"Maybe they *should* take it down," Barry says mournfully, when at last everyone has filed out. "I mean—can't they just put it as a museum display somewhere? If it bothers people so much?"

"Christ, Ng, what's wrong with you?" Virginia snaps. "Don't you *dare* tell me you're on their side. As if they even cared about the statue in the first place! It's an excuse—you know it is."

"I'm not on their side!" Barry protests. "It's just—"

"Just what? You just want to sacrifice your ideals—the second you experience a modicum of resistance?" Virginia scoffs. "Sebastian Webster," she says slowly, "would be ashamed of all of you."

The chapel doors slam behind her when she goes.

• • •

Two days after the Evensong protest, the St. Dunstan's administration puts out a press release, announcing that the faculty committee has voted to remove the Webster statue over spring break.

Dr. Charles's son, Richard, who is a senior in Tamara Lynd's English class, tells her the whole story. She tells Ursula Thale, who tells Gabe Meltzer, who tells Ralph.

Reverend Tipton was the deciding vote.

Laura is the one to tell Virginia.

She doesn't react. She remains, straight-backed, against the edge of Bonnie's bed, which she has now made her own. She bites her lower lip.

"It doesn't matter," she says. "The rest of this whole pathetic school doesn't matter. They can think whatever they like—about him. About us."

She closes her eyes. She leans back against the wall.

"As long as we stick together. One choir. One family." Her smile twitches. "We swore an oath, remember?"

"I remember."

Virginia rises. She goes to the window. She stands there, for a moment, her face to the glass, considering the muddy darkness of the quad. She touches her fingers to the windowpane. She yanks the window up. She leans out onto the quad, so far Laura thinks, in momentary panic, that she will fall over. She inhales the frost in a sharp, single breath. Then she turns back to Laura.

"I have an idea," she says.

Virginia does not tell Laura what it is.

"It's a surprise," she says.

It is the last week of Candlemas. The frost has only just vanished from the quadrangles, from the trees; there are puckered buds on all the branches, and there are green shoots among the corpse-yellow remnants of last autumn's grass.

"Midnight," Virginia says, the morning of the final Friday of term. "I've already told the others." They have run all the way to Howlham and back. Laura is soaked through with sweat; Virginia is triumphant.

"It'll be just like Michaelmas," she says. "Just like the old days. Only *more*.

"The whole family," she says. "Together against the world."

Laura waits, once more, until midnight. She watches the high slice of moon over the water; she watches the wind shake loose the buds of the trees.

She tells herself she has no reason to worry. Whatever Virginia is planning, she thinks, it will be wonderful; it will be like that time they sang Compline on Bethel Beach; it will be like that first morning in the Grinning Griddle; like their first Evensong; it will be like baptism. Virginia knows, Laura thinks, she *always* knows, precisely how to create a world for them, *out* of them, transforming their dull afternoons and ordinary bodies into vessels for transcendence, the way the lighthouse Madonna is always shot through with evening light.

Laura dresses warmly. She lets Virginia wrap her in one of her fur collars, lend her a pair of her black leather gloves. She watches Virginia take an enormous backpack.

They wait for the lights to go out in Mrs. Mesrin's apartment. They check the corridors. They tiptoe out, down the stairs, across the Desmond common room, out the window.

But this time Virginia does not lead them around the back, toward the chapel.

Instead, she points seaward.

"Come," she whispers, and leads them to the woods.

•   •   •

The woods are so different at night. In the morning, on their runs, even the silences feel promising, even before sunrise; the footsteps of chipmunks, the rustling of roots, all incipient with the day to come. But now, the stars studding the sky and the moon bearing down slanting light, the woods are fuller, darker, stranger.

Laura shivers. She hopes Virginia doesn't see her.

She tells herself she's not afraid. Sebastian Webster would never have been afraid.

He would have relished this, she thinks: this world beyond the real.

They come to Farnham Cliff.

"Hideous." Virginia slips her hand into Laura's. "Isn't it?"

She approaches the Webster bust. In the darkness Laura can barely make out more than the outline of his features: his high aquiline nose, his tousled hair, the artistic dishevelment of his clothing.

Virginia reaches out, her fingers outstretched, and touches the cold bronze of his cheek, fingers the plaque on the base: *Come, shipwreck my soul!*

"This is what they want to take away from us."

Laura has never before noticed how loud the waves are when they thrash against the rocks.

Virginia removes two large candles from the bag. She lights them both, and places them on either side of the bust. She rises.

"Do you remember the part," Virginia says, "where the boys all jump off the rocks?"

"Of course." Shrimpy almost drowns.

"We did it once, you know."

She turns back toward the water.

"Izzy, Brad, and me. The lower rock—down there. We stripped off all our clothes, and—"

She leans against the statue. Her smile is strange.

"It was the best night of my life," she says.

Laura tries not to feel jealous. All the best nights of her life, she thinks, have been with Virginia.

The leaves rustle. Virginia looks up.

"Gentlemen!"

They are all there, all shivering.

"What are we even doing here?" Ralph asks. "Christ, it's cold."

"You know you can regulate your body temperature with your mind," says Anton. "If you're disciplined about it." He read this whole blog about it, he says. He offers to send it to them.

Ivan huddles next to Barry.

"Hello, Strauss." Brad's voice is low. "Hello, old pal." He claps the statue on its shoulder. He turns to Laura. "Really, Stearns," he says. His nose twitches. "What's a nice girl like you—doing in a place like this?"

But Virginia is on him before Laura can answer.

"Don't you remember, Noise?"

She nods toward the lower cliffs.

"It was that one, wasn't it? The one that splits in two."

It takes him a moment to realize what she means.

"Yes," he says. "It was that one."

"Gentlemen." Virginia's smile flicks on. "I wanted to bring us out here tonight." Her teeth glitter in the moonlight. She bobs, a little, in a parody of a bow. "To say goodbye."

"Fucking philistines," mutters Anton under his breath.

Virginia raises her voice a little. "A toast," she says, "to the great, lost mystic of American letters. To the Prep School Prophet himself."

"A toast?" Ivan wrinkles his forehead. "But we don't . . ."

"Always come prepared, Dixon."

Virginia goes to her backpack. She takes out an enormous, unopened bottle of whiskey. She hands it to Barry. "Do you approve?"

He inspects the label. "*Lagavulin?*"

"From the well-tended sideboard of Dr. and Mrs. Strauss. They had a twelve-year and a sixteen-year. I brought both."

She passes out plastic cups. She cracks open the top. She pours out seven abundant measures.

The eighth she pours on the ground between the candles.

"I like to think," she says, "that he's drinking with us."

She turns back to them.

"Did you know," she says, "that I've never been drunk before?"

She lifts the glass to her lips.

She downs the whole thing in a single gulp.

They drink. They drink slowly, at first; now more quickly; now the burning on Laura's lips gives way to an ember-like glow in her gullet; now the stars are more numerous and more beautiful than before; now Barry's mutters about the quality of the whiskey dissolve into comfortable murmurs, and the last of Laura's fears evaporates into the sea air.

Virginia keeps refilling their glasses. They keep drinking it down.

Then, when the bottle of whiskey is half-empty, Virginia stands.

She takes a step toward the cliff's edge. She scans the horizon for a moment. Laura thinks quickly of Bonnie and then tries to repress it.

Methodically, meticulously, Virginia removes her scarf, her black peacoat. She unties her fur collar. She takes off her gloves, folding them neatly on top of the rest of her clothing. She unlaces her boots. She removes her stockings.

She unzips the back of her dress.

This, too, she removes so slowly, keeping her face turned away from them, as the whole dark garment flutters to her feet.

Virginia removes her bra, her underwear.

She turns back toward them.

Anton's mouth falls open.

It is the first time Laura has seen Virginia naked.

She is almost childlike in the firelight. Her navel is the color of the moon. There are goose bumps on her arms and legs; her veins are visible. She stands like she doesn't notice their eyes on her, like this is just her natural skin.

Laura tries not to look. Laura keeps looking anyway.

Laura doesn't know if what she's feeling has to do with sex. She knows she doesn't want to touch this body, exactly; or else it's that she only wants to touch this body, to be able to push her hand against Virginia's waist, to touch Virginia's back without being afraid of what else it might signify, without it being *about,* in some sense, touching her in all the other ways that still feel so alien to her. She just wants to touch her, she thinks; that's all.

Virginia watches them watching her. Anton is panting; Ralph is gaping; Ivan is blushing. Barry is laughing nervously.

Brad can't take his eyes off her.

He is not looking at her with desire. Laura doesn't understand how you can look at Virginia without desire.

No, she thinks, what he's looking at her with is appalled fascination, like he's watching a car crash in slow motion.

"Don't you remember?" Virginia's voice is only slightly slurred. "The first time we did this?"

She clambers down onto the lower cliff ridge, the one cleft in two. She gestures toward the others.

"He couldn't stand it," she says. "It made him sick. Living such a dull, dutiful little life—thousands of miles from anything real. He'd have lost his mind, if he'd stayed. It would have killed him before the Republicans did."

Her voice echoes over the water. She turns back toward them. "Don't you remember, Noise?"

"I remember."

She takes a step forward, then another.

"Gentlemen."

Then, in a single motion, she dives.

For a moment there is only the thud of the waters opening.

Then they hear her crying out: ecstatic, triumphant.

Now Anton is stripping off his clothes; he is throwing them on the rocks; he cannonballs in. Now it's Ralph, downing his whiskey; now it is Ivan; now it is Barry, folding his clothes neatly beneath the weight of a rock, closing his eyes at the cliff's edge—as if, Laura thinks, in prayer.

Now only Brad and Laura are left.

She watches him strip naked before her.

He walks with military precision to the cliff's edge.

He turns back toward her with a corkscrew smile. "What's the alternative?" Then he, too, is gone; the water open beneath him.

Laura removes her clothes. She watches them in the water.

For a moment, she thinks—braver with the whiskey, the night sky, with all of them, together—everything is almost how it was.

She closes her eyes. She tries to squeeze out the memory of *almost*.

She jumps.

. . .

They swim; they freeze; they stumble back to shore; back to Webster's feet, back to the candles, still flickering; they throw on clothes haphazardly.

"Drink," Virginia cries, shivering in Anton's coat, refilling their glasses, and they do.

They drink another round, then another, their clothing only half restored. Virginia downs each cupful without flinching.

"Good God." Virginia tips her throat back. "God, this is glorious!"

She staggers to her feet. She pours Laura a glass so full that whiskey spills out onto her fingers. "Go on, drink! D-drink! God, we'll do him proud!"

Laura takes a sip. Her head is swimming; there are so many stars, hovering above her in the night sky, and she no longer knows which are real and which she has drunkenly invented. "I can't."

She can barely make out the words.

"Come on—of *course* you can! I dare you!"

Virginia grabs Laura's cup. She gulps some down. She hands it back to her.

"Finish it!"

Laura swallows it down. The flames are moving so much more slowly now; everyone's faces are melding; Virginia lifts the glasses to all of their lips; she lets all of them look at her.

Now Barry is asleep in Ralph's lap; now Ivan is laughing and crying and then laughing again; now Anton is shouting *Fuck Chairman Zhao, fuck the barbarians* alone at the stars; now they are singing, again, the words of the Compline hymn; now Virginia's building a bonfire; now suddenly, there is a nest's worth of flames licking the sides of the Webster statue; now Virginia is calling out to them.

She shrugs off Anton's coat.

She is standing on the higher cliff, which towers over the lower rock they have just jumped from: veering out in a stark line over the frothing waves.

"Who's ready for round two?"

They all sit up, looking at one another.

"Come on—it's too high!" Barry calls. "You'll kill yourself."

"Too high?" Her voice notches upward.

She throws her plastic cup straight at the Webster statue.

It bounces off the side.

"*He*'d have done it." Her smile spreads across her face. "*He*'d have done it—and a lot more, too—and you want to tell me it's too high?"

"Strauss—"

Brad's voice is low with warning.

"Cowards," Virginia yells. "Cowards, the lot of you!"

She staggers higher up the cliff, still swaying.

She turns to them, eyes shining, waiting.

They all look so uneasy.

"Gallagher? Ervin?"

But even Anton is looking down awkwardly at his empty glass.

"Come on, Strauss," he murmurs. "It's too high. You'll break your neck."

"Nobody?" She looks around. Her breasts are white in the moonlight. "Come on, show me what you're made of!"

They all look at one another in silence.

Ivan squeaks.

Virginia looks at them, for a moment, uncomprehending.

"*The rocks and the harbor*, right?" Virginia slurs. "Come on. Harbor. Rocks. Get it. Get it? Rocks!"

"Strauss." Brad's voice is low. He does not move. "Please."

She rounds on him.

"What? I thought you liked this!"

"Not from up there."

She meets his gaze. She lets her smile widen.

"Fine. Stearns!" She pierces through Laura's stupor.

"What is it?"

"Get over here."

"Come on, Strauss," Barry starts. "Don't make her—"

"She wants to! Doesn't she?" Virginia's eyes are blazing. "Come on—I double-dare you!"

Laura feels herself rise. She feels herself walk, her feet barely supporting her weight, across the narrow path; she feels the squelch of moss beneath her bare feet. There are two Virginias now, beckoning her; two long sets of spiderlike arms reaching for her wrists; two triumphant smiles.

"You're not scared, are you?"

Laura feels herself shake her head.

How can she be afraid of anything, she feels herself so dimly think, when Virginia is there? How can she be afraid of anything, when they are with Webster, when they have sung the Compline hymn, when it's almost dawn, when there's mist on the rocks, when the whiskey is so hot and glorious like she is suffused with it, when she has been baptized, in the name of the Father and the Son and the Holy Spirit, and whoever else Virginia saw fit to call upon; when Virginia is smiling at her, when Virginia is so sure?

"Strauss!" Brad calls in the distance. "Don't."

She is hard, she thinks; her body is so hard now; Virginia has made her hard; Virginia has made her strong; her body can bear the waves, she thinks, just like it can bear the cold.

She feels Virginia catch her as she stumbles; she feels Virginia's naked body pressed against hers.

It feels so good.

"The rest of you cowards," Virginia spits, "could learn a thing or two."

She pulls Laura even closer to the edge.

I can do this, Laura thinks; *I will do this.* She will plunge into the darkness, where the rocks and the harbor are one; she knows what to do; Virginia is with her. The waters will open up beneath her; they will clasp her like hands—

"Jesus—Strauss, wait!"

Brad's voice rings out across the rocks.

Virginia looks up in surprise.

"Let me go first," he says.

He marches so steadily toward them. He doesn't stagger once. His face is hard, is cold. He looks, Laura thinks, like a man condemned.

"Get back," he says to Laura, and then all of a sudden Laura is ten feet away from them, Ralph wrapping his coat around her, Barry warming her arms.

Virginia doesn't seem to notice. She can't take her eyes off Brad.

He pushes past her.

"Christ, Strauss, just get out of the fucking way!"

He takes off his blazer. He thrusts it at Virginia without looking at her.

Virginia takes another step toward him. She seizes him by both shoulders; she pulls him to her.

She kisses him.

At first Laura thinks that she has imagined it, that it is just the whiskey, or the morning mist, or a play of the firelight in the dawn.

But Virginia stays there: her hands like talons on Brad's cheeks, her mouth biting into his, her hair still dripping beads of water down her bare back.

At last, she pulls back in triumph.

Laura sees Brad's face.

He is looking at Virginia with such a strange expression. It is almost, Laura thinks, like disgust.

Then the searchlights come.

"Christ," Anton says. "Security!"

"Come on," Ralph is calling, blowing out the candles. "Move it, let's go!"

Brad leaps back onto the path, dragging Virginia with him, and starts throwing the bottle of Lagavulin and all the glasses over the side of the cliff.

"Don't bother," Virginia's words flow into each other. "Let them come!"

"Strauss, come on—"

"I said, let them come!"

Then Ivan is pulling one of Laura's arms, and Barry is pulling on the other, and they are racing through the woods, and then she hears the sound of falling; now Brad is with them, too, and Brad is running faster than they are, and they are running all the way to campus, and they can see the flashlights, across the trees, coming closer and closer to Farnham Cliff; now Barry is yanking her behind a tree, and Laura is looking back to see Virginia, still naked, on her hands and knees at the base of the Webster statue.

"Come and get me, you fuckers," she cries, and then Laura can no longer see her.

Part III

TRINITY

8

THEY HOLD VIRGINIA'S DISCIPLINARY HEARING THE WEEK AFTER spring break.

She has been out of the dorm at night. She has been drinking. Either of these on its own is grounds for expulsion.

It doesn't have to be this way, they tell her. Virginia is a good student—projected first in her class that year. Virginia has the American Institute for Civic Virtue before her, and then probably Harvard after that. Virginia's parents donate.

Also, campus security heard other footsteps in the woods.

If, they tell her, she were willing to name her coconspirators, an arrangement might be come to. They could consider the incident under the category of *problematic drinking*—a medical issue, not a disciplinary offense. They could send her to Dr. Vance, in the health center, for therapy. She might be able to avoid punishment altogether.

"I told them where they could shove it," Virginia tells Laura. "It's a matter of principle. Nothing's worth giving up one's honor for."

In the end, Virginia's parents call the school. A deal is made. Virginia isn't told the details.

They put her on probation for the entirety of Trinity term. Early curfew on weekends—exceptions for studying in Carbonell; no extracurriculars—no exceptions.

Not even choir.

· · ·

Virginia doesn't react when the disciplinary tribunal presents its verdict—*suspended from all extracurricular activities until next Michaelmas.* She doesn't even flinch. She simply sits, straight-backed, in that horrific and rickety wooden chair in the Mountbatten third-floor meeting room, with her hands, in long black lace gloves, gathered at elegant angles in her lap.

They call Laura as Virginia's peer character witness. She watches the whole thing happen.

Virginia rises. Virginia swallows. Virginia keeps her chin up.

Virginia removes the bronze key from around her neck. She marches so gracefully to Reverend Tipton, sitting with Dr. Charles and Mrs. Mesrin across the room. She places the key down right in front of him.

She turns on her heel and glides out without a word.

"It's fine," she says to Laura that night, her knees huddled to her chest. "I expected it." Her cheeks are hollow; her eyes are dark. "Besides—it's almost senior year." She bites her lip. "It's time to put away childish things." She sits up straighter. "I might even have quit myself, this term. You don't start an ideological revolution with aesthetics, you know. It's time to get serious—focus on schoolwork, on things that matter. Plus I've got to prepare for my internship. I doubt DC people care about chapel choir."

Laura gapes at her.

But Virginia doesn't meet her gaze.

"We all have to grow up sometime," she says.

After a long silence, she adds: "It's what he would have wanted."

.   .   .

Virginia has it all planned out.

She will spend Trinity term focusing on her academics, polishing up her various white papers. She'll spend the summer at the American Institute for Civic Virtue. She'll run for student council president and spend her senior year in office—"They didn't say anything about running for *next* term's extracurriculars," she determines, and in any case Isobel Zhao is probably running again, and it's a moral imperative that Isobel Zhao never be allowed to be in charge of anything.

"It's about time I got serious about political life," Virginia says.

Plus, she can devote more time to her running.

They run so much harder, now, and so much farther. They go all the way past Howlham some mornings; most mornings, to the Risetown border: fifteen miles, total, before breakfast. They run at night, trying to outpace the early curfew bell. They run until Laura's lower back feels like it is splitting like an overripe fruit; until her knees give way beneath her.

They no longer stop at the Grinning Griddle.

"It's a waste of time," Virginia decides. "We can just eat at Keble. There's only so many hours in the day."

Virginia grows frail. Virginia grows drawn. Virginia stops sleeping. She drinks black coffee by the thermos-full in Desmond Hall, reading until three, four, five in the morning—schoolbooks, at first, and then volumes of political philosophy, Hobbes and Locke and Hume, and then more Hegel, then Julius Evola, her scratches like a prisoner's in the margins, ink all over her hands.

Laura witnesses the whole thing.

Virginia lives in Laura's room now. She sleeps in Bonnie's old bed.

Laura does not remember agreeing to this, exactly, but one morning, in the first week of Trinity, Virginia appears with a little steamer trunk full of clothing and a larger one full of books.

"I've talked to Mrs. Mesrin," she says. "She's said it's fine."

She spills out the books all over the bed.

"So long as *you* don't mind, of course," she adds as an afterthought.

"I don't," says Laura. It is almost true.

That strange, unsettled feeling that has dogged Laura since Bonnie's accident has only gotten worse since that night in the woods. She remembers it only in fragments: Virginia's naked, goose-bumped body in the light of the moon, the piercing coldness of the water the first time it enclosed her; the proximity of the fall.

Laura would have jumped. She knows that now. She will do anything Virginia asks her to. It is a fact beyond assessment or adjudication; it is a law of nature. It's not her place to have an opinion on it. She will go where Virginia goes. Virginia will tell her what things mean.

It's not that Laura resents this. Laura has always known, deep down, that her role in this life is to be the Boswell, the Sancho Panza, the Gus Parnell. Virginia needs her, in this capacity; it is so much better to be needed than to be in control. Laura doesn't want—no, she has *never* wanted—to be World-Historical in her own right; whatever flashes of anger or exhaustion she might feel (on the Howlham coast, in Desmond at four in the morning when Virginia's desk lamp is shining bright) are only vestige instincts of primordial selfishness, something base and competitive and animal, probably neoliberal.

Laura tells herself that there is something wrong—broken, even—in that hard-cloistered part of herself that barricades against Virginia's rages: surely, Laura thinks, to have a true *shipwreck of the soul*, you have to open up all of yourself, fling it open like a window on a misty morning, to welcome in the daylight.

It is our sclerotic modern world, Laura tells herself, *that makes me doubt her. That's all.*

It's just that when they sing Evensong now, Ivan Dixon trying and failing to do that high soprano line all on his own, it no longer feels the same. They get the notes right; they all follow the tide of Reverend Tipton's conducting fingers, but all they are doing now is singing. They might as well be the Dewey Decibel System, Laura thinks, chirping "Build Me Up Buttercup" under Langford Gate.

Virginia never tells Laura, specifically, that she is dating Brad. As far as Laura knows, Virginia hasn't told Brad this, either. It is simply something—like their oaths, like their cliff dives—that Virginia has called into reality by sheer force of will. Virginia and Brad walk hand in hand on Devonshire Quad. Virginia and Brad kiss under Langford Gate. Virginia wears Brad's blazer to Latin class, slung over her increasingly bony shoulders.

Brad is such a gentleman with her. He carries her books for her on her way to class; he kisses her cheek whenever they part ways. He drapes his arm, idly, around her on Devonshire Quad.

But, Laura can't help noticing, there is something perfunctory, even resigned, about his attentions. His eyes are always just a little bit mournful when Virginia is with him; when she addresses him it always takes him an extra moment to respond, as if he has been lost in thought elsewhere, as if the most wonderful, the most brilliant, the most hideously World-Historical girl at St. Dunstan's has not chosen him, out of all of them, as hers.

Plus, he never calls Virginia by her first name.

· · ·

At last, Laura gets up the nerve to ask Virginia about it.

"Are you in love with him?"

They are standing at the edge of Risetown, looking back along the coast toward Jarvis Lighthouse. They are both out of breath. The dawn is breaking.

"He's in love with *me*," Virginia says. "He always has been, you know. Since freshman year."

She huddles against the breeze.

"You'd think he'd be pleased." Her voice is only a little bit melancholy. "After all that."

"But are you in love with *him*?"

Virginia watches the shoreline a little longer. She bites her lower lip.

"I don't know," she says at last, "what that means."

She brushes her hair out of her face.

"I've committed to him," she says. Her pause is half-breath. "Isn't that the same thing?"

She turns to Laura, waiting for an answer.

"I mean," Laura fumbles, "aren't you supposed to just, I don't know, *feel* it? *Just know?*"

Virginia tosses a pebble into the water, watching it get eclipsed.

"He would have jumped," Virginia says. She smiles at the memory. "Hideous, wasn't it? He would have jumped. If I'd asked him to." She exhales. "I remember when he was a sad, silly little freshman, sniveling that his parents never called him, getting solid Bs and blow jobs from Tamara Lynd in the Cranmer common room. And now look at him." She swallows. "He makes a fine choir president, doesn't he?"

She throws another stone into the water.

"You see," she says, "nothing much has changed." Her smile twists. "Brad's got the chapel keys now, so we can sing together anytime we want to. And I don't have to spend several hours a week letting Tipton tell me what to do." A sharp intake of breath. "It's all worked out perfectly. I'll be student council president in Michaelmas. Brad will go on being choir president—I'm *sure* Tipton will keep him on; it's too late to recruit anybody new. Brad wants to go to Yale, you know. New Haven isn't *so* far from Boston." She meditates on this for a moment. "I've arranged for us all to go to the Mayfair dance together next month," she says. "Me with Brad, obviously. You with Gallagher. A double date. It'll be"—she pronounces the word like it's foreign—"fun."

"Gallagher?"

Laura cannot imagine anyone she'd like to go on a date with less. She knows, of course, that he is technically attractive—he's probably one of the most conventionally attractive boys in the school, when she thinks about it; nevertheless, she's always been faintly repulsed by the way Anton invariably smells of sweat, of the garlic smoothies he assiduously drinks, about the way she can always see a small, hair-needled patch of skin through the bulging buttons of his undersize shirts.

"Why not? He's Brad's roommate, so it makes sense. And he's always had a bit of a crush on you."

"Me?"

Even Laura knows this is ridiculous. Anton has always been thoroughly, pigheadedly, devoted to Virginia.

"Why not you? You're very beautiful, you know."

It is the first time Virginia has said anything about Laura's looks.

"I just thought . . . you and Anton . . . I mean, that Anton kind of liked *you.*"

"Please," Virginia scoffs. "Anton's—I told you. He's all instinct. I could never. It'd be like loving your rottweiler." She throws another stone into the water. "I think you should do it. It'd be so tidy, you know. Both of us. With the boys. Double dates. Very *Seven Brides for Seven Brothers.*"

It is only when they are halfway back to Weymouth that Laura thinks this through.

Even Virginia thinks Anton would choose her if he could.

Laura has little time to dread Mayfair. The first weeks of term are inordinately busy, between schoolwork and SAT prep, regular running, and the launch of Virginia's student council campaign.

Virginia predicted rightly: Isobel Zhao is running, once again; within two days of the nomination period being opened, she garners the fifty necessary signatures to be put on that spring's election ballot for the coming year.

But Virginia is a more difficult sell. While she's able to get signatures from the boys, of course, and their friends in Cranmer and Morris, and from a few generically loyal girls in the Desmond common room, who don't particularly know or care about Virginia but find a Desmond student council president preferable to a Latimer one, more often than not people respond to Laura's clipboard with something between an eye roll and a scoff. Gabe Meltzer calls Virginia a self-involved snob; Matt Azibuike calls her a frigid, self-serving ice queen who's only doing this for her Harvard applications; Tamara Lynd says that the student council election is just a reification of the corrupt, bourgeois values of New England prep schools more generally, and that she won't be nominating or voting for anyone at all in protest.

Yvette Saunders just gives Laura a look of astounded disgust until she hurriedly gathers up her clipboard and scampers away.

Laura does what she can. She wheedles Ursula Thale, Rachel Goldstein, and a whole bunch of girls from Lyndhurst into signing by bringing them a box of Boston creams from Donut-ism on Main Street; she prevails upon her and Jasper Piedra's shared memories of Candlemas Calculus; she even flirts a little, to her own surprise, with ruddy-cheeked Teddy Kelting, who makes sure to tell her twice that he's *only* doing it because she asked him *very* nicely. But, by the day before the nomination period ends, Laura is stuck on forty-seven signatures.

She doesn't tell Virginia.

People don't know Virginia, she reminds herself, the way she knows Virginia. They do not see her kindness, nor her loneliness, the way her face lights up when she talks about Webster, the way she goes—*used* to go—into such raptures, singing. They don't see how her cruelty is only the coin turn of her capacity for love.

She will just have to convince them.

Samuel Johnson, Laura reminds herself, Don Quixote, Robert Lawrence, Alexander the Great, Joan of Arc, all those scions of the World-Historical—none of them would have gotten fifty signatures, either.

Laura spends the Tuesday night before the end of the nomination period walking from table to table in Keble Hall, clipboard in hand. She manages, at last, to talk Dr. Charles's son, Richard, into signing, in exchange for two weeks' worth of Laura's Topics in European History notes.

But then it's eight o'clock, and the staff are putting away the heated trays of shepherd's pie and viscous lasagna, and the final dinnertime stragglers are gathering up their crumb-covered plates, and Laura is still short two signatures.

"Oi! Laura!"

Isobel Zhao is sitting alone in the corner, her face half-obscured by a mountain of SAT prep. Her hair is pure silver.

"Isobel. Hi."

Laura hurriedly looks down. She and Isobel haven't spoken since before the Evensong protest.

"What've you got there?"

"It's nothing," Laura says. "Really."

"How many does she have?"

Laura reluctantly shows her.

"Will wonders never cease." A smile spreads across Isobel's face. "St. Dunstan's getting a conscience." She arches an eyebrow. "How the mighty, et cetera."

"You don't have to gloat," Laura says softly. "You've already won."

Isobel's smile fades. "You call *this* winning?"

"The statue's gone. You're running unopposed." Laura's cheeks burn. "What more do you want?"

Isobel considers Laura for a moment. "You really don't get it, do you?"

"You're right," Laura snaps. "I don't. Explain it to me."

Isobel sighs a long and exhausted sigh.

"I want," Isobel says so slowly, "to save her."

"Save her?"

Isobel keeps her eyes on her empty plate.

"Yeah," she says, a little louder, with a little more certainty.

"From what? From the *boys*? From God?"

"Jesus, Laura, just give me the clipboard!"

Isobel all but yanks it out of her hand.

Isobel makes two quick, neat signatures. "*Robust debate in a public forum*, right? Isn't that what she wants? I'm putting Miranda down, too."

"I . . ." Laura stares at her in astonishment. "But—why?"

"She's not the only one," says Isobel, "who gets to have principles."

• • •

"You shouldn't have accepted it," Virginia says, when she sees the signatures. "I don't want to accept anything from either of them. Cross them out."

"But—"

"Find someone else—I don't care who. That idiot Saunders—just promise her an Instagram photo and she'll be happy."

"Virginia—"

"Go down the hall and ask Thale and Lynd; they're probably still up. Or—"

"Virginia!"

At last Virginia looks up at her.

"Nobody else would sign."

Virginia's mouth falls open. For a moment she stares at Laura in shock, not even blinking, her electric-blue eyes widening; for a moment, too, Laura thinks she might cry. But Virginia just swallows and sits up straight.

"I see," she says. She forces a scoff from her throat. "Typical. High school. Not a serious person in this whole place. I mean, except for us, obviously." Her mouth twitches. "You know what they say about a prophet in their own land. Anyway . . ." She rises and goes to the window. "It'll be different, this summer. At the institute. People there understand the importance of seriousness. They're not too busy nursing petty grudges over . . ." Her voice trails off. "Anyway, I told you I wasn't likable."

Virginia hands in the nomination form. Virginia keeps running. Virginia keeps dating Brad.

Virginia continues to sit with the rest of the choir, in Keble, her arm flung over Brad's shoulder, or else her hand twining his. She continues to opine about Reverend Tipton's music choices. But something has changed.

The boys are so awkward now whenever Virginia bounds over to join them, almost embarrassed, as if she has caught them doing something they shouldn't. Brad doesn't make eye contact when he kisses her—so lightly, on the cheek or on the lips. Anton—whom Laura can't look at without blushing—no longer breaks in at once at the end of Virginia's sentences, bellowing agreement before she has even gotten to her point.

Laura doesn't know if it has to do with the chaos of that final night of Candlemas, or with the absence of the statue, or with the fact they've seen Virginia naked, or with the fact that Virginia is no longer in choir, or if it has to do with the fact that Virginia is now dating Brad. All Laura knows is that something none of them can name is different, and that she no longer looks forward to Friday nights.

Trinity continues. The buds burst open. Devonshire Quad turns pink with scattered petals; Ivan gets allergies. Laura keeps her vigil. She studies with Virginia; she reads over Virginia's white papers; she follows her on the runs that stretch longer and longer, toward the Canadian border.

Laura helps Virginia record her campaign video.

They try to do it professionally. Virginia borrows a tripod and a camera from Carbonell, ignoring Freddy's barbed *good luck* at the checkout desk; Laura films her in the rare-book room, against the shelves, telling St. Dunstan's how G. K. Chesterton once said tradition was the democracy of the dead.

"There's no point," says Virginia, scrolling through the footage. "I look like a corpse and sound like a bureaucrat."

It's true. Virginia's magnetism doesn't translate to video. On-screen, Virginia is stilted and awkward; her overflowing allusions come across mannered and pretentious. Her skin looks sickly, and a little green.

"We'll do it again," Laura says. "It just takes practice, that's all."

"You just need to relax," Laura says. "Then everyone will see what I see."

"From your mouth to God's ears," Virginia says.

The Friday before the Mayfair dance, when the choir all files out of chapel for rehearsal, Virginia is not there waiting for them. Laura comes back to Desmond to find her curled on a corner of her bed, scrolling through her phone.

"You know she's got fifty-two thousand followers now?"

Bonnie has dyed her hair black. She wears lots of eyeliner and talks at length about the problem with private prep schools, particularly private prep schools in New England, and also about the moral and spiritual failings of organized religion. She reads a three-card Tarot spread for everyone who donates to her Patreon. She makes three thousand dollars a month.

"I heard."

Virginia doesn't look up. "Who'd have thought it? Bonnie di Angelis, goth witch queen of the Internet." She snorts. "Do you think she Facetunes? I'm sure she Facetunes." She nods to herself. Then she lifts her head. "Or is she just—like that naturally?"

"I don't know," Laura says. "Maybe a bit of both."

She comes to sit by Virginia.

Bonnie is in a cemetery. Bonnie is standing in leather boots. Bonnie has cut her hair into a flapper-girl bob and is spray-painting a pentagram and an anarchy symbol on the side of a Nyack church wall. Four thousand people Like that one.

"Do you think she's happy?" Virginia says suddenly. "I don't mean back in Westchester; obviously, nobody could be happy in Westchester. I mean—existentially."

"No," Laura says.

"Why not?"

"Come on." Laura nestles closer to Virginia. "You know why. She . . . has no transcendence. I mean—maybe she's happy like how, you know, Natasha is happy, at the end of *War and Peace*. . . ."

This makes Virginia smile. "That's not true happiness," she says. "It can't be."

Laura hopes, deep down, that Bonnie is experiencing true, existential happiness, even in Westchester. Virginia scrolls through more of Bonnie's photographs: Bonnie in a leather choker; Bonnie in a corset; Bonnie in black lingerie with spiderwebs on it.

"It's not fair," Virginia says. "Beauty is wasted on her."

She is silent for a while.

"You know, Brad hasn't tried to sleep with me yet."

"What?"

"It's been a month. We've only kissed. And even then—" Virginia swallows. "I suppose he's nervous, you know. Because it's functionally my first . . ." She bites her lip. "I mean, it's *different* with us. Because we were so close before. It's primarily"—she draws herself up against the wall—"a union of souls." Her eyes fall briefly to her phone.

"Do *you* want to?"

Virginia doesn't say anything.

"I'm curious," she says at last, "what it feels like."

"But I thought . . . I mean, what about the God stuff?"

Virginia looks up at her. "What God stuff?"

"I mean—" Laura tries to find the right words. "Do you feel like, I don't know, you're *allowed*?"

"Don't be ridiculous," Virginia says. "It's one thing to have meaningless high school fucking on the squash courts, or something. That's pornographic. It wouldn't be like that. Not with us. Brad—I mean, Brad understands about Webster, and about—about seriousness, and hideousness, and . . ." She stops herself. "He'd be a good person to do it with. If I were to do it. Not that I want to do it. It'd probably be horribly boring and we'd both repent."

Laura doesn't say anything. The idea of Virginia having sex disturbs her more than she wants to admit. It would be like if gravity suddenly stopped working, or if the sun set in the south. There are constants that keep the world turning, Laura thinks; Virginia's chastity is one of them.

She immediately feels guilty for thinking this.

"I'm sure," Virginia says firmly, "that Brad knows that, too. It's why he's barely tried anything. We watched the *whole* of *Fanny and Alexander*, in the Cranmer common room, and he didn't even try to touch my breasts. Of course, there wasn't much time, what with early curfew and everything. But I'm off it for Mayfair, they said. Everyone is. So we can stay out late."

She keeps scrolling through Bonnie's feed.

"Mayfair," she says. "Spring. Flowers. Bees. He'll try then."

At last, Mayfair comes. They put out a tent on Devonshire Quad; they gird the poles with vines. They put out tables with lace tablecloths and plastic vases overflowing with silk flowers; they garland the outsides of the dorms. They put down a little dance floor, right outside Mountbatten Hall, and hire a swing band all the way from Kittery.

225

Virginia has nothing to wear.

The dress code is, officially, all white; in practice girls wear pastels; boys just wear their ordinary button-downs and slacks, and floral ties if they're feeling creative, except for Teddy Kelting, who famously turned up one year in nothing but tighty-whities and a terry-cloth bathrobe. But Virginia's closet is hanger after hanger of black: lace and silk, sensible cotton, moldering furs.

"What did you wear last year?" Laura managed to find a vaguely floral dress she likes from the Treasure Chest in town; it hangs loose and gauzy over her calves.

"We didn't go last year." Virginia fingers the edges of a fur coat. "I wouldn't let them."

She gets to the white-sequined dress her father has bought her, hanging untouched since Thanksgiving. She brushes her fingers over it.

"This is all I have."

She considers it for a moment: the tight-stretch fabric, the hemline that barely skims below the boyish line of her hips. She takes it off the hanger. She holds it so gingerly, as if she is afraid of it.

The dress doesn't suit her.

It is too short, and it is too tight, and it pancakes her small breasts just above the nipple, pressing a scar-like line into her flesh. The color washes her out.

Her hair and makeup are equally disastrous. She has tried to curl her long, fine hair with Laura's curling iron, succeeding only in frying it into various uneven ringlets; she has tried, too, to contour, smudging dirty shadows on her face that even Laura—attending meticulously to YouTube tutorials—can't fully remedy. She can't walk in heels.

It is the first time, Laura thinks, as Virginia totters down the Desmond stairs, holding the banister so that she does not fall over it, that she has seen Virginia look anything but beautiful.

At six, Brad and Anton come to the common room.

Brad is wearing a tuxedo two sizes too big, along with a pink polka-dotted bow tie and cummerbund to match. Anton is wearing a hideous white blazer over a black shirt and a black tie, which makes him look like an extra from *Saturday Night Fever*.

"You look nice," he mutters to Laura without looking at her, and Laura wonders what Virginia had to promise to get him here in the first place.

Brad takes in Virginia—her hobbling deerlike legs, her red Kewpie lips—with flustered astonishment.

"You, uh. Well, look at you, Strauss," he says. "Uh—here. This is yours."

He hands her a rose like he's delivering a pizza.

Virginia's smile collapses in on itself.

"Thank you, Brad," she says quietly.

They make their way onto Devonshire Quad. The swing band has already struck up; everyone is already dancing; Reverend Tipton is standing by the punch table, hiding his face in a Solo cup of cherry cola.

The others are already there. Ralph is standing by one of the garlanded poles, his arm brushing around Yvette Saunders's waist; Ivan is gazing mournfully across the dance floor at Freddy, who is at the floor's edge taking pictures, her scrawny arms emerging doll-like from the puffed sleeves of an appalling seventies prairie dress. Barry is the only person there who is actually well dressed, in a white linen summer suit Laura is sure he's had tailored; he watches the band, tapping his feet with the music.

They all look up, in something between shock and horror, when they see Virginia approaching.

"*Strauss?*"

Ralph doesn't even try to hide his amusement. Beside him, Yvette's smile calcifies into something cruel.

"Gentlemen!"

It sounds so much less authoritative, now that Virginia has to balance on Brad's arm.

"Virginia." Yvette drags out every single syllable. She air-kisses Virginia before Virginia can stop her; Virginia recoils, wobbling against the tentpole. "I just want you to know . . ." She puts a hand over her heart. "How deeply sorry I am to hear about choir." She pauses. "I hope you're able to fill the time somehow."

"I manage."

Yvette puts a determinate hand on Ralph's shoulder. "Ralph's been telling me how *great* the lineup is this term. We're even talking about, like, a collaboration, maybe?"

"A—collaboration?"

"Between the Dewey Decibel System and choir. We were thinking a sing-off, maybe, under Langford Gate? Adorable, right?"

Virginia's nostrils flare.

They hear the click of a camera.

"Move in closer," Freddy says. "I want to get everyone together." She looks Virginia over. "You'll have to crouch in those shoes."

"Freddy! You're looking—" Ivan begins, too eagerly, before Ralph shoves him.

They all move in together. Anton thrusts his arm around Laura's shoulders. Brad straightens his back.

The band plays a louder chord; Virginia looks up.

Isobel and Miranda are kissing on the dance floor.

Isobel is in a white three-piece suit, her hair dyed platinum to match. Miranda is wearing a 1950s party dress, with gauze petticoats and matching long gloves with a corsage. They are dancing, riotously—they must, Laura thinks in surprise, be the only students at St. Dunstan's who actually know *how* to swing dance—Isobel leading Miranda into swivels and dips and Charleston kicks, picking her up and setting her down; raucous with joy.

"God," Ralph says loftily. "It's like everyone here's dressed like Tom Wolfe."

Virginia doesn't even look at him.

She is too busy watching Isobel throwing Miranda into the air.

"I said," Ralph tries again, a little louder. "It's like everyone here—"

Virginia grabs Brad's arm so tightly he yelps.

"Come on," she says. "Let's dance."

Virginia and Brad dance; Ralph and Yvette dance; Anton and Laura dance. Anton is a plodding, methodical dancer, counting time out loud while staring at his feet, and so Laura is able to watch Virginia and Brad over her shoulder. His movements are jerky; he is holding her at such an arm's length. He catches Laura's eye, for a moment, over Virginia's shoulder, and his awkward concentration twists at last into a wry, sad smile; Virginia trips on her heels and stumbles to the ground and does not let Brad help her up.

They dance; they drink punch; Yvette Saunders takes a selfie with Ralph. Barry gets the swing band's keyboardist to let him cut in on "Why Don't You Do Right."

The swing band starts playing a slow dance, to "Can't Take My Eyes Off You." Miranda and Isobel head back to the floor.

Virginia stands up straighter; she looks, so expectantly, at Brad.

But Brad extends his hand to Laura.

"Why don't we switch it up a bit," he says. "You don't mind, do you, Strauss?"

Virginia doesn't say anything.

Laura looks at Virginia in terrified appeal. "No, no," she begins, too quickly, "you should . . ."

"Go ahead," says Virginia.

Laura hesitates.

"I said *go*."

Brad leads Laura onto the dance floor. Out of the corner of her eye she can see Virginia, leaning against the tentpole, watching them.

"Lovely night," Laura tries, too brightly. "Isn't it?"

"Fine . . ." Brad exhales heavily. "Fine."

He is more at ease now; his hands are firm around her waist.

"You know—I think it's just *great*, you and Virginia," Laura tries a little harder. "Just—*great*!"

He nods.

"It's just so romantic, after all this time—"

"Yes," Brad says, steering her out of the way of Miranda and Isobel. "After all this time." His arm is stiff and awkward around her shoulders.

"I think it's always better, when people are friends first. It's more natural that way . . . you have a foundation. A history."

"Yes," Brad says. "We certainly have that."

His hands are so tight upon Laura's shoulders.

It's like, she thinks, he's afraid of falling.

"It was so brave of you," she tries, one final time.

"What was?"

"Offering to jump."

"What are you talking about?"

"In Candlemas. When Virginia went up to the high cliff. Everyone else was so afraid—*I* was afraid. I almost . . . I mean, I don't know what I would have done."

"No." He steers her past Ralph and Yvette. "You would have."

"I just think it was brave of you, that's all. She thinks so, too."

But Brad is looking at her with such a melancholy smile.

"Never let it be said," he murmurs, "that I never did anything for you."

Laura looks up at him in confusion. She opens her mouth to ask him what he means, but before she can speak she sees the empty corner of the tent.

Virginia is gone.

Virginia doesn't answer her phone. She doesn't reply to texts. Laura checks, briefly, Desmond, and she is not there, either.

"She's probably gone running," Brad says. "This isn't exactly her scene."

He slings one arm around Laura's shoulder, another around Anton's. "Come on. Let's worry about it tomorrow."

They keep on dancing. Barry tap-dances to "Brother, Can You Spare a Dime?"; Anton tells them all about this new meditation technique Eric Weinstein talks about in a podcast that allows you to burn twice as many calories just by visualizing flames after you eat lunch. Ralph brings out a flask of gas-station wine product he bought over on Carver Avenue, and Laura and Yvette take turns trying to force it down.

Laura keeps furtively checking her phone.

"Come on, Stearns." Ralph claps her on the shoulder. "We can have one night without our chaperone. Can't we?"

Laura doesn't know how to say no.

•   •   •

Laura dances with Barry. Laura dances with Anton. Ivan Dixon finally gets the courage to ask Freddy Barnes to dance, and she offers him her arm without altering her scowl.

"That I don't get," Ralph announces, watching them. "I mean, I know there's no accounting for taste, but . . ." He sighs. "Maybe Dixon's a masochist."

The sun sets; the stars start twinkling; the air is petal-clogged.

Laura and the boys make their way back to the Cranmer common room, except for Ralph, who offers to walk Yvette back to Desmond and then turns off his phone. Barry turns on *The Great British Bake Off*, and then there is no more talking to him; Anton turns the subject to cryogenics, telling everyone about this scientist in Oxford who is almost certainly going to find a cure for death.

Then Brad's phone buzzes.

He picks it up. He swipes a few times.

All the color drains from his face.

He slams the phone down.

"What is it?" Ivan asks.

"Nothing," Brad says. "Nothing."

He looks, Laura thinks, like he's going to be sick.

"Let me guess," Anton cuts in. "Our Lady."

"No, it—"

"Checking up on you? Making sure you've been good?"

Brad stiffens.

"Making sure you've been *serious* . . . ?"

"Fuck it!" Brad leaps to his feet. "I'm going upstairs."

Barry and Ivan are still watching the whipping of a tiramisu.

"Come on, Stearns." Anton grabs Laura by the shoulder. "I'll walk you home."

They take the back way from Cranmer to Desmond, behind the

parking lots. Anton keeps Laura's hand inside his enormous paw, squeezing it intermittently.

Laura keeps her eyes straight ahead.

"Nice night," she says. "Beautiful moonlight, isn't it? I always love a ..."

Anton shoves her against a dumpster. Anton sticks his tongue down her throat.

It's a brutal tackle of a kiss: unromantic and efficient, as if Anton had determined at the beginning of the night he was going to kiss someone, by God, and is now too stubborn not to see it through. His breath smells like Chateau Diana and onion dip. Sweat seeps through his shirt onto her shoulders.

Laura recoils.

"Anton—" She can barely gasp it out before he's sucking on her lower lip, forcing his hand under her dress.

He doesn't hear her. He is murmuring into her cheek, her neck, between her breasts, scratching her clavicle with the bristling outline of his beard, lost in what he is doing; smearing his sweat on her neckline.

"You want this," he murmurs. "Don't pretend—she told me everything." He reaches his hand up a little further, and Laura yelps.

"Everything? What are you ..."

His finger is against her lips.

"Shh—don't be shy. I know." Laura can feel the flimsy seams of her dress pop, one by one, along her thigh. "I know how much you want this."

"Jesus, *Anton!*"

She shoves him away so violently he stumbles.

He looks at her, for a moment, his eyes blazing.

"What?" His laugh is hollow. "You think you're too good for me, too?"

"No," she says quietly. "I don't think that."

"You know, half this school would die for me to take them to Mayfair!"

"I know."

"You don't!"

He slams the dumpster, just a few inches beside her head. It reverberates against her back.

"They're all not like you, you know. The rest of this whole fucking school. If I wanted—if I asked—anyone else, anyone *normal*!"

"Anton, it's not about you—"

"Instead of a couple frigid, stuck-up cunts!"

The word shatters in the air.

He gapes at her for a moment, as much in shock as she is. His mouth drops open; he fumbles, now, for some kind of apology, but it is too late.

Laura is already halfway to Desmond.

Laura sits for a long time on the bed, her dress torn and her hair undone, shaking, playing it out over and over in her head.

So, Laura thinks, hugging her knees to her chest, Virginia planned this. Virginia had it all decided—her and Brad, somewhere, in his Cranmer dorm, at a suite at the Wayfarer, in the woods—while Laura is left with Anton, to play it out exactly how Virginia wants it. The idea makes her retch.

She did this, she thinks, *knowing how much I want her.*

Laura waits for Virginia to come home. She practices what she is going to say in the mirror, keeping her voice low. She hears, already, Virginia's excuses, the ones that make everything so simple, that make the most hideous things make perfect sense.

She won't fall for it, this time, she tells herself. She'll make Virginia *see*, finally, that you can't play games with people, like that; you can't make everything conform to your vision of how the world should be, just because you're smarter than everybody else, just because you talk about God all the time; just because everybody's in love with you.

But when Virginia comes home, Laura's speeches vanish.

She is carrying the camera, the tripod. She staggers like a sleepwalker across the room. Her eyes and her cheeks are hollow. Her lipstick is smudged. She looks like death.

She puts the tripod down in the corner of the room without looking up. She sits down, on the edge of her bed, as if Laura isn't even there.

"Where were you?"

"Carbonell."

"Why?"

"Student council stuff." Virginia huddles her knees to her chin.

"Are you okay?"

Virginia nods. She is silent for a while.

"Do you think . . ." she says at last. "It's possible to surprise God?"

"What?"

"I mean, He's supposed to know everything about us, right? What we're going to do before we do it? Who we are? He's supposed to have it all planned out."

"I mean—I guess?"

"But we've got free will, too, right? We can do things, we can be different people, from whom we're supposed to be."

"I don't understand."

"Like, if we do something so . . ." Virginia takes a deep breath. "If we do something nobody expects, something totally against our nature, against what makes us who we are. Do you think we can surprise God? Do you think we can make God clap a hand over his mouth and cry out, *Well, gee, I didn't see that one coming?*"

"What are you talking about?"

"Nothing." Virginia kicks off her stilettos. "Nothing. Christ, I hate these things."

"You left the dance."

"I was tired."

"We were worried."

Virginia doesn't say anything.

"Anton stuck his tongue down my throat."

Virginia doesn't react to this, either.

"He said you said I liked him."

"Oh." Virginia unzips her dress. "Did I?"

"He called me a cunt!"

Virginia blinks, for a moment, confused. "Why?"

"Never mind," Laura says. "It doesn't matter."

Virginia crawls into bed. She pulls the coverlet up all the way to her chin.

"Are you going to tell me what's wrong?"

"Nothing's wrong."

"Are you mad at me?"

Virginia stares for a long while at the foot of her bed.

"Maybe," she says softly. "I never know when I'm angry. I can never tell when I'm angry or when I'm just bored." She swallows. "When I just want *something* to happen, and it doesn't even matter what."

At last she looks up at Laura. "I'm sorry," she says. "I'm not making any sense. I'm just tired. God, I'm so tired."

"Do you want to sleep in tomorrow?"

Their alarm is set for four forty-five.

"No," Virginia says. She draws herself up. "Don't be ridiculous." She takes a deep breath. "I'll be all right in the morning," she says.

She turns out the light.

Virginia spends the next two days in a somber mood. They barely speak at all on their morning runs; Virginia says nothing about Mayfair. She does not mention Brad, or ask about Anton; she avoids Keble altogether.

Laura is relieved. She doesn't want to face the choirboys again, at least not until she can greet Anton with a straight face. Nobody has reached out to her, either, since the dance, although when she and Virginia walk to Latin class on Monday morning, Ralph and Ivan stop short when they see them on the quad, lowering their eyes and flushing bright red before turning on their heels and scurrying away.

"What's wrong with them?" Virginia asks.

Laura hopes that it has nothing to do with her and Anton.

"You know—they really are horribly immature."

Virginia lifts her chin.

"I don't know why you're doing choir at all, to be honest."

"What?"

"It's just—it's not like you want to be a professional singer, or anything. Especially with senior year coming up. It's a real waste of your time. It's not exactly serious, any longer, not with Tipton at the helm."

Laura knows exactly what will happen next.

Virginia is going to make her leave choir.

Even now, Laura still loves it. There are moments when she sings, her voice knitting together with Barry's on *Glory be to the Father and to the Son*, or when the eerie particularity of her solo is swallowed up in the greater harmony, that she feels the same astounded shiver that she felt on her first Evensong.

But Laura knows she will do whatever Virginia asks. She no longer remembers how to do anything else.

The next day, at Assembly, the student council candidates all gather to present their videos. Laura shuffles in, alone. Virginia is already backstage.

The choir in their usual spot, under John Devonshire's portrait. Yvette Saunders is with them, Ralph's hand on hers.

Laura takes a few tentative steps toward them.

They all freeze when they see her.

"Hello . . . guys . . ."

Yvette bursts into peals of laughter.

"Everything okay?"

Yvette laughs even harder. Anton doesn't even look up.

"Fine," Brad says, so quickly. "Absolutely fine. Take a seat, Stearns."

She considers them.

"O-kay?"

"You're just in time," Brad says, checking his watch. "Strauss is about to tell us all what miserable sinners we are."

"*Sure* she is," Yvette murmurs.

Ralph shoots her a look; she falls silent. Laura sits as far away from Anton as possible.

Isobel goes first. She uses "Black Sabbath" as her campaign theme song, sauntering onto the stage to near-unanimous raucous applause.

"Morning, fuckers," she says, while Mrs. Mesrin gesticulates in horror from the side podium. "Let's do this."

Mrs. Mesrin launches her video from the St. Dunstan's computer. It flickers across the screen at the back of the auditorium.

It is a catalog of her various successes at St. Dunstan's: the removal of the Webster statue, the ongoing faculty reassessment of Evensong, the abolishing of the paternalistic rule that students can't be unsupervised in the private dorm rooms of the opposite sex.

"*All this*," says Isobel in the video, dressed in a boy's rowing blazer and a bow tie, "*without holding any political power whatsoever. Imagine what we can do with the apparatus of the state.*

"*We're gonna burn the whole thing down.*"

Half the room gives her a standing ovation when she's done.

Now it's Virginia's turn.

There are a few scattered cheers from across Assembly Hall.

To Laura's surprise, even the choir's applause is perfunctory: a vague *whoo* that dies on their lips, Brad and Ralph's muted *Hear! Hear!* as they tap the arms of their benches. Anton doesn't applaud at all.

Virginia marches to the front podium.

She clutches a copy of her speech to her chest. Her skirt goes all the way to her ankles. She looks straight out at the audience.

"Gentlemen," she says. "And ladies," she adds, a little too late. "I'm pleased to present to you my vision for St. Dunstan's."

She nods at Mrs. Mesrin.

The video starts playing.

Virginia is sitting on the table of the rare-book room in Carbonell. She is wearing her white-sequined dress, which she has hiked up almost all the way to the top of her thighs. Her lipstick is smeared, and her mouth is open in a sultry half pout.

Her underwear is visible.

Brad stiffens. "Jesus . . ."

"*I want you to know*," Virginia-in-the-video murmurs, in a high, kittenish voice Laura has never heard her use before, "*how much I'm looking forward to our first time together.*"

Virginia, onstage, freezes.

"Oh no." Brad grabs the arm of his bench. "*Oh* no."

Virginia in the video hikes the dress further up her hips. She splays her legs. "*I want you to know,*" she goes on.

"Well, fuck me!" Ralph is leaning in, his eyes shining with insalubrious glee.

"What *is* this shit?" one of the Morris boys mutters behind them.

The real Virginia does not move. Animal horror spreads across her face.

The video keeps playing: "*What I've been thinking about,*" this ghost-Virginia murmurs, "*what I've been waiting for. I've dreamed of you discovering . . .*"

She opens her legs. She traces her fingers up her inner thigh.

Laughter drowns out the rest of her words. The Morris boys, the Lyndhurst girls, everyone is laughing, or else screaming in some combination of horror and delight; somebody cries out stop to the video, but nobody does.

Virginia remains frozen onstage, looking wildly from the screen to the audience and back again. Mrs. Mesrin, too, is frozen: staring at the laptop as if she can simply will it to stop.

Isobel moves first.

She strides across the auditorium; she yanks the cord from the laptop so violently it clatters off the podium and smashes on the floor. The video flickers into pixels.

Virginia just stands there: watching the absence where her face has been.

People's titters syncopate into silence.

Virginia bolts.

"Did you guys see—" Ralph begins, but Laura is already running out of Assembly Hall, down the corridors of Mountbatten, out onto Devonshire Quad. Virginia is ten paces ahead of her; Virginia long and lithe and so unlike that painted figure on the screen: pursing her lips, tracing her fingers.

"Virginia—wait—please!"

Virginia keeps running.

Laura catches up with her, at last, at the edge of the woods.

"Please just talk to me!"

Virginia rounds on her. Her eyes are glassy with tears. "What do you want?"

"What *was* that?"

"I checked," Virginia gulps. "A million times. What I sent to Mrs. Mesrin—there's no way . . ."

She staggers against a beech tree.

"I *checked*!"

"Breathe!" Laura grabs Virginia by the shoulders. "Please, you have to breathe."

Virginia collapses into her arms.

"Tell me what happened."

"I'm careful." Virginia is shaking so hard Laura can barely hold her. "God, I'm so careful, I'd never have—God, I'm going to be sick!"

She retches. Nothing comes out.

"He was the only one who had it. The only one—oh God!"

"Who?"

"Brad!"

Virginia's whole body convulses, then grows still.

Finally Laura gets it.

She remembers Brad's face, after the Mayfair dance; she remembers all their faces; the way even Ivan Dixon blushed when she sat down.

They've seen it, she thinks. *All of them.*

Her stomach lurches.

It would have been so easy. Anyone with access to the Assembly laptop could have done it, in those frantic minutes when everybody was still finding their seats—slipped to stage right, stuck a USB stick into the computer, switched the files, switched the names.

It couldn't have been them, she thinks. *I know them; I know them.*

"It's not your fault, Virginia."

"It *is* my fault."

"It's not; listen to me—you did *nothing* wrong, you—"

Virginia slaps her.

Laura falls back into the dirt.

"God, you're *pathetic!*"

Virginia leaps up. "*You did nothing wrong, don't worry, it'll be okay, don't you dare feel bad*—God, you're like a little dog!" Her face is as white as the trees. "Just a little yapping lapdog begging to be loved. That's all you are. You never understood a goddamn thing!"

"Virginia, I—"

Virginia's just angry, Laura thinks, so desperately. She's angry; she's just lashing out; she doesn't mean—

"Everything we talked about—everything we believed—you didn't mean a single word, did you? You just smiled and nodded and pretended, and said *Yes, Virginia*, and *No, Virginia*. Don't you *dare* tell me it wasn't my fault. My God. You little fool. You make me sick." She catches sight of Laura's face. "What?" Her laugh is horrible. "What is it now?"

Laura doesn't say anything.

"I'm going for a run. Don't you dare follow me."

She leaves Laura in the dirt.

• • •

Laura doesn't know how long she stays like that: mud-covered, disheveled, with bits of twigs falling from her hair.

She is barely conscious of crossing back across Devonshire Quad, of entering Desmond, of sitting down at her desk.

She is barely conscious of pressing her computer keys: of the email, from an anonymous account, that has appeared in her in-box that afternoon.

Virginia Strauss sex tape, the subject line reads. It's been CC'd to the entire St. Dunstan's student body.

There is a link.

Laura sits there for a while, staring at the screen, deciding what to do.

She doesn't delete it.

It's not that she's not going to delete it, she tells herself. Of course she'll delete it. Every single law Laura knows demands that she delete it. There are things you do not look upon, in this world, without turning into salt, or stone, and your best friend half-naked, trailing her fingers up her thighs, is one of them.

Only, there is a bruise on Laura's lip.

Only, Laura wants to.

It's not that she wants to see Virginia get off. The idea repulses her. Virginia is not supposed to get off, not ever, except if you count vague holy ways where you see the saints in ecstasy; that's the whole point of Virginia; that's why Laura worships her.

There are two kinds of people in this world—how many times has Virginia told Laura this?—there are the ones who matter, and the ones who don't, the Robert Lawrences and the Gus Parnells, the World-Historical and residents of Ordinary Time; there is transcendence, everywhere, and the heavens crack open like an egg every time a priest tells you to go to a Sunday-night class in Howlham, every time a girl joins choir who shouldn't, and that is why it is acceptable to send love notes to priests, that is why it is acceptable that Bonnie di Angelis fell off a cliff, that one time, and that is why it is acceptable to slap a person who is just trying to help you and call them a *little yapping lapdog* who never understood anything, anyway, and Virginia understands this, better than anyone, which is why Virginia is better than sex, except when she's not, and if Virginia isn't better then everybody, then Laura doesn't have to be, either.

That's what Laura tells herself when she stares at the screen.

She is not a fool. She is not weak. She is not Gus Parnell.

She has something on Virginia at last.

Laura tells herself that she is only going to look at the beginning. She is only going to see whether it's just some kind of virus, or a deepfake, or spam.

It's not that she's watching the video for sex reasons, she tells herself, watching the video.

It's just she wants to understand.

It's just that Virginia would never do something like this, and Virginia has done something like this, and Virginia having done something like this means all the times she has made Laura ashamed of thinking about doing something even a little bit close to this make no sense any longer, and nothing makes sense any longer, and this video is the only thing that could explain why.

Somewhere in the video will be the thing that makes Laura understand the video.

It is not Virginia's white dress, with the sequins popping off. It is not the spines of books, running up the back wall. It is not the look on Virginia's face; it is not the lilt in Virginia's voice, it is not how Virginia pantomimes pleasure when her fingers trail up her inner thigh;

it is not how Virginia has set the whole thing up, with a tripod and equipment from the AV library, because of course, Laura thinks, with unfamiliar bitterness, if Virginia Strauss is going to make a sex tape *of course* she has to make it so much better than an *ordinary* sex tape, and the satisfaction Laura gets from thinking this out loud keeps her watching, a little longer, and then a little longer still, and although the angel in her breast beats its wings in vain, trying to stop her, all Laura can think is that this might be the one hard, strong thing she has ever done in her whole life.

Virginia, she thinks, would never expect her to.

Laura watches all two minutes and thirteen seconds without stopping.

Laura hears the door close.

"I came back to tell you I was sorry."

Virginia is standing in the doorway.

Her face is drawn. Her eyes are red.

Laura's pleasure curdles into shame.

"Virginia, I—" She scrambles to close the browser tab. "I—someone sent it to me. I don't know who, I—"

"They sent it to everybody." Virginia's voice is very calm and very quiet. "The whole school's probably got it by now."

"I'm so sorry."

Virginia's face is blank. "Don't worry about it. You might as well watch it." Her nonchalance is more unnerving than her rage. "Everyone else did."

"Virginia, please, I—"

"I'm very tired," Virginia says. "I don't want to talk anymore."

She goes to the bed. She turns out the light.

"I'm going to bed now," she says. "Sleep well."

They lie there, like that, in silence, for a few hours, and then at dawn Virginia rises, wordlessly, and slips out of room 312, and although Laura rushes to the window, and thrusts it open—overflowing with the sorrowful, penitent things she wants to say—she knows, as she watches Virginia vanish into the woods, that Virginia will never hear them.

9

VIRGINIA DOESN'T GO TO CLASS FOR THREE DAYS.

By then, the whole school has seen the video.

If it were a *normal* sex tape—Yvette loudly explains to Gabe Meltzer at Keble breakfast—just an *actual* horny person being actually horny—people might actually feel sorry for her. It's not that people don't know you're not supposed to share sex tapes people make for you.

But to check out a tripod, and one of the AV library's cameras, to do it in the rare-book room of Carbonell, in front of all those old copies of Webster, to monologue through it like you're doing performance art—all this, the St. Dunstan's population collectively decides—is such a profound self-own that normal campus sexual etiquette can't possibly apply.

"Complete cringe," Yvette Saunders concludes.

Besides, Virginia brought it upon herself—with her whole God thing, her performative objection to *pornography*, what she did to poor Bonnie di Angelis (those rumors, pulled under by time, resurface). The truth—that Virginia is not just a stuck-up, frigid bitch but also a hypocritical one—is a matter of public interest.

It's like those Republican politicians caught cruising in men's bathrooms, everyone says. People have a right to know.

Not that anyone knows, exactly, who replaced Virginia's campaign video with the sex tape. Nobody pays attention to that part. The prevailing theory—which gains tractions first among the girls of the Dewey Decibel System, then spreads to the rest of campus—is that Virginia did it herself, out of some strange psychosexual compulsion to punish her own horniness, or else out of a desperate need for attention.

"Daddy issues," Gabe Meltzer decides. Tamara Lynd thinks she has a humiliation fetish.

Once you're willing to make a sex tape in Carbonell, there's no telling what other sick, demented things you might do. After all, Matt Azibuike half recalls, didn't she send a bunch of dirty messages to a priest, way back when?

Even if it *had* been one of the boys who leaked it, everyone collectively decides, Virginia would still have deserved it.

"If you're smart enough to get straight As every term," says Julia Feinstein, "you're smart enough to know boys *always* spread your nudes."

Laura racks her brain trying to work out which of them did it.

She rules out Brad immediately. Brad loves Virginia, Laura thinks, maybe as much as she does; he is the only one who would have jumped, that night, on the rocks of Jarvis Point. Ivan Dixon, who bursts into tears at Compline, would never hurt anybody on purpose; Ralph would find the whole thing tacky; Barry doesn't even have a smartphone.

Even Anton could never have done it. Sure, Laura thinks, he is brutish, and impulsive, and thoughtless—this Laura knows—but he is never deliberately cruel. Cruelty, Laura thinks, involves foresight; it takes initiative. Anton needs Virginia to fill out his college apps.

None of them, she keeps desperately resolving, could have done it. None of them *would* have done it.

Only, she keeps thinking, one of them did.

Virginia goes running at dawn. She stays out until curfew. She says a few perfunctory words to Laura—about laundry, or leaving the light on; the rest of the time, it's like Laura isn't even there.

Laura tries to apologize again, of course, with halting, mealy-mouthed vagueness, but Virginia doesn't even let her finish her first sentence.

"It's fine," she says. "Forget it." She won't.

Laura knows their friendship is over. There is nothing she can do, no excuse she can come up with that will make her, in Virginia's eyes, any less culpable than whoever sent out the tape in the first place. She has looked on Virginia's beauty bare. There are things you pay with your life for seeing; this is one.

She is, she thinks, no longer a lapdog, overflowing with yapping love for everything that comes near her.

The thought doesn't comfort her.

There are worse things to be, it turns out, than a fool.

The worst part? Laura didn't even have the guts to betray Virginia straight out.

No, Laura thinks, she'd stored up, mouselike, her little nest of small resentments; she'd delighted—when the time came—in trading them in for one big transgression.

Virginia runs alone now.

Brad comes to Desmond on Friday afternoon.

"Strauss, please!" He has been knocking on the door to room 312 for ten minutes. "I know you're in there. Mrs. Mesrin said—"

Virginia is sitting in bed, reading with her earbuds in. Laura is at her desk, trying to ignore the insistent thuds.

"Just let me explain!"

Laura can hear the music blasting through Virginia's earbuds.

"Just give me one minute!"

Virginia yanks out her earbuds. She picks up her phone; she fiddles with it; she goes, at last, to the door.

"Fine," she says. "One minute."

Her phone is counting down.

"Look, Strauss, I swear—I have no idea who swapped the video." He casts around wildly to Laura in appeal.

"Fifty-five seconds."

"It wasn't me, Strauss. I swear. I had nothing—nothing to do with what happened."

"So who was it?"

"I don't know! A hacker, maybe?"

"A hacker. Seriously?"

"Strauss, I swear!"

"Who was it, Noise? Was it Gallagher? I always knew he was a loose cannon. Or Ervin? Material for his *novel*, I bet."

"It wasn't anybody! Strauss, I swear, they promised. . . ."

"Work it out. Do the math, Noise. If it wasn't you, then it's whoever you sent it to." She lifts her chin. "You did send it to somebody, didn't you?"

Brad doesn't say anything.

"What, you sent it to Gallagher, for his *wank bank*? You sent it to Ng as a joke—what? Who did you send it to?"

"I don't know," he says.

"What do you mean, you don't know?"

"All of them," he says at last. "I sent it to all of them."

Her silence curdles.

"Virginia, I—"

Virginia doesn't let him finish.

"Five seconds." Her face is bone white. Her spine is so straight Laura thinks it will snap. She lets the clock tick down to zero. A bell goes off. "Thank you. You can go now."

He does.

Virginia watches the door long after he has gone.

"All of them," she says softly. She bites her lower lip.

"Virginia, come on, you can't think—"

"All of them," she says.

She puts her earbuds back in.

Laura resigns from choir the next morning.

She tosses her robe and surplice onto the Keble table, where Brad sits alone with his chemistry textbook. There are bags under his eyes. His lips are gray.

"You don't have to do this," he says.

"I do."

"We can't have choir without any girls. We'll have to bring in the Dewey Decibel System." He tries and fails to smile.

She shoves the pile toward him.

"Why did you do it?" she says.

Brad grits his teeth.

"I've never pretended," he says slowly, "to be better than I am. Strauss knew that." His shrug slumps.

"She loved you."

"She's not capable of love."

"She trusted you. She sent you that—that video because she trusted you."

"You think that's what that was? Trust?"

"She trusted you not to show it to the whole school."

"I didn't plan that."

"Someone did."

"Listen, Stearns. I've talked to the others. They all swear they had nothing to do with it."

"And you believe them?"

"They're my friends, Stearns!"

"And Virginia? She's not?"

"It's not that simple."

"Of course it's that simple!"

"Christ, Stearns, she should have known!"

"What, that you'd leak it?"

"That it'd get out. Somehow." Brad sighs. "Sometimes people just do dumb shit—for no reason. Because they can. I don't know. Because it feels good. Because—it makes you feel like you've got a semblance of control."

"Is that why you leaked it? To show her you were *in control?*"

They stare at each other for a while.

"Come on, Stearns. You can't pretend she didn't enjoy it. She got off on the fact we all wanted her."

"She chose you."

"Is that what you think?"

His voice is hollow and cold.

"You'd have laughed at me, you know, if you'd known me freshman year. This idiotic freshman, barely five foot four, jumping off rocks, declaring my undying love: declaiming Webster, naked on the sands of Bethel Beach." His laugh dies in his throat. "Oh, she was very nice about it, of course. She let me down easy. She had this whole explanation: pornography, profanation, God, World-History, revolution— I'm guessing you know the drill."

He blows out his lips.

"I told myself I didn't mind. It was good for me. Courtly love, right? Like those knights who used to joust for roses. Love without sex. *Transcendence.*" He grimaces. "I'd have done anything for her. Hell, I broke up with a sweet, kind girl—someone I actually, genuinely liked—via a goddamn text message because Virginia Strauss told me I could do better. I went along with her plans, her schemes, making a fool of my-self, all of us making fools of ourselves, because *Reverend Tipton was an unserious person*, because we don't hold Virginia Strauss to ordinary standards, do we?" He sighs. "Turns out—all it takes to get Virginia Strauss into bed is to stop caring what she thinks."

Laura doesn't say anything.

"I did love her," he says. "But there's only so much a person can put you through."

"So now you got your revenge."

"Jesus, Stearns, it's not like I planned it! Gallagher came back from whatever the hell went on with you, ranting furiously about the unreli-ability of women; Ervin gets back from Desmond; we get to talking. Man to man. I didn't plan to *show* it to anyone, at first; it was just a funny story. Guess what? Turns out the virgin queen's grubby and horny as the rest of us. Only—they didn't believe me. Ervin said I was making it up, dared me to show it to them, *pics or it didn't happen*. Ob-viously I refused. Only Gallagher . . ." He leans his cheek on his palm. He keeps looking at Laura. A slight, mocking smile crosses his lips. "Well, Gallagher pointed out—*very* convincingly—quite how whipped I'd become." He shrugs. "What's a man to do? Right?" He swallows. "It's what we do, isn't it? Unserious boys and porn."

"Anyway, we all watched it together," he says. "The five of us. Cast it to the Cranmer common room television. Right after *The Great British Bake Off*."

"Are you trying to make me hate you?"

"I don't know. Maybe. Do you?"

Laura does.

"I just didn't know," she says at last, "how much you'd always hated her."

Brad doesn't say anything.

• • •

Virginia stops showering. She doesn't comb her hair, or brush her teeth; her dirty clothes fester in the corner of their room. She sits, glowering and disheveled, in the corners of the classes she perfunctorily attends, handing in no homework, refusing to speak when called upon, even when Mrs. Mesrin throws her a softball about bird imagery in *Macbeth*.

She leaves earlier and earlier for her runs, now, dispensing altogether with the five-o'clock rule: sneaking out the Desmond common room window at four thirty, then four fifteen.

Also, she quits the American Institute for Civic Virtue.

"I wrote them an email," she tells Laura, one day, as she tosses her running clothes on the floor between their beds. "I explained everything."

"You told them?"

"They were going to find out sooner or later. They might as well hear it from me."

"You didn't have to do that."

"It was a matter of principle." She considers Laura, huddled on the bed. "I doubt you'd understand."

Isobel turns down the student council presidency.

She writes an op-ed in the *St. Dunstan's Chronicle* about it. Without getting into specifics, she informs the St. Dunstan's student body that any election won by unjust or unethical means is illegitimate, and that any *irregularities* that may have occurred are further evidence of St. Dunstan's brokenness as an institution, and a sign that it's not worth governing at all.

The values of this institution, she concludes, *can't be reformed.*

They can only be rejected.

It's the first constitutional crisis in St. Dunstan's history.

After days of deliberation, the administration announces it will rerun the election in Michaelmas.

Virginia spends an hour with the *Chronicle* on her lap, tracing the words with her fingers.

Laura is so lonely now.

She'd never noticed, in the choir days, how few her friendships had been. It hadn't mattered.

It's not that anybody is unkind to her. Some Desmond girls let her sit with them at lunch. Tamara Lynd walks with her from Topics in European History, and they make idle chatter about how Dr. Meyer spits when he talks. Teddy Kelting, learning Laura has dropped out of choir, asks her on an Evensong date. (She invents, on the spot, a Nevada boyfriend named John.)

There is nothing wrong with them, Laura knows, except that nobody shipwrecks her soul.

Tamara Lynd would never jump off a cliff at three in the morning; Teddy Kelting would never swear a blood oath in a crypt.

Nor can Laura bring herself to throw herself on the mercy of Miranda and Isobel. They would ask her, she knows, to mix together the things she loves with the things she cannot stand, to admit that the boys of choir shared the video *because* that's just the kind of things that boys of choir do.

Laura can give up choir. She can't give up remembering it. She can't think of the time they sang Compline on Bethel Beach and think only that it was just the inevitable prelude to a bunch of boys laughing about a sex tape in Cranmer Hall.

Remembering is all Laura has left.

• • •

Laura takes to solitude.

She sits alone at Keble; she walks alone to class; she tries and fails to reread Webster, only now Robert and Gus and Shrimpy all have the boys' faces; only now Webster has Virginia's voice.

She sits alone, too, at Evensong: nestled in the back row, trying to pretend that Gabe Meltzer doesn't have his hand underneath Tamara Lynd's skirt, trying to pretend the boys don't still sound beautiful.

Virginia doesn't attend.

Brad's prediction comes true. Reverend Tipton can't convince any girls to commit to a full season of choir this late into term, and so instead they have a rotating cast of girls from the Dewey Decibel System subbing in each week. What they lack in seriousness, they make up for in skill. An ordinary student, sitting in a pew like this one, might never know there was any difference at all.

Maybe, Laura thinks, filing out of her second Evensong without Virginia, there never was any difference at all.

She opens the chapel doors right onto the boys. They are all milling on the steps, in their choir robes; Laura avoids their gaze, shuffling straight through them.

"Stearns," Barry tries; she ignores him. "Listen, Stearns, please—"

Then a voice comes from behind them.

"Oi!"

Isobel is standing, waiting for them, on Devonshire Quad.

"*Shit.*" Ralph Ervin rolls his eyes. Laura scampers out of the way.

"Oi—I want to talk to you."

"Come on," Anton says. "Let's get out of here."

They make their way across the quad. Isobel follows them.

"Hey! I'm talking to you! Hey!"

She gets in Anton Gallagher's face and shoves him.

He staggers back.

"What the *fuck*?"

"Which one of you did it?" She shoves Anton again. "Huh? Was it *you*, Anton?"

Ralph rolls his eyes. "Christ, Isobel, fuck off. Nobody did—"

"What—was it you?" She rounds on Ralph. "You wanted to impress your new girlfriend, is that it?"

"Hey, listen," Barry cuts in. "What happened, we know it was awful, and we're so sorry it happened, but it has nothing, nothing to do with us, okay? So just—"

Ivan is staring at the ground.

"Let me guess—you were all in on it? Did you decide together that it would be hilarious, just hilarious, to share the most intimate moments of a person's life—"

"Yeah, sure," Anton bellows. "Real intimate."

"She deserved it? Really? That's how you're gonna play it?"

She shoves him a third time.

"Look, Zhao, I don't like to hit women, but . . ." He shrugs. "God, like you even fucking *count*."

"Go ahead!" Isobel spreads her arms wide. "Take a shot." Her smile glints. "I dare you."

Brad just stands there, his hands in his pockets, saying nothing.

He looks up at Laura; he lifts his shoulders in a barely perceptible shrug, as if to say, *What else would you have me do?*, as if Laura should have known this all along, about them, as if she should have always expected this of them.

"Go on," Isobel says. "What would Sebastian Webster do?"

"Fuck it." Anton throws up his hands. "Let's get out of here."

They all cross the quad toward Cranmer.

Isobel remains, her arms outstretched, on the quad. She looks up. A smile inches across her face; she touches her fingers to her forehead, in a parody of salute.

Laura follows her gaze to the Desmond windows.

Virginia is watching them.

Virginia does not say anything to Laura about what she has seen. She doesn't say anything to Laura at all. She spends the evening curled up on her phone, her earbuds in, typing furiously, biting her lower lip.

At last, at three thirty in the morning, she turns to Laura, who is pretending to still be doing her Calculus homework.

"I'm going for a run," she says. "Don't wait up."

"*Now?*"

"What's the problem?"

Laura doesn't say anything. She watches at the window as Virginia spikes across the quad.

Laura doesn't sleep that night. She spends it sitting against the window, her textbook in her lap, her heart flinging itself against her ribs, dread clenching her lungs.

She knows, already, what she will see.

They come back together right before first period, sweat-drenched and exultant: Virginia's tall, lanky frame and Isobel's small, sprightly one, their shoulders touching.

They come to a stop in front of Latimer, directly across the quad.

Virginia takes Isobel's hand. She squeezes it. They stand together, like that, for a moment, and then Isobel unlocks the door and goes inside.

. . .

"You're running with Isobel now?" Laura tries to make it sound so casual.

Virginia shrugs. She takes off her running clothes. She folds them, neatly, and puts them away. "God," she says. "It smells in here." She shoves a few rancid sports bras into her laundry bag.

"I mean—you don't even like her. Do you?"

Virginia doesn't even bother to turn around.

"Isobel Zhao," she says, "is a fine runner. One of the best in the school, in fact. You know, she did the New York marathon when she was fifteen?"

She wraps herself in a towel.

"It's important," she says, "to train with people who challenge you." She pushes past Laura.

"I'm going to take a shower," she says.

Virginia and Isobel run every morning after that. Laura watches them.

She watches them meet on Devonshire Quad. She watches Virginia take Isobel's hands, rubbing them to warm them in the chill preceding dawn. She watches them turn together toward the water, toward the woods, maintaining the same quick and even pace, Virginia never outstripping Isobel for more than a moment. She watches them return, their faces flushed, their heads thrown back in laughter. She watches their bodies touch.

She watches them sit together, at breakfast, in the corner of Keble, leaning forehead to forehead over one of Virginia's books of political theory; she watches Virginia vanish into Latimer Hall, on weeknight evenings, and not return until the curfew bell.

For weeks, Laura tries, in varying and inutile ways, to bring up the subject as lightly as she can manage, as if it is an ordinary thing that Virginia and Isobel spend all day, every day, together; for weeks, Virginia acts like she's crazy for noticing.

"I don't know what you're so worked up about," Virginia says. "I'm allowed to have other friends, you know."

Laura tries to be brave about it. It's not like Virginia's *wrong*, she thinks—after everything she's been through, maybe it's good for her to have other friends, friends who have nothing to do with choir. And they were friends before—but when she remembers this she remembers, too, that Isobel was once in love with Virginia, remembers all the vague innuendo she has spent the past year shutting out.

It's just that when she watches Isobel punch Virginia lightly on the arm; when she watches them sit together, side by side, on Devonshire Quad, Virginia's hair falling over Isobel's shoulders, all Laura can think is that there are two kinds of people in the world: people who watched the video and people who didn't.

Isobel, Laura thinks, might be the only good person in the whole school.

Laura can't even bring herself to hate her.

She tells herself she can stand it. There are only a few weeks left of Trinity now; then it will be summer; then it will be senior year and everything will start all over and maybe she'll have a new roommate who will show her a new side of St. Dunstan's, who will show her how to live. Ralph and Anton will have graduated by then, and maybe there will be new people in choir, and maybe the others will get bored of it and resign; maybe by then, seeing Virginia won't hurt so much.

Laura focuses on schoolwork. She takes her SATs. She spends her evenings in the library, avoiding Desmond, avoiding any chance of running into choir on the quad.

"So, what, you just live here now?" Freddy says the next time Laura returns a textbook.

"Just take it, Freddy."

"Happily."

Freddy scans it.

"Let me guess," she says. "They put a sock on the door." Her eyes flicker over Laura's face. "Well, it's spring, right? Everyone fucks in spring. Why shouldn't Virginia Strauss? You know, it's funny; I haven't seen Isobel and Miranda together in ages."

"I'm not—" Laura's cheeks burn. "I mean, *they're* not . . ."

"Sure." Freddy puts the book in the returns basket. "Whatever you say."

"They're just friends."

"I believe you." Freddy's lips curl. "The proverbial millions, though . . ."

"Virginia isn't even . . ."

Visions of Virginia's hair, falling over Isobel's lap, flash behind Laura's eyes.

"Virginia Strauss will try anything once," Freddy says. "I think we all know that by now."

Laura tells herself it doesn't matter. If Virginia and Isobel *are* together, like that, she thinks, she should be happy for them. A good person would be happy for them. Virginia deserves to be with someone who challenges her (*You*, Laura thinks bitterly, *could never have challenged her*); she deserves someone who knows what she thinks (*You never knew what you thought about anything*); she deserves someone capable of calling her out on her shit (*You could never do that, either*, Laura thinks, *not for very long*).

Only, all those nights she's spent in Virginia's bed, all those times Virginia has pressed her hand against Laura's lips, all that devotion she has given, so freely, that Virginia has taken, so lightly, thinking, *this is the most she can ever have of Virginia, the most Virginia can give.*

Maybe she's no better than the boys.

You could stand not having her, she thinks, *so long as nobody else could.*

Maybe it's all about sex, after all.

She hates how everything's always all about sex, after all.

Virginia and Isobel keep running. They leave earlier and earlier now, until Virginia stops sleeping at all, sneaking out straight after Mrs. Mesrin turns off her lights.

Then comes the day they come back soaked through.

It's the end of May. The grass is halfway up their calves. The apple tree outside Keble has grown ripe with fruit. There is seaweed in Virginia's hair.

They walk across Devonshire, arm in arm. Their running clothes are waterlogged, like they haven't even bothered to remove them; Laura can see Virginia's nipples beneath her shirt. Everybody stops to look at them.

Virginia doesn't stop smiling once.

That night, an hour before curfew, Miranda bangs on Laura's door.

"Where is she?"

Her hair is disheveled; her makeup is smudged; there are bags under her eyes.

"I don't know," Laura says.

"Were they here? God knows they're not in Latimer—they're not in Carbonell—I've checked every single carrell."

"I don't know, I swear."

Miranda looks at her for a moment.

"Right," she says. "Right—sorry, I'll go, then."

"Wait!" Laura is so lonely. "You can come in, if you want. They—" It's so hard to say it. "They're usually not back until curfew."

Miranda nods. She enters.

She turns to Virginia's bed. She fingers the edge of the blue-striped pillows.

"So," she says softly, "this is where she sleeps." She swallows. "Pretty basic, isn't it? I'd have expected something more from her. A coffin, maybe?" She tries and fails to smile. "I don't know."

She sits on the bed.

"Look, they're probably out running. They—"

"You think I'm stupid, don't you?"

"I—no."

"Let me guess. *Nothing's going on. They're just running. Just gals being pals.*" She snorts. "I've been hearing a lot of that lately. How *hard* it's been for poor little Virginia Strauss. How she finally *gets it.* How *she wants to change.* How she's *on the side of the angels*!" Miranda shrugs. "*Vive la révolution,* right? Hell, maybe she believes it. You can believe anything, if you want to badly enough."

She scans Virginia's bedside table, Virginia's books, Virginia's things.

"You know they've already fucked, right?"

Miranda says it so simply.

"What are you talking about?"

"Freshman year. Why do you think Strauss left Latimer like that?"

Laura tries to protest; she can't. She knows, at the pit of her stomach, it is true.

"First they went cliff jumping," Miranda goes on. "Izzy, Virginia, Brad Noise. She told me the whole story."

She leans back on her elbows.

"They swim naked onto the beach. Izzy goes to take a piss in the woods. Brad takes the opportunity to confess his undying love. Virginia turns him down flat. *No interest in men*, you see.

"They go back to Latimer, they start talking; out of nowhere, literally, nowhere, Virginia grabs her face and lunges at her, kisses her, one thing leads to another . . ." She shrugs. "It was Izzy's first time, you know. She didn't even *know* what she was. Anyway, first thing next morning, Virginia goes to Mrs. Mesrin, demands a transfer, and doesn't talk to Izzy for a year. The whole time, LARPing as St. Dunstan's resident nun."

"I didn't know," Laura says. "I'm sorry."

"You know what the worst part was? Izzy never even blamed her. She always had *some* excuse—it was the God thing; it was the boys; it was her horrible parents; it was her eating disorder; it was that stupid fucking book.

"Tragic, right? Poor, repressed Virginia Strauss couldn't just *accept herself* and *just be happy*, and tell God to fuck right off."

Miranda wipes her eyes with the back of her hand.

"Maybe it's true?" Laura doesn't know whether she wants it to be true. "Maybe—maybe she feels like she's free now?"

"So—what? God's not real—so now she gets to fuck my girlfriend as a consolation prize?"

"I don't know," Laura says. "I'm sorry."

"I matter, too, you know!"

"I know," Laura says, like she hadn't completely forgotten Miranda existed until five minutes ago.

"I'm sorry," Miranda says. "I should go."

She waits against the doorframe. Then she leans forward and kisses Laura on the lips. Her lip gloss tastes like ginger.

Laura doesn't have time to react before Miranda pulls back.

"There," Miranda says, with a deep breath. "Now we're even."

She leaves Laura's lips burning.

· · ·

Miranda breaks up with Isobel at Keble the next day.

She comes up to the table where Isobel and Virginia are sitting. She slams down her tray. Laura can't make out the words, but Isobel is pleading, and Virginia is smirking, and then Miranda slaps Virginia straight across the face and storms off.

The boys all start shouting applause.

Anton bangs on the table; Ralph makes catcalls.

"Called it!" Ivan Dixon crows, standing on a chair. "I bet she liked that."

"Dyke drama," Anton says. "Typical." Barry coughs, awkwardly, and shuffles. Brad doesn't say anything.

Virginia and Isobel look at each other.

Virginia slips her arm through Isobel's elbow.

They march out of Keble together.

Laura can't stop thinking about Isobel and Virginia together.

So Miranda's right, she thinks; so they're together; so they're happy; maybe they're in love, and liberated at last, and nothing can touch them; maybe Isobel kisses between Virginia's breasts, maybe she trails her lips down her navel; maybe she tastes like ginger, too; Laura can't stop thinking about those maybes.

She doesn't know if the alternative is worse.

Laura keeps track of Virginia and Isobel's movements. She notes down their runs. She calculates exactly how long they have been gone; calculates, too, the mileage; tries to imagine whether they are *this* morning at the Grinning Griddle, *that* morning at the Breaking Grounds; looks on a map on her phone, the night they leave at twelve thirty, to calculate how far they could have made it; to calculate, too, which cliffs they might have jumped from, or else how long it might take—if they stopped for a while in the woods, Isobel's fingers on Virginia's collarbone, Virginia's mouth on Isobel's waist.

Finally Laura can stand it no longer.

Virginia slips out on the last Tuesday of term, at twelve fifteen in the morning.

She waits for Isobel on the quad; they head seaward.

Laura will be able stand it, she thinks, once she finally knows for sure.

She will be able to know what to *do* with Virginia, where to put her, in that impossible taxonomy of human relations; she will finally understand how to understand herself. All she has to know is what Isobel and Virginia are doing in the woods.

She watches Virginia and Isobel vanish into the beech trees. She leaves the room, tiptoes down the Desmond stairs. She crosses the quad and follows them.

Laura has not run in so long; it hurts, the way it hurt that first Michaelmas morning; she does not let that stop her.

The pain makes her want to scream; she follows them, anyway. She reminds herself of all the old mantras—*you are hard, Stearns; you are strong; you are not like Natasha, settling for happiness because you lack transcendence*—she whispers them with the little breath she has. She scratches herself on brambles; she cuts herself with thorns.

There are coyotes howling in the distance.

Laura comes out, gasping, to Farnham Cliff. She turns her head along the coastal road. She does not see them.

Her heart plummets.

They're so much faster than she is, they're so much stronger. What a fool, she thinks, she was to think she could catch up with them at all.

Laura takes a deep breath. She blinks back tears. Time to turn back, she thinks, to accept things as they are. Virginia has finally gone where Laura can't follow.

Then Laura sees them.

They're descending the downward slope past Bethel Beach.

They're heading to the lighthouse.

She watches them scramble along the path. She follows them.

Laura creeps across the back of Bethel Beach; she slips behind beech trees; she tiptoes through pines. Once, she steps too loudly on a branch, and its crack echoes beneath her feet—ahead of her, they look up, waiting, but then at last, hearing nothing more, they turn back ahead and move onward.

She follows them all the way to the lighthouse base.

A car is waiting for them.

Laura darts behind a tree.

A figure emerges with a flashlight. Laura recognizes him. It's the old man who runs the Grinning Griddle.

He turns to them, flooding Virginia's and Isobel's faces in light. Their expressions are certain. They know exactly what they're doing.

They nod at the man in recognition.

He goes to the trunk of the car. He opens it. He takes out an enormous cherry-red canister of gasoline, then another, then another still, passing each one to Virginia, who passes them to Isobel, who takes them inside the lighthouse ruin.

When he is done, Virginia reaches into her jacket pocket. She counts out bills.

He takes them. He stands, for a moment, as if hesitating—considering the hour, the lighthouse, their faces. Then he folds the bills into his raincoat pocket and gets in the car.

Laura only just manages to crouch out of the light before he rumbles back toward the main road, casting them in darkness.

Laura can only just make out their outlines, hunched together, in what's left of the lighthouse door.

She doesn't wait to see what they do next.

She runs.

10

LAURA STAYS UP ALL NIGHT TRYING TO MAKE SENSE OF WHAT she has seen.

She doesn't come up with anything.

She watches the quadrangle; she racks her brain; she thinks, dully, idiotically: they must be driving somewhere, but of course Virginia's from New York City—she doesn't drive; Isobel, maybe, but then again there is a gas station on Carver Avenue; then again, they're not old enough to rent a car in the first place; there is no reason, none in the world, why two girls would buy three canisters of gas, in the middle of the night, at the ruins of a lighthouse. Only—

Laura tells herself she's being ridiculous. She is dramatic; she's hysterical; of course there's an explanation, something ordinary, something she hasn't thought of, something she should have thought of, something that will make the jagged pieces of her understanding finally cohere.

Laura paces. She folds and refolds her laundry. She tries to lie down so many different ways; she covers her face with a pillow. Nothing works.

At last, at dawn, Virginia tiptoes in.

She is so quiet, turning the doorknob. She wears her socks, her shoes dangling in her hand.

"Where were you?"

Virginia starts in surprise.

"What are you doing up?"

"I couldn't sleep."

"Oh." Virginia closes the door behind her. "Sorry."

"Where were you?"

"Running."

"Where?"

"Risetown." Virginia pulls her sports bra over her head. "We managed a thirty K."

"What was your time?"

"I don't remember—three hours? Give or take."

As if, Laura thinks, Virginia would ever not remember her time.

"What were you doing with gas canisters?"

Virginia freezes.

"You followed us?" Her color is gone.

"What are you planning to do with them?"

Virginia doesn't say anything for a moment. She bites her lower lip, creating a purple bruise around her teeth.

"God, Virginia, please—tell me what you're doing!"

Virginia closes her eyes.

"We're running away," she says.

"Running away?"

"Listen, Stearns, you can't tell anybody—you understand me? Anybody. Nobody else knows."

"But—where?" Laura stumbles over the words. "Why?"

"You know why."

Virginia sits, so slowly, on the bed; she still holds Laura's gaze. It is the first time, Laura thinks, that she has looked Laura in the eye since Laura watched the video.

"God, Stearns, there's nothing for me here. You think—you think I like walking through this place, knowing there isn't a single person who doesn't see, looking at me . . . God, even Dr. Charles watched; he can't even look me in the eye." She folds her hands in her lap.

"You could go home."

"To Dr. and Mrs. Strauss?" Her laugh is hollow. "I'd rather die."

"Then—where?"

"One of the islands, maybe. Canada. The border's only twenty miles off." Her voice is steadier. "We bought a boat. It's nothing fancy—it's a piece of shit, really, from that crusty old geezer at the Griddle. It's docked in town." Her stare is electric. "Anyway—he came back to sell us gas. Please, Stearns, swear to me, you won't tell anyone." She sighs. "Even—if you won't do it for me. Do it for Isobel. God, her family—they'd try to track her down, they're horrible, they don't even know she's . . ."

"Then." Laura tries so desperately to make sense of this. "The two of you. You're . . ."

Virginia sits up a little bit straighter.

"Lovers. Yes."

Laura's heart constricts. "Oh," she says. "I see."

"Her parents would never allow it. If they found out they'd make her come home; they'd never let her see me again—she kept Miranda a secret for years; she's always planned to run away the *second* she turns eighteen. . . ." She is speaking more and more quickly, her words tumbling over themselves. "And—God—what would we *do* here, Stearns?" Her voice notches higher. "I don't want, God, what? *The American Institute for Civic Virtue?*" She scoffs. "*Harvard?* And Zhao's too good for this place; she's too good for whatever dull, *sclerotic* values they try to brainwash you with here. Christ, Bonnie was right. This whole place is rotten, inside out." She bites her lip again to stop it trembling. "Besides—it's pretty Websterian, right? Taking a boat, running off, in the middle of the night . . . ?"

Virginia is leaving.

That's the only part of this that matters.

Virginia is going away, and Laura will never see her again. Fat, hot tears coagulate on her cheeks.

"What will you do?"

"Change our names. Write. Make money—I don't care how. I'm not too proud." Her mouth twitches, a little. "Start a revolution, in exile? Zhao wants to squat in this commune she read about in Toronto."

"When?"

"Friday night."

"*Friday?*"

Two days. That's all she has.

"Please, Laura."

Virginia gets up and crosses over to Laura's bed. She takes Laura's hands in hers; the feeling of her skin shakes Laura through.

"You can't tell anyone."

"I won't."

"Promise me!"

"I—"

Virginia's eyes are glass. Virginia's nails are digging into her wrists. Virginia needs her.

"I promise," Laura says.

Virginia closes her eyes.

"Thank you," she says.

She presses Laura's hands to her lips. Her tears flow onto them.

"Virginia?"

"What?"

"Do you love her?"

Virginia swallows. A shadow flickers over her face.

"Yes," she says.

Laura's heart breaks.

Of course, she thinks, Virginia would love someone like Isobel.

Someone hard; someone strong; someone who knows her own mind. Someone who didn't watch the video.

"Okay," she says.

She swallows down her pain.

"Okay," Virginia says.

She rises; she goes to her dresser; she wipes away her tears.

"There's something else," she says.

"What is it?"

"I need your help."

"Of course," Laura says. "What is it?"

"I want to say goodbye." Virginia takes a deep breath. "To him. You know . . ." She nods at the copy of *All Before Them* on Laura's desk. "But I can't stand—God, I can't even ask, to have to face them."

"What do you need?"

"The chapel key. Brad has it. Just borrow it for a while, okay? Tell him you want to practice down there or something. I'll give it right back to you. I promise."

Laura's stomach knots. She hasn't spoken to Brad in weeks.

"You remember, don't you? How it was? All of us together, our little family. You know—that night—I really did believe in . . ." She takes Laura's hand. "You know. God. Webster. Everything."

"I did, too."

"They believed it, too," Virginia says. "In the things that mattered. Only—they forgot." She shrugs. "People always forget." She lets Laura's hand fall. "That's the problem with this whole filthy world."

"I'll get the key," Laura says.

You deserve this, Laura tells herself. *You betrayed her.*

She'd watched the whole video, beginning to end. She'd enjoyed it. She'd enjoyed that brief, perverse moment of power she'd had over Virginia; she'd traded everything for it.

Now Virginia and Isobel are lovers; now Virginia and Isobel are running away; now Virginia and Isobel are going off to be World-Historical, to launch ideological revolutions, to do whatever Webster would have done, if he'd been born now instead of then, while Laura remains useless on the threshold of her own life.

Only, Virginia has trusted her, once again, for the last time, for the only time that matters.

This much, she thinks, *I can do for her.*

This, at least, she thinks, *I can do.*

Wednesday night, Laura goes to Cranmer.

The boys are all sitting in the common room. They titter when they see her.

"Stearns!" Ralph is splayed out on the sofa. "Miss us already, huh?"

"Let me guess . . ." Ivan says, in a strangely performative voice, like a child pretending to be an adult. "Your girlfriend's got a girlfriend."

"Don't worry," Anton says. "I'm sure she'll let you join in."

"Just make sure to film it," Ralph says.

"I'm here to talk to Brad," she says. "That's all." She doesn't make eye contact with any of them. "In private."

Brad swings his legs out.

"Come on," he says. "Let's go upstairs."

Brad's room smells faintly of cigarette smoke and more prominently of raw garlic.

"Sorry for the smell," he says, nodding to an uncleaned juicer molding on a bookshelf. "Gallagher's." He takes a heavy seat in his swivel chair. "What do you want?"

"I want to borrow the chapel key."

"What for?"

"That's personal."

His mouth twitches. "It's for her, isn't it?"

"No."

"You're the worst liar I've ever met."

Laura meets his gaze.

"It doesn't matter," she says, "who it's for. *I* want it."

He considers her for a moment. Then he opens his desk drawer, and takes out the small iron key. "For my sins," he says. "Just have it back by Evensong." He hesitates. "We were planning to do Compline, Friday night." His voice wavers slightly. "Just like last year." He sees her face. "Hey, tradition, right?"

As if, Laura thinks, anything is like last year.

"As if," she forces the words through gritted teeth, "a single one of you believed it."

Brad fingers the key in his palm. "You know, it's a lot more enjoyable," he says tightly, "when nobody's demanding you believe it."

Laura grabs the key.

"Thanks." She turns to go.

"Wait—Stearns!"

"What do you want?"

"How is she?"

"Do you care?"

"I—" He sighs. "Look, I'm not a bad person, Stearns, okay?" His voice notches a little too high. "I just—I mean, I didn't know what was going to happen." He leans back in his chair. "That's not very convincing, is it?"

"No. It's not."

"Well, I didn't."

"And you still don't know who did?"

"They all still swear it wasn't them."

"And you believe them?"

"What else do you want me to do?"

"What's right."

He looks up at her.

"Good old Stearns," he says. "Sitting on my shoulder. Telling me right from wrong. A real Jiminy Cricket. A person needs that, you know. You notice, once it's gone."

"Don't tell me you miss her."

He shrugs.

"It was nice," he says. "Believing."

"Nobody stopped you."

"You really hate me, don't you?"

"Why should you care?"

He stares at her for a moment.

"Come on," he says at last, with a resigned laugh. "Don't tell me you didn't know."

"Know what?"

"Really. Really?"

"Look, Brad, I don't know what you're talking about."

"Come on. Admit it. Even Strauss knew—she must have—deep down; she's got a sixth sense about this kind of thing; why do you think she was so desperate to keep her claws in me?"

At last Laura understands.

"You're joking."

He rises. "What can I say? You're good, Stearns. Poor Stearns." He laughs a little. "Too good, too pure, for this cruel world."

He takes a step toward her.

"I'm not," she says. "Really."

"Never let it be said," he says softly, "I don't have a type."

"I really should—"

"Look, I'm not asking you to run off into the sunset with me. I'm not even asking you to forgive me," he says. "I'm just asking you not to hate me—too much."

"I can't do that."

"Just say you don't hate me," he says. "That's all I'm asking for. Please."

It unnerves Laura how badly he wants this from her.

"If I'd sent you a video like that," she says, "would you have done the exact same thing to me?"

He doesn't answer her.

She opens the door. She slams it behind her.

Laura gives Virginia the key that night.

"He said he needs it back by Evensong," she says. Virginia takes it.

Laura can't stop herself. "Do you want me to go with you?"

"No." Virginia swallows. "No, I need to go alone."

She slips the key into her purse.

Virginia returns it the next afternoon.

"Thank you," she says to Laura. "It was exactly what I needed." She touches Laura's cheek.

Laura can't stand how good it feels.

"Of course," she says. "Whatever you need. Only—"

"What?"

"Are you sure? I mean, couldn't you, I don't know, get through the summer, stick it out, wait until Michaelmas, to know if this is what you really want?"

Virginia is still for a moment.

"I won't go home again," she says. "And I can't stay here." She swallows. "So, you see—I've got nowhere else to go."

Laura leaves the key in an envelope in Brad's pigeonhole. She doesn't leave a note.

The final Friday of term comes. The administration puts out a press release, with the result of the faculty committee's yearlong deliberations. As of the coming Michaelmas, Friday Evensong will be optional, just like any other extracurricular.

"Just as well," Virginia says, shrugging, when Laura tells her.

"Zhao was right," she says. "Nobody should go—not unless they believe it." She lifts her chin.

"It's a profanation," she says softly.

Virginia and Laura get ready for Evensong together.

Virginia laces up her boots; Virginia buttons up her collar to the throat; Virginia puts on her gloves.

It is the first time Virginia has been to Evensong since the video came out.

She braids her hair. She checks herself in the mirror. Laura tries not to think that in twelve hours she will no longer be here.

"Is—" Laura keeps her voice even. "Is Isobel joining us?" She says it so casually, like she's talking about brunch.

"No," Virginia says. "She's—she's sitting with Miranda. She wanted to leave things on a good note." Her lip twitches a little. "I suppose I can understand that." She turns to Laura. "So it'll just be us." She smiles, and at once Laura feels relief flood through her.

At least, she thinks, they'll have one last Evensong together, just the two of them, the way things used to be.

"I was thinking," Virginia says. "Maybe we could go to the Grinning Griddle, tomorrow morning. To say goodbye." She interlaces her fingers with Laura's. "I want one more Lime of the Ancient Mariner, for the road. Zhao and I could take the boat, even—dock for a little while. Have breakfast. Talk? What do you think?"

"I'd like that," Laura says. "More than anything."

Virginia's smile flickers for a moment; then it fades out, replaced by something dark and still.

But then the bells start ringing from the chapel spires, flooding the quad with sound.

"Come on," she says. She takes Laura's arm. "Let's go."

They walk into the chapel together.

Virginia keeps her head held high. She ignores the stares, Julia's and Tamara's whispers, Teddy Kelting's chuckles when she passes his pew. She sails all the way down the nave, to the front pew.

"Excuse me," she says to Yvette Saunders. "This is our seat."

She pushes her way past her. She doesn't even notice Yvette's glare.

Reverend Tipton almost drops his Book of Common Prayer when he sees them; the boys, too, turn red. Brad looks resolutely at the floor. The lighthouse Madonna gazes down, in the pink summer light; her cheeks flushed; her eyes shot through with sunlight.

Reverend Tipton fumbles with his pages.

He reads out the bit from that Psalm about how, to God, there is no difference between darkness and light.

They kneel. They confess their sins, in droning breaths, and when they get to the part about *the devices and desires of our own hearts*,

Laura stops thinking about God at all, because her heart has no room, right now, for anything else.

Virginia leans her forehead against her fingers. She whispers so quietly; she beats her fist between her breasts.

And Laura, she tries so hard to hold on to the moment, to remember everything, to take in exactly what the incense smells like, that melancholy sweetness that turns bitter at the back of the throat, to take in every flickering angle of the candles, and what shadows they make; she must remember everything, she thinks, so that when she is an old woman, when she is living the tail end of a life without Virginia in it, a dull life, an ordinary life, a life that she now knows will never be World-Historical, she will at least be able to remember that the air smelled like frankincense; that Virginia wore her braids as a crown; that Laura could see, when she kneeled, the whiteness of her neck. The boys sing the Magnificat.

This is the last time, Laura thinks, *we will all be in the same room together.*

She watches Brad carry the melody, his chest puffed out, his eyes bloodshot.

For a moment, she almost feels sorry for him.

But now they're onto the readings, the Apostles' Creed, the Nunc Dimittis, the prayers; then Virginia is sitting straight-backed in the pew, her eyes fixed on the altar; now Laura sees Isobel, out of the corner of her eye, sitting next to Miranda, their bodies no longer touching, Isobel's face wan and pale, her lips drawn in, her head completely shaved, and Laura's heart constricts.

Virginia slips her hand into hers.

Don't let this end, Laura prays. She doesn't know if there is a God, or if He looks anything like Virginia's God, but she prays, anyway, to whatever is out there: *Do not make me do this without her.*

· · ·

Now it's all over. Reverend Tipton puts out the candles. People file out the nave, their heels clatter on the marble. The choir comes down from the stalls.

Virginia approaches them.

She glides to the altar.

"Gentlemen," she says, as they gape up at her. "I wanted to say goodbye." She extends a hand to Brad. He stares at her a moment, flabbergasted, before taking it. He shakes it tentatively, as if he's waiting for the catch.

"Have a good summer, Strauss."

He nods at Laura without looking at her.

"Stearns."

Brad turns back toward the others.

"Let's get out of here," he says.

Virginia turns back down the nave. Laura follows her.

At last, at last, they are alone in Desmond, listening to the sound of the curfew bell.

"Are you packed?"

All Virginia has is a small duffel bag.

"We don't need much," Virginia says. "We'll buy what we need when we get there." She nods to herself, and for a moment Laura wants to fall on her knees, again, to beg her to stay, to beg her to take her with them—she has a frantic, senseless vision of herself, living with them, like some sort of stalwart spinster in a nineteenth-century novel, making them breakfast, laying out their clothes, typing up their papers. She swallows it down.

"It'll take us a while," Virginia says. "To get the boat ready. I should go ahead, first, as soon as it's safe. I'll meet you at the Griddle. It's got to be well after curfew. One thirty?"

Laura has never done the run alone before.

"One thirty."

"Order me a Lime of the Ancient Mariner?" Now Virginia smiles. "And a black coffee, of course."

"Of course."

They sit, for a while, in silence on Virginia's bed. Virginia draws her knees to her chest.

"Nineteen," she says suddenly. "God, just *nineteen*."

Laura looks up at her.

"I used to think," Virginia goes on, "how sad it was that he died so young. *What he could have been*—that's what they always say. . . . All the books he could have written . . ." Her voice trails off. "I don't think that anymore." She swallows. "He must have *known*. You know?"

She turns to Laura.

"Known what?"

"That he was going to die—one way or another. That he didn't *fit*. That the world, the whole rotten world, wasn't worth living in, if it wasn't . . . I mean, if nothing actually mattered? If you had to, just, I don't know, bend the knee to the way things were, learn to compromise, to take things less *seriously*, and become someone who— God, I don't know . . ."

Laura has never seen Virginia fumble for words before.

"Had to grow up?"

Virginia's smile twitches.

"One great act," she says. "One great World-Historical act. One great, World-Historical middle finger to everything he despised. He couldn't have done anything else."

"Maybe," Laura says.

"It's funny, isn't it?" Virginia says. "Growing up."

"What do you mean," Laura says.

"All the things they tell you when you're little, right? Fairy tales, fables, things like that. Cinderella and her prince. Wicked stepsisters with their eyes pecked out."

"Yes," says Laura. "I remember."

"And then you grow up—and you realize it isn't like that at all. You do things—good things, bad things, *cruel* things, and they all just—I don't know—evaporate. Like rain. And you're just supposed to accept it."

"You know," she says at last. "In a way, I'm glad the video got out."

"What?"

"It would have been so much worse," she says, "if it hadn't. Knowing I'd done that, that I was *that* kind of person, at least for a little while, having to stand that *nobody* knew that about myself but me. Not knowing what I know now, about the b—" She swallows. "My whole life would have been a lie."

"Virginia, I'm so—" Laura opens her mouth, again, to say all that she is so desperate to say: about the video, about the pleasure she took in it, about how she has regretted it, every day since, but Virginia stops her.

"It doesn't matter," she says. "I want to forget all about it." She collapses into silence.

"Nineteen," she says a minute later. "What would *we* even do at nineteen, Stearns?"

Laura can't even imagine being nineteen.

"You'll—" She tries to tell herself about the wonderful life Virginia will have, with Isobel, away from St. Dunstan's, away from her parents, away from everything sclerotic and mediocre and dull; she can't stop her tears. "Well, you'll be World-Historical by then, won't you?"

Virginia's voice wavers only a little. "From your mouth," she says, "to God's ears." She shakes herself loose from the silence. "Anyway," she says. "Let's not get sentimental. Not before breakfast?" She goes to the window. "Mesrin's turned out her light. I should go." She turns back to Laura. "One thirty?"

"One thirty."

"Lime of the Ancient Mariner. Don't forget."

"I won't."

Virginia hoists the duffel bag onto her shoulder.

"Don't forget," she says again, and leaves.

Laura watches Virginia cross the quad. She watches Isobel emerge from Latimer a moment later and follow her. She stays at the window a while longer, watching its emptiness, trying to accustom herself to it.

This, she tells herself, is how it is always going to be, from now on.

She watches the clock tick. She calculates the distance. She swallows down the lump in her throat.

At last, at twelve forty-five, she leaves.

She slips down the stairs, as she has done so many times before; she creeps out the window; she shivers at the night wind on the quad.

She makes her way through the woods.

It is so much harder without Virginia to guide her; the brambles are so much thicker; the shadows much darker. She runs through the beeches, to the coastal path, to the clearing where the Webster statue once stood—overgrown, now, with wildflowers and weeds; she runs along the coastal path, down the hill, to where the intermittent lights gleam on the Weymouth dock.

It is only when she makes it to the Weymouth harbor that she realizes she has done it in her shortest ever time.

Laura gets to the Grinning Griddle early—it's only one fifteen; the owner grunts in recognition when he seats her.

She orders two coffees. She orders a Call Me Fish-Pail and a Lime of the Ancient Mariner. She sits by the window, watching the dock, the few fishing boats bobbing, steaming her hands with the coffee, checking the time. She can't eat. She barely swallows her coffee.

One thirty comes. Laura scans the horizon. Wind is whipping up the water; rain echoes syncopated on the boardwalk. There is no sign of a boat.

In the distance, she sees a bolt of lightning streak the sky; thunder comes a moment later.

"Storm's coming," the owner says.

Wild hope overtakes her: maybe the water's too rough; maybe it's too dangerous; maybe they've changed their minds—maybe they'll stay, for another day, another two; maybe she can still convince them not to leave at all.

She watches the waves wash clean over the dock.

No, she thinks, tracing her fingers on the window. Nothing would stop Virginia. Not even a storm. Not even God.

One thirty-five. One forty.

Virginia does not come.

Laura's coffee gets cold. Both plates lie untouched on the table. Rain batters the dock; the thunder rolls on; the red plastic clock on the wall keeps ticking; a fire truck rolls by, its blaring lights illuminating the entire street.

"Excuse me?" Laura turns, at last, to the owner, who is staring, too, out the horizon.

"Uh-huh?"

A second fire truck passes them.

"How long would it take to take a boat from Jarvis Lighthouse to here? Give or take?"

He raises an eyebrow.

"Why would you take a boat from Jarvis?"

"My friend, she's docked there—"

"You can't dock at Jarvis Lighthouse. Much too shallow, you'd have to be crazy to try."

A third fire truck passes them; its siren drowns them out.

At last, at last Laura understands.

"You want me to pack those up for—"

Laura doesn't let him finish. She runs.

Laura runs through the rain, through the storm, faster than she's ever run before; the only thing in the world that matters, now, is that she does not stop; she prays, with every part of herself, that it isn't true, that she has made some mistake; that there is an explanation; that there is something, *something* else that will make this night make sense. She can't feel her limbs; she can't hear her heartbeat; the sirens are getting louder; she can no longer form words.

She runs to the edge of campus without stopping.

She hears it, first: that great, infernal sound, the one that shakes the ground.

It is the collapsing of the bell.

At last she looks up.

The smell clogs her nostrils. The ash obscures the stars. Someone in the distance is screaming; the firetrucks flood the chapel with their strange, red light: indistinguishable, in the smoke, from the flames.

11

THE BODIES WASH UP ON THE NEXT MORNING.

Campus security finds them on Bethel Beach: two girls, blue-lipped, bones broken, seaweed in their throats. They take them away before the students can see them.

They put them with the others.

The rumors cross campus before they hit the press. The boys must have been in the crypt when the fire broke out; there was gasoline, canisters and canisters full, poured on all the pews, on the wooden staircase to the choir loft, on the organ casing, on the banisters.

They find their bodies—all five—on the stairwell between the chapel and the crypt. Smoke inhalation, most likely, or else the heat.

By noon the next morning the campus shares an understanding. Virginia Strauss and Isobel Zhao set the fire—because of the video, because of politics, because of a secret lesbian sex-and-death pact, nobody knows exactly; it doesn't really matter. What matters is they killed the boys; they killed themselves afterward, jumping from one of the high cliffs; they'd have died as soon as they hit the water; they must have known nobody could survive a fall that high.

Laura does not remember the hours between when she ran, still screaming, toward the flames, and when she woke up, in a clean white bed with hospital corners, in the Mountbatten health center, with Reverend Tipton at her side, telling her that all of them are dead.

"I'm sorry," he'd said—she does not remember this part very well—"there's been an *accident*," as if the only wicked things that happen in the world are the ones that happen by mistake.

She doesn't remember slapping him in the face, either, but she's told she did that, too.

She remembers, vaguely, the statement she's told she gave to the police, Saturday morning: the boat, the gasoline, the gasoline that Virginia swore—she *swore*; of course Laura believed her—was for the boat, their breakfast at the Grinning Griddle, the Lime of the Ancient Mariner, Virginia's favorite, black coffee; Evensong; the key; oh God, oh God, that little, stupid key, that Virginia had for eighteen whole hours; what does the key have to do with anything; why are they asking her about a key; Virginia didn't even have the key; she'd returned it, a day before; she'd only wanted it to go to the crypt to say goodbye.

And you believed her? the inspector asked her, and Laura kept saying, *Yes, yes.*

It had to have been an accident, she must have said that twenty times.

They said something about the gas station on Carver Avenue. How a person could copy a key there—twenty-four/seven, at one of those little machines—or didn't she know that?

She didn't know, Laura kept saying when they told her that the crypt door was locked from the outside. *She couldn't have known they were there.*

She remembers the police car dropping her off, at Desmond, late Saturday night, maybe even Sunday morning; how she almost collapses on the threshold, until Julia Feinstein comes to take her by the arm, and hauls her up the stairs, and presses a cold compress to her forehead.

She remembers the smell of smoke, of roasting meat.

They put the fire out. They couldn't save the chapel. What is left of it stands behind cordons of yellow tape: the lighthouse Madonna, sheared in two: standing headless under an empty sky, under a rain of ash. The wood has splintered in on itself and then calcified; only stone remains: what's left has turned black. Laura can see it from her window.

It is the last day of Trinity term.

There will be a service, that evening, for the boys: something makeshift, on Devonshire Quad, with candles, with their photographs. Reverend Tipton had asked her to sing. That's the only part Laura remembers.

"You see"—that was when his voice broke—"you're the only one that's left."

There will be nothing for Isobel, for Virginia. The papers don't even print their names.

Laura sits alone, huddling in her half of the room. It is Sunday morning. The police have taken everything else already: Virginia's books, Virginia's running clothes, Virginia's furs and lace collars and black gloves; the room doesn't even smell like her anymore.

They've even taken her sheets.

Laura sits like that, for a few hours, staring at the wall. She's still numb—they told her to expect that part, in the health center; she can't remember what they gave her, exactly, except that they told her not to drink alcohol with it, which she remembers thinking was a ridiculous thing to say to a seventeen-year-old girl who barely looks fifteen and has never had a fake ID in her life.

Then again, she thinks, she'd drink a whole bottle of Bonnie di Angelis's sweet vermouth if she could.

She thinks again about the key.

The police have told her not to think too hard about the key.

It'll kill you, they warned her, *if you let it.* They believed her—that was the worst part—they looked at her with such animal pity; *of course* she hadn't known; *of course* she hadn't even guessed; you couldn't think that, could you, of poor, sweet, dumb Laura Stearns, who worshipped the ground Virginia walked on; of course poor, sweet, dumb Laura Stearns would believe that Virginia Strauss only wanted to go down to the crypt, to pray, Virginia Strauss who isn't like other people, Virginia Strauss who is noble and pure and too good for everything except burning five boys alive.

She needed to say goodbye, she keeps telling herself. *That's why she needed the key.*

She didn't know.

She keeps telling herself that, too.

Yvette Saunders is sobbing in the corridor.

"I was finally going to meet Sadie!"

Then it's all real.

Brad and Anton and Barry and Ralph and Ivan are all dead; then the shock of it comes over her again like a fever and she has to put a pillow over her mouth so Yvette won't hear her scream.

• • •

Laura forces herself to pace the room (*Keep moving*, they said at the health center, *it's good for you*). She forces herself to fold and refold her laundry; to move all her pencils from one side of the desk to the other; to rearrange her books.

It's then that she sees the envelope, tucked in a corner of the shelf, between *All Before Them* and *Paradise Lost*.

It is small, delicate, calligraphed: addressed in Virginia's fine slanting hand.

For Laura.

Laura almost tears it in two.

My dearest Laura, it says.

By the time you read this, you will know why I have written it. You will probably already hate me, although I hope a part of you already understands, without my having to explain.

Those boys deserved to die.

Laura stops reading.

The lines don't form letters. The letters don't form words. The paper comes apart and reassembles, kaleidoscopic and nonsensical, in her hands.

Virginia didn't know. Virginia couldn't have known. Virginia would never. Virginia always would.

Of course, of course, Virginia would.

Virginia always does everything to the limit of what a person can do.

That, Laura knows, is why she loves her.

The words re-form before Laura's eyes.

Those boys deserved to die. You must know that already, deep down. I'm tired of pretending that they don't.

Virginia lays the whole thing out. She explains about World-History,

and Ideological Revolution. She explains about Good and Evil and Realism and Relativism; she capitalizes every other noun. She explains
how the whole world is rotten, from the inside out, because it wants
you to forget every immoderate thing you ever believed, if you want to
survive.

I don't accept that, Virginia says.

If I leave you with one thing, she says, *let it be this:*

*That's not the world I want to live in. That's not the world I want
for you.*

*You may not understand, yet, that what I have done I have done for
you. But I promise you, one day, you will.*

I want you to live in a world, Laura, where things matter.

That is the only way I know how to love you.

Laura crumples the letter and throws it to the floor.

She stares at it, for a while, as if she expects it to rise up and vaunt
itself between her fingers.

Then, slowly, gingerly, she picks it up again.

Laura reads the whole thing through three times.

She reads the postscript.

PS: You have my permission to share this.

It's the *permission* that gets her.

Like the whole world is going to be clamoring for the manifesto of
prep school prophet Virginia Strauss.

Like Laura is going to be the one to give it to them.

Laura needs air. God, how she needs air! It is Sunday afternoon now.
The drugs are wearing off, and all Laura can think is that they jumped,
the two of them, from one of the high cliffs, and Laura needs more

than anything she's ever needed to know which one it was, to see it, with her own eyes, the place where they fell.

She crosses the quadrangle; she doesn't look—doesn't let herself look—at the ruins of the chapel; she turns straight toward the woods, just as she did early yesterday morning. God, could it really be yesterday morning; there is so much yellow police tape here, too, but she just vaults over it without stopping; what's the point of police, she thinks, when everyone's already dead.

She cuts her way through the woods. Somewhere she scratches her arm on a bramble and starts to bleed, but she doesn't know when; she doesn't notice until she's all the way out at Farnham Cliff.

Miranda is standing by the edge.

She is in a ratty black fur coat, even though it's June. Her hair is tangled, and falls all to her waist. She is smoking.

She looks up when Laura approaches. She doesn't say anything. She hands Laura a cigarette; Laura takes it; Miranda lights it.

They stand, side by side, for a while, smoking, not talking, saying nothing about the fact that they are both looking out at the outlines of bodies, drawn in upon the sand.

At last Miranda lifts her chin.

"She didn't know," she says, "that they were in there." Her voice is hollow. She swallows back tears. "The police asked me—they kept asking. I told them. They didn't believe me." She casts her eyes from cliff to cliff. "Showed me her op-ed for the *Chronicle*, all that stuff about revolution. Made out like Izzy was some sort of dyke harpy who just wanted to kill all men. Like the whole thing was her idea."

The cigarette trembles in her hand.

"Did she know?"

"Yes," Laura says. Her own voice sounds so strange to her.

Miranda nods.

"The door—it was—"

"She had a key." Laura can't bring herself to say why.

Miranda takes another puff of her cigarette.

"Izzy didn't know," she says again. "I'm sure of it. When we talked, the night before the—she—" She lets the words die on the wind. "She said—she said she was planning something. Something big. CAME and CREWS—they *were* child's play, she said; *unserious.* She said she didn't mind being expelled; even being arrested. It'd be worth it, she said, just to know she'd taken action." She turns to Laura. "She said *expelled.*" She lets the word echo. "You don't talk about being expelled," she says, "if you're about to burn five boys alive."

She lets the ash fall onto the rock.

"What did she tell you?"

"That they were—lovers. That they were running away together; they'd bought a boat; they were going to sail to Canada, somewhere they could be together, away from their awful families." It all seems so foolish when she says it out loud like that.

"*Lovers?*" Miranda snorts. "Please."

"You don't think . . ."

"I don't know," Miranda says. "I don't know—and I don't care. Not anymore. If they did, if they didn't, what does it matter? Not when it comes to her." She lights another cigarette. "Sex was just how she got people to do what she wanted."

She shakes out more ash onto her coat.

"I hate her," Miranda says suddenly. "I hate her, and I'm glad she's dead." Her voice notches dire. "I hate her, and I hope she goes to hell, and I hope there *is* a hell, so that people like her can go there!"

And Laura thinks, *Me too.*

God, she thinks, *me too.*

Miranda's right, she thinks; Miranda's always been right; there is nothing, has never been anything, about Virginia worth saving. It is all so clear, now—at last, at last, too late—Virginia was a liar; Virginia was a sociopath; Virginia spat in the faces of the people who loved her; Virginia wanted nothing but to be worshipped, like some dark, bloodthirsty goddess of war; Virginia tormented Bonnie; she tormented Reverend Tipton; Virginia burned five boys alive, just because she could.

Laura's foolishness overwhelms her. Her weakness overwhelms her. All the excuses she has made for Virginia, for so long, all the *you don't know her* and the *you have to understand* and the *Virginia isn't like other people* come crashing down.

Virginia killed those boys, she thinks. She killed Isobel, she thinks; it is still murder even if she only dared Isobel to jump. How easy it would have been, she thinks: for Virginia to plan it, to seduce Isobel with the image of a purifying blaze; to *dismantle the master's house*—she always had a way with rhetoric—to forget to mention the boys inside.

She wonders which of the cliffs it was; Virginia's wrists digging into Isobel's shoulder, as she whispered, *Jump.* She wouldn't even have made it out like it was suicide at all. *Consecration,* she'd have called it. A baptism. *I dare you.* The only thing you could do, really, once you'd set a church aflame.

How easy it would have been, Laura thinks, to jump.

She would have jumped, too.

Laura wonders how long it took them to die.

She hopes Isobel died quickly. She hopes Virginia died slow.

It's wicked, Laura knows, and vengeful, but Laura wishes for it anyway: Virginia, in the water, her bones shattered and her lips turning blue; Virginia changing her mind, when it is too late, when the water is already closing over her; Virginia knowing, in her last knowledge on this earth, that everything she'd done had been for nothing at all.

Miranda puts out her cigarette on the rock.

"Burn in hell," she murmurs, "you vengeful bitch."

She spits over the water's edge.

Laura throws the last of her cigarette off the cliff. She watches it sink, until there is nothing left.

They sit for a while longer, in silence, watching the light fall lower on the lighthouse.

"Word of advice," Miranda says after a while. "Turn off your phone."

Laura has been getting news notifications for hours. It was a sex thing; it was a death thing; it was a pagan rite gone wrong; it was Catholicism; it was Satanism; it was a frame-up and the girls had nothing to do with it; it was what the social justice warriors have been planning all along. Five journalists have already left voicemails.

"Predictably, Bonnie di Angelis has managed to make this all about herself."

Miranda hands Laura her phone.

Bonnie is all in black. Bonnie's eyeliner is running down her cheeks. Bonnie is staring at the camera with wild, unfocused eyes.

"*I would just like to say,*" she says, through tears, "*that Virginia and Isobel are the heroes we deserve.*"

"What is this?"

"Keep watching."

Bonnie goes on: "*I knew those boys. I loved them. And that's why I'm the only one who can tell you the real, unvarnished truth—they deserved everything they got and more.*"

She has a whole manifesto written out in the caption section. There are two kinds of people in this world, she says: the ones who take action and the ones who don't. Angry women, everywhere, she says, should rise up and burn the patriarchy once and for all, how there isn't a single man alive who probably doesn't deserve it, deep down. After all, she says, Virginia Strauss wasn't the only girl whose sex tapes they passed around. She'd loved Brad once, too. She'd made videos for him, loving him. Only, after they broke up, somehow half of St. Dunstan's had seen them, too.

Boys like that, she says. Doing things like that to women. It's how it's always been; it's how it is; it's how it'll be, right up unto the end of the world, until we finally work up the nerve to do something about it.

Two thousand people have Liked it. Three thousand more have left comments about how Bonnie's a terrible person. She has six thousand new followers.

"Do you think she believes it?" Miranda keeps her eyes on the screen.

"Maybe."

The truth is, Laura thinks, Bonnie always believes in everything.

The thought makes her feel even lonelier.

"I used to feel sorry for her. Freddy, too." The tears have dried on Miranda's face. "Izzy always told me not to bother. Of course she needed Freddy. Because of the library job."

"What do you mean?"

"How do you think we pulled off that Evensong prank? Freddy had all the admin passwords."

"What?"

A vague thought digs into the edges of Laura's consciousness.

"I mean—that's how you do check-in and checkout. She gave us the codes for the chapel computer, paired it with the Bluetooth speakers ..."

Laura is already on her feet.

"I have to go," she says.

. . .

It is almost dusk by the time Laura gets to Carbonell.

Freddy is sitting at the checkout desk, tapping her fingers, staring at the monitor screen.

She's editing one of Bonnie's videos. She's applying a filter to Bonnie's face that lengthens her lashes and contours her cheek.

"Do you know," she says, when Laura approaches, "I've talked to six different news stations today?" She keeps her eyes on Bonnie's cheekbones. "This place really is rotten."

"You switched the videos," Laura says. "At Assembly."

Freddy still doesn't look up.

"So?"

"So—seven people are dead!"

Freddy keeps fiddling with Bonnie's upper lip. "Not my problem," she says. "I wasn't there."

"Jesus—Freddy!"

She yanks the monitor so quickly Freddy's earbuds tumble out of her ears.

"What do you want?"

"Why did you do it?"

"After the shit she put Bonnie through"—Freddy's smile is thin and cold—"people deserved to know the truth. She was a sociopath and a fraud. And a hypocrite."

"How did you get the video?"

"Ivan sent it to me." Freddy shrugged. "Poor idiot. Probably thought it'd impress me. It didn't."

"You got them killed!"

Freddy looks up at her.

"Look," she says, "I didn't do shit." She taps her fingers on the counter. "All I did was show people who Virginia Strauss really was. We're all just lucky she didn't set a bomb under Mountbatten Hall." She turns the monitor back around.

"You don't even feel bad."

"I'm not saying what happened wasn't sad. But it's not like they were saints, either. You think they didn't share plenty of private videos? You think they didn't all send around Bonnie's, too? Believe me, Brad made sure everyone in Cranmer knew he was finally getting laid. . . ." She gnaws on her lower lip. "You really want to tell me, if he'd lived, he'd have woken up one day and become a decent human being?"

Laura opens her mouth to protest.

She realizes, too late, she has nothing left to say.

She can't defend anybody.

On her screen, Bonnie is lighting candles and intoning. She has it all worked out: they're Thelma and Louise; they're Bonnie and Clyde; they're Valerie Solanas for the twenty-first century; they're the spirit of the—

"Don't judge. People find it cathartic."

"Tell her to take it down."

"Someone donated a grand to her Patreon, you know. Felt *seen*."

"Take it *down*, Freddy."

"Please." Freddy looks back up at her. "You assholes made Bonnie's life a living hell while they were alive. Shedding crocodile tears over *wasted potential* won't bring any of them back, either. So, tell me—why shouldn't she finally get something out of it?" She leans back in her chair. "It'll be the only decent thing any of them ever did for her. Strauss should be on her knees—thanking her. Wherever she is," she says softly. "Admit it. Bonnie's giving Virginia Strauss what she always wanted. Her name in lights."

Laura can't.

• • •

So, Laura thinks, this is how it ends: everybody deserves what they get, one way or another. So Virginia was a fraud; so Isobel was a patsy; so Laura's a fool; so the boys were just coddled, callous idiots who circulated a sex tape of the girl they couldn't fuck, until poor, stupid Ivan Dixon sent it to Freddy because he couldn't fuck her, either; so Sebastian Webster wrote a mediocre book and died on the wrong side of history, for no reason but that he was rich, and young, and bored, and the sclerotic modern world was the same then as it is now, and always will be; world without end; and all Webster ever meant by *the rocks and the harbor are one* is that in the end you die.

So there is nothing, was nothing, special about the night at the crypt, nor the night on Farnham; there was nothing special about Evensong, except that Virginia was hot, and good with words, and they were bored, and all secretly wanted to sleep with her, and she knew how to use that against them, and Laura was so lonely, and it is so easy to convince a person of the things they want to believe, and that is all it ever was, and no matter how many times Laura tries to make excuses, no matter how many times she works it out, the answer will always come back the same.

There is nothing, she thinks, as she watches Freddy adding freckles to Bonnie's cheeks, worth saving in any of them; there is no such thing, not really, as a *shipwreck of the soul*, except the ones when you drown; and the best thing Laura can do now, Laura knows, is grow up and accept the fact that the world is what it is, and nothing will ever change it.

Only, Laura doesn't want to live in that world, either.

Freddy is smirking at her, from across the library counter, and Freddy is right, but also Freddy is wrong, for all sorts of reasons Laura can't even explain or understand, only maybe sometimes you can decide to say no to the world; maybe you can affirm it, even if you don't believe it, deep down, even if you are old and wise enough to know how wrong you are, and maybe, Laura thinks, that's what strength is.

There is another answer, she decides. There has to be. She just hasn't found it yet.

"I don't accept that," she says.

Freddy just looks at her.

"Then you're a bigger idiot than I thought."

Laura can live with that.

The sun is setting when Laura comes to Devonshire Quad.

Reverend Tipton is already there. He has laid out all five of their yearbook photographs, all taken at the start of Michaelmas; Laura can't believe they ever were so young. He is arranging a stack of folding chairs by rows.

"I'm sorry," he says, as she approaches. "I couldn't do anything more for the girls. It was felt it—wouldn't be appropriate." He nods at the chairs spreading all the way to Cranmer. "Not here."

He has a little bruise under his eye where she has hit him. She suddenly feels hideously sorry for him: with his wobbling lip, his twitching nose, his fogged-up glasses. She feels so sorry for everyone, now.

"It's fine," she says. "I wouldn't expect you to."

She takes one of the chairs from the pile; she helps him unfold them, put them in lines; she helps him place a little votive candle on each seat.

"There," he says, when at last they've laid out the row. "Much better."

There are lilies by all the photographs, and by the tentpoles.

He hands her a sheaf of paper. "Here," he says. "Your music. Just a Magnificat, I think."

"Thanks."

He keeps his eyes on the empty chairs.

"I keep thinking," he says at last. "I should have baptized her."

"Yes," Laura says. "You should have."

He leans back upon the table.

"I had an excuse, of course. She needed preparation—I didn't have the time . . . but of course, I had all the time in the world. If I'd wanted to."

"Why didn't you?"

"She annoyed me." His laugh is weak. "That's all it was. She was posh, and irritating, and stuck-up. For a girl like that—nobody else, in her whole life, had ever put her in her place. There was something— pleasurable—about being the first one. Of course, I knew she'd never go to those classes. The commute alone—I told myself, of course, if she wanted it badly enough . . ." He looks up at her. He has an expression Laura has never seen before: it is both softness and fear.

He is not looking at me, Laura thinks, *like he is talking to a child, anymore.*

She folds this knowledge quietly away.

"That wasn't all, though, was it?"

"No," he goes on. "That wasn't all."

"What was it?"

"Jealousy, maybe? Horrible, isn't it, when I say it like that." He keeps her gaze. "But it all seemed so *easy* for her. You know—you suffer, and you pray, even with this. . . ." He tugs, instinctively, at his collar. "And you have those long, dark nights of the soul, when you think it's all for nothing, and half the time you're just going through the motions, and here comes this—God, a child, too clever by half, charging in like Joan of Arc . . ." He stops himself. "She made it all seem very simple."

"Maybe it is," Laura says. "Sometimes."

His smile is wistful.

"I've been wondering all day," he says. "I can't help but feel responsible, in some way. For everything. If somehow—"

"You are."

He opens his mouth in surprise.

"Not only you," Laura says. "Not only anybody." She takes another breath. "But yes. We were."

All of us, she thinks. *All of them*, knitted together, like their voices, until you can no longer tell what belongs to someone else, and what's your own; all of their wanting, their waiting, their hope, for understanding not yet come.

He sighs and is silent for a while.

"You're too wise for your own good," he says at last.

"That's the first time," Laura says, "anyone's ever said that to me."

They hold the vigil on the Devonshire lawn. Yvette sobs in the front row; Tamara Lynd, too, and Ursula Thale; Teddy Kelting and Matt Azibuike and Richard Charles, and Miranda, with her hands in her lap, her eyes forward, bereft of tears. Reverend Tipton says the words nobody knows how to say about death, and loss, and how sometimes God allows senseless things to happen, and nobody knows why.

Laura sings the Magnificat alone.

"*My soul*," she sings, "*doth magnify the Lord.*"

Her voice wavers, at first, in the silence; then she gathers strength; she cannot hide among them now; and so she has to sing for all of them at once; she has to fill their absence with what she has left of them; *he hath scattered the proud in the imagination of their hearts*, she sings, and maybe Freddy is right, Freddy is incontrovertible; there is nothing worth anything in anything, but Laura is stubborn, and at the heart of Laura's softness there is steel, and although she knows, she knows, that maybe everybody deserves to die, in the end, she knows, too, that that isn't the end of it; there is something else, she thinks, there has to be something else, that isn't fire and isn't drowning and still shipwrecks your soul; there are exactly four good words in Webster, and this is enough to love him; there is something, in Evensong, that is not old smoke and Virginia's gloves; there is something, in Virginia, in all of them, that she cannot despise; that she must be too strong to despise; because everybody is right about Virginia Strauss, and still, everybody's wrong; because hidden away from the shame and the sin and the broken bones and the smell of ash and the bodies bloated from drowning, there is something else, something hard and solid and small, like a pebble, that you can close your hand around, or that sticks in your shoe, demanding your attention, something that isn't World-Historical, no, it isn't capitalized at all, that matters, even when nothing else matters, such immoderate hope; and Laura knows how foolish it is, at a time like this, to say that *this is the thing that matters* but Laura is a fool, Laura has always been a fool; Laura no longer minds; her foolishness is different now.

As it was in the beginning, she sings, *is now, and ever shall be.*
World without end, she sings. *Amen.*

They file off the quadrangle, in silence, holding their candles.

Laura is the last to go.

She waits, for a moment, on the Desmond threshold. She turns toward the water.

Laura walks alone again through the woods; she comes once more to Farnham Cliff; she turns left and walks farther, to the absence, where the statue once had been. She considers, there, for a while.

She reaches into her pocket.

Virginia's letter is still there, folded away. She takes it out now; she reads it again.

It is the only way, Virginia says, *I know how to love you.*

Laura goes to the water. She has a sudden, animal urge to rip the letter up; to tear it into pieces; to let it blow away in the wind, like ash.

She stays there, for a while, deciding. Then she folds the letter in half, and then in half again, and then in half again, making it smaller and smaller until she can slip it, just beneath her collarbone, into her bra; she feels it, unmistakable, between her breasts.

It is one of the graduals she thinks of, one of the ones they sang in Michaelmas, one of those days when Ivan was overwrought and Anton was ebullient, when Barry was enraptured by the final cadence and Ralph made Brad stop and repeat whatever joke he was making about the end of the world so he could note it down for the World-Historical novel he was going to write, one of those days that Virginia caught Laura's eye, and looked at her, and then at them, and back at her again, and smiled with such overflowing grace that the whole room was suffused with it, and anyway, anyway, they sang that bit from Isaiah: *All these may forget, but I will not forget; look*, it goes, *I have written you on the palms of my hands*; and that is the thing Laura thinks of, as she presses the paper into her breast, as she turns toward the harbor, as she starts to run.

Acknowledgments

I'M SO PROFOUNDLY GRATEFUL TO EVERYONE WHO BORE WITH me through the near-decade it took to tell this particular story, and to everyone who thoughtfully read and gave feedback on the half-dozen drafts that culminated in this one. I'm particularly thankful for the incisive comments—and incredible patience—of my editor, Carina Guiterman, who tirelessly helped me draft and redraft this book until it at last resembled the story I wanted to tell; for the incredible work of the whole production team at Simon & Schuster; and for the support of my agents Emma Parry and Rebecca Carter for tirelessly working to bring this story to life.

Thank you too, to my husband, Dhananjay, for supporting me as I wrote draft after draft of this novel (in a pandemic, no less): always my first—and best—reader.

About the Author

TARA ISABELLA BURTON is the author of the novel *Social Creature* and the nonfiction *Strange Rites: New Religions for a Godless World*. Her fiction, essays, and religion journalism have appeared in the *New York Times*, *Granta*, *The Wall Street Journal*, *The Washington Post*, and more. She is a contributing editor at *American Purpose* and a columnist in *Religion News Service*. She holds a doctorate in theology from the University of Oxford, where she was a Clarendon Scholar. She lives in New York City.